"Be my woman, Rae."

Suddenly she wasn't sure what he was really saying. Was he just asking for a hot and frenzied roll in the blanket to celebrate old times? Or did he want something more?

All at once she was scared witless. Scared witless that she would accept his offer—whatever it was.

This was exactly why she'd gone on the run and hidden from him for so many years. The fear that he would return and hold out his hand, and she would take it. Forgive him his sins and set herself up for an even greater heartbreak—never knowing when he would decide to walk out on her again for whatever reason, real or fabricated.

"It's not possible."

"It is."

Then she whispered the words she knew would keep them apart forever.

"I was pregnant when you left me."

Dear Reader,

"In like a lion, out like a lamb." That's what they say about March, right? Well, there are no meek and mild lambs among this month's Intimate Moments heroines, that's for sure! In *Saving Dr. Ryan*, Karen Templeton begins a new miniseries, THE MEN OF MAYES COUNTY, while telling the story of a roadside delivery—yes, the baby kind—that leads to an improbable romance. Maddie Kincaid starts out looking like the one who needs saving, but it's really Dr. Ryan Logan who's in need of rescue.

We continue our trio of FAMILY SECRETS prequels with *The Phoenix Encounter* by Linda Castillo. Follow the secret-agent hero deep under cover—and watch as he rediscovers a love he'd thought was dead. But where do they go from there? Nina Bruhns tells a story of repentance, forgiveness and passion in *Sins of the Father*, while Eileen Wilks offers up tangled family ties and a seemingly insoluble dilemma in *Midnight Choices*. For Wendy Rosnau's heroine, there's only *One Way Out* as she chooses between being her lover's mistress—or his wife. Finally, Jenna Mills' heroine becomes *The Perfect Target*. She meets the seemingly perfect man, then has to decide whether he represents safety—or danger.

The excitement never flags—and there will be more next month, too. So don't miss a single Silhouette Intimate Moments title, because this is the line where you'll find the best and most exciting romance reading around.

Enjoy!

Leslie J. Wainger
Executive Senior Editor

Please address questions and book requests to:
Silhouette Reader Service
U.S.: 3010 Walden Ave., P.O. Box 1325, Buffalo, NY 14269
Canadian: P.O. Box 609, Fort Erie, Ont. L2A 5X3

Sins of the Father

NINA BRUHNS

Silhouette®

INTIMATE MOMENTS™

Published by Silhouette Books

America's Publisher of Contemporary Romance

SILHOUETTE BOOKS

ISBN 0-373-27279-0

SINS OF THE FATHER

Copyright © 2003 by Nina Bruhns

This edition published by arrangement with Harlequin Books S.A.

® and TM are trademarks of Harlequin Books S.A., used under license.
Trademarks indicated with ® are registered in the United States Patent
and Trademark Office, the Canadian Trade Marks Office and in other
countries.

Visit Silhouette at www.eHarlequin.com

Printed in U.S.A.

NINA BRUHNS

credits her Gypsy great-grandfather for her great love of adventure. She has lived and traveled all over the world, including a six-year stint in Sweden. She has been on scientific expeditions from California to Spain to Egypt and the Sudan, and has two graduate degrees in archaeology (with a specialty in Egyptology). She speaks four languages and writes a mean hieroglyphics!

But Nina's first love has always been writing. For her, writing for Silhouette Books is the ultimate adventure. Drawing on her many experiences gives her stories a colorful dimension, and allows her to create settings and characters that are out of the ordinary. Two of her books won the prestigious Romance Writers of America Golden Heart Award for writing excellence.

A native of Canada, Nina grew up in California and currently resides in Charleston, South Carolina, with her husband and three children.

She loves to hear from her readers, and can be reached at P.O. Box 746, Ladson, SC 29456-0746 or by e-mail via the Harlequin Web site at http://www.eHarlequin.com.

Chapter 1

At last he'd found her.

Roman Santangelo roared through Lone Pine on his Harley with just one thing on his mind.

RaeAnne Sommarby.

He didn't pay too much attention to the way the townsfolk stared at his outrageous hair and leather gear as he floored the bike and pointed it north. Having looked like an extra for the *Road Warrior* movies for years, Roman was used to being stared at. Even back when he was eleven, his best friend Cole had given him the nickname ''Renegade'' because of his tough-guy appearance. The name had stuck through his school years as well as the decade he'd spent in the Navy. It wasn't until he'd joined the FBI that he'd reverted to his real name. But the image hadn't changed. It was the reason the Bureau kept sending him out on all those sensitive, risky jobs. His ability to blend in with the bad guys.

Okay, maybe blend in was the wrong phrase. Perhaps more apt would be that he stuck out like such a sore thumb that nobody in their right mind would ever believe he was the best undercover agent the FBI had west of the Rockies. At least that was his theory.

And as for RaeAnne, well, like the old song said, she was always on his mind. Had been for the past eighteen years. Ever since he'd walked out on her without a word three months before her high school graduation.

But this time was different. This time, he'd found her.

The smells of the high desert spring filled Roman's lungs as he swept down the highway—the scent of sage baking in the bright morning sun, the rich spice of soil growing warm after the long winter rest, the fresh tang of snowmelt flowing into the Owens River in the distance. If his stomach weren't threatening to turn inside out from sheer nerves, he'd be enjoying this May ride up US 395.

But seeing sweet RaeAnne Sommarby's—now RaeAnne Martin's—distinctive signature on that Forest Service permit at the Lone Pine station after all this time, had him breaking out in a cold sweat. Was it a coincidence? RaeAnne showing up here of all places, within sixty miles of where he grew up and the very spot his father had betrayed everything he'd always stood for? Probably not. More likely it was some kind of weird karma, or cosmic justice, at work. Roman was big on justice, but usually of the more earthly variety.

He forced himself to throttle up the Harley even faster, devouring the gently curving ribbon of asphalt leading him to his own moment of judgment. Damn, he was shaking like a leaf.

Would she recognize him? Hell, would she even remember him? True, after what he'd done to her, what woman wouldn't? He just prayed she had it in her to forgive him.

For that was the whole purpose of this trip. To beg her forgiveness. He'd carried the guilt for eighteen years now, and just like the situation surrounding his father's betrayal, he needed closure. And to move on.

I'm sorry I broke your heart, he'd say to her. *Sorry I ruined your graduation, and destroyed all the plans we had together. I'm sorry I made a mistake and screwed up so badly. I'm so sorry.* Then he'd throw himself on her mercy, hoping for a word of forgiveness.

And if he got it, maybe, just maybe, it would give him the strength he needed to confront his next task—proving to himself that he hadn't turned traitor to his family and his people without good reason. That he'd had no choice, justice had demanded it.

The miles flew by, and pretty soon he spotted the turn-off that would take him to RaeAnne's small archaeological dig at Cleary Hot Springs. He pondered that bit of news as he swung off the highway and bounced onto the rocky, washboarded dirt road heading over the coral-colored hills and up into the steep rise of the Sierra Nevada. RaeAnne an archaeologist. What a surprise.

Cresting the ridge of a hill, he brought the bike to a stop and gazed up at the magnificent mountains towering above him. Stark, rugged, awe-inspiring, the snowcapped peaks scowled down at him, as though standing guard over the woman whose world he was about to invade, ready to do battle with the man who would surely bring renewed heartache to their gentle explorer.

"I swear I won't hurt her," he promised the silent sentinels. "All I need is ten minutes. Fifteen max. To explain and apologize. Then I'll be gone and you can have her back again, safe and sound."

It was absurd talking to mountains. He knew it was absurd. Though full-blooded Paiute, he wasn't one of those mystical Native Americans who went around speaking to totems and spirits and such. He'd been brought up in the bustle and chaos of Southern California, and was firmly rooted in modern reality. He was an FBI agent; it was his job to stick to the tangible facts. But at that very moment, a chilly wind kicked up, lifting the ends of his long hair below his helmet, sending a shiver up his spine, and he could almost feel the mountains hunker down to watch his penance. To make sure he kept his word.

Giving himself a firm mental shake, he gunned the bike

down the back side of the hill, and made the final turn, following the Forest Service guy's directions. The last leg was just a track, barely two shallow ruts which led down into a hidden valley.

But what a valley! It was one of those magical places only California could produce, a tiny, secret paradise harbored in the nexus between lush alpine forest and the living desert. Tall pines and budding cottonwoods blended in an open tapestry with winnowing grass, fragrant sage, and colorful Indian paintbrush. And there, nestled next to a gurgling creek in the midst of this peaceful Shangri-La, was RaeAnne's ancient stone cabin.

No wonder she had picked this spot for her solitary dig. A person could easily fall in love with this place and stay forever.

Suddenly the tranquil air around him was shattered by a loud yell in a crude male voice. Roman whipped off his helmet and snapped his head toward the sound. A series of whoops and shouts shrilled through the narrow valley, making his blood run cold.

RaeAnne!

Gunning the Harley into action, he instinctively felt for the stainless steel Colt Python holstered at the back of his waistband, then reached down and flicked the snap off his boot-knife's sheath. Within seconds he was peeling around the cabin, tires spitting gravel and dust.

His heart nearly stopped at the sight that greeted him.

A half-dozen angry youths were running around in a frenzy, shouting and hoisting cardboard boxes into two dilapidated trucks. A woman stood under a tree, screaming and jerking at the ropes that held her wrists, which were tied over her head to one of the tree's low branches.

The woman was RaeAnne.

RaeAnne Martin banked her fury with an iron will and screamed again at the boys who were ruining eight hard weeks of work and possibly destroying bits of their own history in the process.

"Toby! Listen to me—you have to be careful with that stuff! Don't—!" *Oh, jeez,* she cursed silently as another box of fragile archaeological finds was slung into Toby Benson's rustbucket truck. "You are *so* going to regret this!" she screeched.

"Yeah, sure. Tell it to your sheriff," Toby yelled back. "Have him come and arrest me."

RaeAnne ground her teeth at both the reference to her sheriff—Sheriff Philip O'Donnaugh was *not* hers, at least not officially—and at the inference that he'd be able to do squat. Big Pine Reservation was out of the sheriff's office's jurisdiction, and they all knew it. If the kids made it to the reservation, the only ones who could mete out punishment to these hooligans were the Tribal Council and the FBI. RaeAnne was well aware of the chances of interesting the FBI in her measly archaeological artifacts—slim to none. That left the Tribal Council, and there she was sure to lose. Didn't matter if she had all the right government permits and married Sheriff O'Donnaugh to boot.

Wonderful. Two years of planning and eight thousand bucks in grants down the drain. Not to mention the black eye to her professional reputation.

"You don't understand," she yelled at Toby. "I am not messing with Indian burials. This was just a hunting camp, shared by both Paiute and whites. That skeleton is Caucasian!"

"You know that for sure?" he shot back.

Honesty compelled her to answer, "Ninety percent. We'll know for certain when it comes back from the lab."

"No way. My ancestor ain't gettin' sent to no damn white man's lab to be desecrated."

She was completely out of patience. Hanging from a tree by her wrists tended to drain what little she possessed. "Goddammit, Toby, he's not your ancestor! He's got a bullet in his skull!"

"Oh, and that would be so unusual?" Toby mocked, five hundred years of evidence to the contrary clearly written in his youthful bronze face.

This was not the time to get into a debate over Indian-white relations, or the historical accounts of the Cleary Hot Springs shoot-out. "You've read the stories about what happened here—"

"Stories!" he spat out. "Bull—"

Suddenly a huge black motorcycle came careening around the cabin into the clearing, spewing a shower of rocks as it roared to a halt.

"Hey, what's going on here?" shouted an equally huge man as he dumped the bike and sprinted toward the boys.

Stunned, RaeAnne could only watch helplessly as the kids jumped whooping into their trucks and jammed them to life. The man waved his arms, trying to head them off, making the silver chains dangling from his black leather jacket shimmer and tinkle.

The stranger's hair was outlandish—short on the sides but long on the top, hanging halfway down his back. When he turned his head, a single long braid swung from over his ear. The man looked like an outlaw!

A sudden spurt of fear pierced her daze. The kids were leaving. Leaving her there, all tied up and alone with the stranger. They might be punks, but they were nonviolent punks.

"Toby!" she screamed. "Don't you dare leave me like this! Come back! I swear I'll—" She stopped, realizing she was yelling at a cloud of dust. Where the hell was O'Donnaugh when you needed him?

The outlaw slowly turned to faced her. A tremor went through her whole body, leaving her knees weak and her mind numb. He was watching her, closely, in the way a mountain lion might eye a fluffy kitten. Focused, fascinated, wary. Not sure whether she was friend or foe. Whether to walk away...or eat her for breakfast.

Oh, God, please don't let him hurt me.

RaeAnne swallowed the knot of panic lodged in her throat. "Who are you?"

"Are you okay? Did they hurt you?"

"No, I'm—" her words stalled when he whisked off his leather jacket and tossed it at the bike, then reached down to his boot. When he straightened, he held a dull black dagger in his hand "—fine." The word came out in a thready whisper.

"You sure?"

She swiped her tongue over suddenly parched lips. "What are you going to do to me?"

His eyes narrowed and his fingers tightened around the dagger. "Cut you down."

Sounded reasonable. So why was she still trembling?

He took a single step toward her, then stopped. Treating her to a full, unhindered view of his body.

It was impressive. Tall, broad-shouldered, biceps rippling under a sleek black T-shirt. Trim waist, lean hips, long, muscular legs encased in tight black leather. *Oh, God.* The man was gorgeous. And the most dangerous-looking man she'd ever seen in her life. Despite the balmy morning, she was suddenly freezing.

He continued to stare at her. She shut her eyes. Tried desperately to get her knees to start working again. So she could run like hell when he cut her down.

If he cut her down.

She refused to go down that path. Just as she refused to think about how her own body was reacting to him. Traitorous, capricious flesh. How could shivers of fear turn so easily to quivers of excitement?

She burned with shame and embarrassment, yet there was something oddly familiar about this stranger. Something that spoke to her on a deeply elemental level, telling her that he didn't threaten her life, but her peace of mind. Or worse.

Nonsense. Dangerous nonsense. There was nothing familiar about him. She'd never seen him before. Had she? Surely she would remember someone who looked like this man.

The soft crunch of footsteps approached, halting directly in front of her. She squeezed her eyelids tighter.

"RaeAnne. Don't be afraid," he whispered.

She whimpered, telling herself she didn't know that voice. That deep, gentle rumble of tones. Didn't know his touch. Those strong, steady fingers skimming up her arms. Or the press of his hard male brawn against the yielding softness of her breasts.

No.

She took a shuddering breath, wanting, needing, to deny it all. And found herself filled, surrounded, by the unique, musky spice that would forever haunt her memory. Her senses saturated with the scent of the boy who had taken her young world and crushed it so thoroughly she had never fully recovered. The one man in the world she never wanted to see, ever again.

"Roman."

His name tore from her lips, half curse, half supplication. He cut her bonds and she collapsed into his arms, unable to stop the flood of emotions that turned her limbs to liquid.

"Yes, it's me."

A million conflicting feelings raged through her. Joy, despair, love, hate. A whole rainbow of every emotion she'd experienced over half a lifetime, all centered around this one horrible, wonderful, deceitful man.

"I don't believe it," she murmured.

Elation, passion. *Anguish, hurt.*

"I don't quite believe it myself," he quietly answered.

Especially hurt. Pain razored through her heart, making her gasp with the agony. Even the breath in her lungs stung with bitter misery.

Reaching deep down into herself, she somehow found the strength to take a step backward, out of his arms.

She looked him in the eye. "Well, I hate to cut short this touching reunion, but I've got to go after my artifacts."

Forcing herself to turn, she strode toward her Jeep, which

was parked at the side of the cabin. *Damn. Keys.* She veered to the door and reached inside to grab her purse.

"Wait."

She stopped, but didn't look at him. She couldn't do this. It was taking all her willpower to walk away. "What?"

"I need to talk to you."

But she couldn't talk to him. Didn't want to rip open all those old wounds that had taken her so long to heal over. It would kill her.

"It's been a long time, Roman. There's nothing to talk about."

"Please, Rae. Let me say this. Then I'll go."

If possible, the pain cut an even bigger swath through her heart. After eighteen years, she only rated a few words, then he was just going to take off again. Just as he'd done back then. A minute or two, then, so-long-sweetheart-catch-ya-in-another-eighteen.

Well, what did she expect? That he wanted to reminisce over old times? Find out what she'd been doing since he disappeared so utterly and completely from her life? Or maybe that he'd finally seen the light, realized he loved her, and had come to beg her to go back to him?

Yeah, right.

She fisted her hands around her purse and turned to face him. "Okay. What is it?"

She hated that his eyes were plaintive, twin pools of raw vulnerability. He had no right to be vulnerable. He was the hard one, the one who had thrown away everything they'd had for no reason she'd ever been able to discern.

"I'm sorry, Rae. I'm so damn sorry. I was wrong to leave you without a word."

"Okay. You're sorry." She made her leaden legs move to the Jeep. Away from him. "Apology accepted."

His sculpted lips parted. "But I want to explain—"

"No need," she interrupted. *Too late. Years too late.*

"Yes, there is. I have to explain. I need you to forgive me—"

"No problem," she said over her shoulder as she jumped into the Jeep and raised a hand, as if flicking away a pesky fly. "Bygones. Well, I'd love to stay and chat, but I really have to catch those guys before they make it to the rez."

Firing up the engine, she caught a glimpse of his face in the rearview mirror. Slack-jawed, uncertain, pale as her own skin. She thought about what she'd gone through because of this man, about the incredible losses she'd suffered, and steeled herself against feeling sorry for him. He didn't deserve her sympathy. Not one minute of it. Not after—

She stopped the thought before it even formed. She would not put herself through that particular hell. Not now. Not in front of him. He'd long since forfeited the right to know about her private burdens.

The Jeep lurched forward under her shaky foot. She had to get out of there. Fast. Before she did something she'd regret. Like break down. Or consent to listen to a single word Roman Santangelo had to say. Either way would be her undoing. Either way would prolong the number of minutes and seconds she had to spend in his company. Would exponentially increase the chances for true disaster.

Grinding the gears from reverse into first, she headed for the road leading away from the cabin. And prayed Roman Santangelo wouldn't climb onto his damned motorcycle and follow her.

Naturally he followed her. But not on his motorcycle. To RaeAnne's alarm, Roman shook himself out of his stupor and loped after the Jeep, his long legs making short work of the small head start she'd gotten on him. In a lithe motion worthy of a Hollywood stuntman, he jumped cleanly into the passenger seat.

"What do you think you're doing?" she demanded, slamming on the brakes.

"Coming with you," he said calm as pudding. "I'm a witness."

"Witness to what? This was just a little misunderstanding. Toby and I are friends."

"Misunderstanding?" He looked at her incredulously. "Woman, you were tied up and left to an uncertain fate with a possibly dangerous stranger. If nothing else, the kid deserves to have the tar whipped out of him. And I didn't exactly get the impression he had permission to take those boxes."

She clamped her jaw.

"Drive. They're getting away."

She clutched the wheel tightly.

"I'm a card-carrying Paiute, RaeAnne. Big Pine is a Paiute reservation. I can help."

It was true. Even though they'd both grown up on Rincon Reservation, one of the Luiseño settlements north of San Diego, Roman was Paiute. And his father was a certified Paiute hero, a man who'd died defending his people against the hated FBI. If anyone could help her case with the Tribal Council, it would be Roman.

She girded herself against the temptation. "I don't need your help. I've done this before. I can't—"

She snapped her mouth closed. Her fragile wall of self-control was starting to crack. She had to stop that dam from bursting. Because once the words started trickling out of her, she knew she'd never be able to stop the flow.

"Fine," she growled. "But don't say a thing. I can only deal with one crisis at a time."

He nodded, apparently taking her literally. Thank God. Buckling his seat belt, he leaned his head back against the headrest, a grim expression settling on his face as they sped toward the highway.

She tried not to look. Honestly she did. But against her will, when the tires rolled onto the smooth pavement, RaeAnne's gaze was drawn to the exotic angles of his cheekbones and jaw, to the fanned lines radiating from the corners of his tired eyes, to those lusciously sensual lips that had given her such dazzling pleasure when love was new and life was a splendid, unpainted canvas.

What had happened? They'd been so incredibly happy together. So totally, hopelessly, irrevocably in love. She had fallen hard for Roman Santangelo the first time she'd laid eyes on him, at the tender age of nine. He'd been eleven, new to the reservation where RaeAnne's mother taught high school, and an instant celebrity because of his father. It had taken him seven long months even to notice the skinny blond bookworm giving him moon-eyes, and seven even longer years to finally make love to her.

But in between those two memorable events, they had formed an unbreakable bond of friendship, sharing everything, hiding nothing, growing up and growing closer with each passing day of those turbulent years. He was going to be a veterinarian, and she wanted to be a teacher, until they had kids of their own. Theirs was the love of a lifetime, born in childhood, forged by the true, pure love of innocence, untouched by the sorrow and ugliness of the world. They would never part, mated for life.

At least that's what she'd thought.

Until the awful day when the sorrow and ugliness had closed in, squeezing the life, the love and the happiness from her forever.

Oh, God. She couldn't stand it a second longer. She had to know, even if it killed her. She screeched to a stop at the side of the highway, her foot trembling on the pedal, her knuckles white from gripping the wheel.

"All right. Explain it, then," she whispered into the wind. "Why did you leave me?"

Chapter 2

God help him, this was it.

Roman took a calming breath and glanced over at Rae-Anne. Suddenly he wasn't prepared for this moment. He couldn't think what to say to make that sad, wounded look in her eyes go away. He desperately needed her forgiveness. Needed her to look at him the way she used to, back then.

The curtain of mountains drawn high against the sky seemed to move closer, leaning in with their bald, craggy pates as if to eavesdrop. He drilled a hand through the short strands of hair above his right ear.

"Do you have any idea how long I've been searching for you?" he began.

Crossing her arms over her chest, RaeAnne focused on a distant point, where the highway disappeared in a shimmering smear of black and yellow into the horizon. "No."

She wasn't going to give him an inch. Not that he deserved one. "Seventeen years," he murmured. "Almost eighteen. I came back for you that same fall, just a few months after I left. But you'd already gone. You're a hard woman to find."

With a snap of the seat belt, she slid out of the Jeep and leaned her hips against the hood, her back to him. "I guess I didn't want to be found."

He followed suit, but hung back at his door. "So I gathered. Nobody at Rincon knew what had happened to you. Not even Tanya or Cole."

He, RaeAnne, Tanya Proudhomme and her cousin Colton Lonetree had been inseparable in high school. Cole was still his best friend. Roman had been floored when she hadn't kept in touch at least with Tanya.

"I wanted a clean break, after…everything. First you left, then Mom died."

Of their own volition, his legs carried him to her side. Her sad eyes pooled, and he had to physically restrain himself from reaching out to her. He could only imagine what she'd gone through at such a young age. Guilt scaled down his body like strips being flayed from his flesh.

"I heard about your mom. I'm sorry. She was a great lady."

A shudder racked through her, and she swiped at her eyes. "Yeah."

"You get married?" he asked, striving for a neutral voice. Inwardly preparing himself for the blow.

"What?" She glanced at him uncertainly.

"Your name's Martin now." He shrugged with false detachment, jamming his hands in his pockets. "I figured you'd gotten married."

She returned her gaze to the horizon. "Martin was my grandmother's maiden name. At seventeen it's easy to become someone else. There were few records, hardly anything to change, except the name on my college application."

Total, irrational relief swept through him. He had no business being glad she hadn't ever married. Just because he'd never found anyone else to fill her place in his heart…

"Well, you did a damn good job of disappearing. You could give the FBI lessons." He leaned his butt against the hood, too, feeling the heat of the engine through his leather pants. It had been a source of supreme frustration that he'd not been able to track her down. Over the years, he'd tried everything in the book, to no avail. She'd been thorough.

"How'd you find me?"

"High school reunion committee." The corner of his mouth lifted at the irony. It was always the most insignificant details that nailed the bad guys. And they'd caught her, too.

She stared at him, scandalized. "Reunion committee?"

"You requested high school transcripts last year. The secretary routinely sends names and addresses to the committee. The address was fake, but the name turned out to be real enough."

She took two strides away from the Jeep and let out a sigh. "Unbelievable."

"Was the thought of seeing me again so terrible?"

The silence stretched out so long he had plenty of time to brace himself for her answer. But it was still like being gut shot when she softly said, "Yes."

"I guess I deserved that."

"So, what was it that drove you away?" she said, chin lifting as she turned to face him. "Got tired of me? Or maybe there was another woman?"

"No! How could you— God, no." He took a step toward her, but she backed away. "There was no other woman. And you know I could never get enough of you."

"What, then? What did I do to deserve you leaving like that?" She looked at him and his heart simply broke in two.

"Nothing," he whispered. "You did nothing. It was my—" He rubbed a hand over his face. "Do you remember that last night, when I dropped you off after—"

After the most incredible night of his life. The prom had ended hours earlier. It was nearly dawn and they'd spent the whole night—

Ruthlessly he cut off the memories. It would do him no good to go there. To recall the warmth of her body cradled against his, the smell of her hair fanning over pale shoulders in the moonlight, the crinkle of her stiff formal as it was crushed beneath—

Damn! He swallowed heavily and forced himself to go on. "After your prom."

She nodded at the ground between them, face awash in her own memories.

"Do you remember hearing about a car crash that night out on route 76?"

Her gaze slowly lifted and focused on his. "Yes. But what does that have to do with anything?"

"It was awful. I saw it happen. A car full of teenagers was hit by a drunk driver. Thank God they were okay, but the drunk guy was in bad shape. There was blood everywhere, and he was trapped, unconscious, hardly breathing. I could tell he needed help or he'd die."

"What did you do?"

"Broke out a window. Sliced my arms up pretty badly in the process, but I never even noticed, what with all the blood." He fingered the thin rope of a scar that cut clear across his forearm. "Pulled the guy out. Gave him mouth-to-mouth and CPR until the ambulance arrived."

"Did he live?"

"Yep." Roman's whole body went weightless, his vision tunneling to a single, spinning image of RaeAnne, much as it had that night, when he'd learned—

"I don't understand. Why are you telling me this? What did it have to do with us?"

"He had AIDS, RaeAnne. They told me at the hospital, the man was dying of AIDS."

RaeAnne stood there, feeling like a jackrabbit in a flash flood. Deluged by unexpected emotions, bombarded with unforeseen confusion. A thousand times she had played this scene with Roman in her mind, and in not one of them had she ever imagined this explanation.

"Do you— Are you—" The words leaped out, her immediate distress over his health overriding all else.

"No." He shook his head, almost reluctantly. "It's a miracle, but I'm still testing negative."

"Thank God." Her profound relief belied every homicidal thought she'd ever entertained about him...and over the years there had been many. If only she had known....

That's when the anger began to percolate through her. Slowly at first, then overwhelming in its speed and extent.

"*Cara,* wait—"

His hand reached out, but she shrank from his touch, and from the sound of his favorite endearment, adopted from an old Italian movie they'd seen together. Her anger was like a living thing, consuming in its outrage the brief moment of horror and sympathy she'd felt for him.

"You *bastard!* Why didn't you tell me?"

"I couldn't—"

"Couldn't what? Be honest? Be fair? Give me a chance to support you? Or at least a chance to say goodbye!"

"Baby, I—"

She slapped him. She'd never raised a hand to a living creature in her life, but it just burst out of her like an explosion.

"Don't you *dare* 'baby' me, Roman Santangelo." The word almost choked in her throat, so great was the pain it caused her to say it. "You have no idea what you did by walking away."

"Rae—"

Spinning on her heel, she stalked to the Jeep. "Get in." Barely giving him time to jump in, she jerked it into gear and tore down the highway toward Big Pine. "Of all the selfish, arrogant..."

"I thought I was a dead man, Rae. Worse, I thought if I saw you again, you'd be dead, too."

"That's ridiculous."

"I know that now. But in the mid-eighties, nobody really knew what caused AIDS or how you got it. I was sure if I so much as kissed you, you'd be infected."

She rolled her eyes.

"How could I say goodbye without kissing you? Or touching you? I couldn't face it. Couldn't face the pity in your eyes. Couldn't face what others would think of me. Couldn't put you through it all. It just seemed better to disappear."

"It wasn't."

"Yeah. I figured that out pretty quickly. But by the time I did it was too late. Only six months, but you'd already left."

She'd often imagined him filled with regrets and remorse, going back to Rincon to find her. And instead, finding her gone without a trace. She'd savored that thought. She'd worked hard at not leaving a trail, and for eighteen years it had paid off.

So why did the triumph of her success taste so bitter now?

"You should have trusted me," she said, stubbornly clinging to that bitterness.

"I know. Can you ever forgive me?"

Suddenly everything was all mixed up, upside down. She didn't know what to think anymore. She remembered those first, scary days of AIDS—the fear, the prejudice, the myths. Could he really have had a justified reason for abandoning her the way he had? Not to her—for her, nothing would *ever* justify what he'd done. But maybe to himself?

No. She refused to consider that possibility. It would mean she understood. It would mean she had to forgive him. And that was one thing she could never do. Because of the baby.

But there was no time now to dwell on the past. More immediate concerns loomed, such as salvaging her career. She skidded into a parking spot at the Big Pine tribal offices and grabbed her purse. Roman shadowed closely behind as she shot through the door. No sign of either Toby or the boxes. Great.

"Was Toby Benson just here?" she asked the receptionist, taking pains to be polite, despite her inner roiling.

"I'm not allowed to give out that kind of information," the woman informed her.

Politeness flew out the window. "Look, a bunch of—"

Roman grasped her arms and gently set her aside. She sputtered a protest, but he commandeered the receptionist's attention by introducing himself in the Indian way, giving the names of his people as well as his own, and letting her know he was born here at Big Pine. When he mentioned Hector Santangelo was his father, the woman's eyes widened. Even after thirty years, the name of the local hero made an impression.

As Roman explained the situation and schmoozed his way into the receptionist's good graces, instead of the gratitude she should be feeling for his help, RaeAnne only felt even more angry.

Roman had no right to waltz back into her life and take over like this. Philip O'Donnaugh regularly barged into her life and took over, too. It annoyed her to no end. She'd thought it was just because he was a sheriff and used to taking charge. Apparently not. What was it with men, anyhow, that they all thought women were helpless?

It was *her* dig that had been sabotaged and *her* artifacts that had been stolen. She was perfectly capable of handling the situation herself.

"Excuse me…"

The receptionist ignored her, bestowing a smile on Roman. "I'm really not supposed to say anything," she said in a confidential hush, "but since you're one of us, I guess it's all right to tell you. When the boys came in earlier, I called the Tribal Chairman and he felt this was a matter for the Board of Trustees. The boxes of artifacts have been taken there."

"To Bishop?" RaeAnne groaned. "If anything is broken, I'm holding the tribe responsible."

"Thanks very much," Roman said as he ushered her toward the door. "We appreciate the information. Come on, let's go."

RaeAnne did not look forward to driving another fifteen miles to the Bishop Reservation where the Paiute-Shoshone

Board of Trustees' offices were located. Not with Roman
filling up the Jeep with his...with his...obnoxiously compelling presence. His legs were so long his knees crammed
into the bottom of the dashboard. His damn shoulders were
so broad they barely fit in the small confines of the front seat.

He'd always had ridiculously broad shoulders. At a traffic
signal she shifted gears, accidentally bumping up against
him, and was thrown headlong into the memory of the very
first time she'd bumped up against those broad shoulders.

It had been on a school bus, on a field trip. Roman was
late as usual, the last to climb onboard, and the only seat left
was next to her. She could still feel the burning of her cheeks
as he'd slid in beside her, delivering one of his meltingly
sexy smiles as his shoulder brushed hers. It was one of those
perfect, elusive moments a young girl lived for. Her heart
beat wildly, and she could scarcely believe her luck. Her
complete and utter thrall must have shown on her face, for
he'd turned and looked at her then, for the very first time
really looked at her. And for the remainder of the trip his
shoulder had rested nonchalantly against hers, quietly sending her into a paroxysm of young girl's fantasies.

All of which had come true.

"Don't worry, we'll get them back."

Roman's words startled her out of the memory, and for a
moment she grappled with a stinging disappointment that he
wasn't talking about lost fantasies.

"I've got my doubts," she mumbled, the artifacts the least
of her worries. What she really wanted back was her righ-
teous fury. The fury that had given her the strength to get
through the past eighteen years. Where had it suddenly gone?
There was no way she'd be able to deal with Roman without
it. Without the fury, there was only pain. Pain, and shattered
fantasies.

Roman and RaeAnne managed to make it to the Board of
Trustees' offices on the Bishop Reservation without drown-
ing in the silence, but to Roman it felt like the punishing

silence of the condemned. He'd surely been tried and convicted in her mind, and this was the sentence. Eternal silence.

She'd never forgive him. This whole idea had been folly. He didn't know what he'd been thinking. He let out a soundless snort. If it had been *her* who'd run out on *him,* would he accept such a lame excuse? Would he ever forgive her? Just because she asked?

In a heartbeat.

He sighed. Big tough FBI agent. Able to haul down the bad guys and take a beating without blinking, but one woman's wordless judgment sends him to his knees. What a wuss.

As they parked and walked up the sidewalk, he fought the urge to grab her and pull her into his arms. Demand she listen. Somehow convince her of his unbounding repentance and contrition. He stuck his hands into his pockets and glanced over at her.

She was still so beautiful it made his throat ache. Others might think her straw-colored hair too plain and unruly, but to him it was a mass of spun sunshine, making his fingers itch to sift through its golden drifts. And her body. The lithe, subtle curves that had sent him into countless throes of rapture as an insatiable youth had matured into the lush and alluring body of a woman. Watching her walk, hips gently swaying in her tight jeans, breasts bouncing softly under her T-shirt, made his fingers itch in a completely different way— one he hadn't felt in years.

Whoa, boy, don't even think about it, he sternly admonished himself. All he needed to do to blow any chance he might have left was to come on to her sexually. That would be a brilliant move. Not.

"So, I suppose you want to do it again?" she said as they approached the front door.

His head jerked up. "Huh?"

His thoughts must have been written all too plainly on his face, for a blush ripped over hers and she quickly looked away.

They had always been totally in sync with each other, knowing instinctively what the other was thinking. Not that there'd been a huge variety of topics. After about age fifteen, they'd been pretty well confined to one.

Some things never changed.

She cleared her throat. "I meant, you'll want to take charge again."

He couldn't help smiling as the blush deepened.

"In the office." Her fluster further increased, but she put an end to it by rolling her eyes. "Tell you what, this time I'll do the talking." She reached for the door.

"Wait. I—" Before he realized what he was doing, he grasped her hand and brought it to his lips. "Oh, *cara.* What can I do? Tell me what to do to make this all better."

"Help me get my artifacts back," she said. "And then—"

She stopped short of saying it, but he knew the words she'd been about to say. "Go away?"

"That would be best."

She said it with such firm conviction he thought maybe she wasn't just trying to convince him, but herself as well. For the first time since the day he'd talked to the high school reunion committee, he felt a glimmer of hope.

"Will you forgive me before I leave?"

She looked away, her expression going fragile. She shivered, as if a chill wind had swept down from the glaciers glittering on the mountains above them. "I don't know," she murmured, and went through the door.

She was holding up pretty well, Roman thought as he watched RaeAnne pace back and forth. All things considered.

Toby and the gang had thrown the place into a bit of a commotion with their arrival and transfer of the stolen boxes. The Board of Trustees wasn't used to dealing with this kind of thing. Their main function was to consider issues that impacted native people in the whole Owens Valley—economic development and broad political questions—not small-time archaeological digs or rogue teenagers trying to flex their cultural muscles. Archaeological concerns were generally dealt with on a state level, or even federally, such as with the Smithsonian's ongoing talks on the subject.

Still, Roman knew firsthand that academics digging up human remains struck a mighty sore spot with most Indian people, so he wasn't surprised that the Board Chairman was reluctant to turn the boxes back over to RaeAnne. And certainly not without very careful consideration by the whole Board. There would be far-reaching local political implications regardless of what they chose to do.

Roman and RaeAnne were waiting for the Chairman to contact the rest of the Board, to see when that meeting might take place. She was hoping for this afternoon. Roman knew better. However, he wasn't about to say anything to annoy her any more than she already was.

The Chairman's office door opened and the distinguished-looking older man appeared. Immediately RaeAnne turned to him, anxious impatience sparking in her eyes, but to her credit, she didn't jump all over him with questions. She waited as he handed a small sheaf of papers to his secretary and spoke a few low words to her, then approached them in an unhurried manner.

"Have you made a decision?" she asked nervously.

"There is one more member I must speak with," he said, his voice pleasant and melodic. "He is a salesman and travels."

"Okay," RaeAnne replied uncertainly. "Any idea when that might happen?"

The older man gave her a smile. "I will keep trying."

She exhaled. Roman felt a touch of pride when she didn't give vent to her irritation, but just said, "Thank you. I know you're very busy."

The Chairman then turned to him, pinning him with a considering gaze. "Roman Santangelo, I would speak with you."

With that he headed back to his office, giving Roman little

choice but to follow. He lifted his palms at RaeAnne, who looked none too happy about being excluded.

"I knew your father," the Chairman began when Roman had taken a seat opposite the desk nameplate that said Robert Campanelli, Paiute Tribal Chairman. "A long time ago."

So that's what this was about. His father. Roman made an effort not to look pained. He just nodded and accepted a small cup of coffee.

The old man studied him for a long while, so Roman took the opportunity to do a little studying of his own. The Chairman's silver hair was even longer than Roman's, but unlike his, was caught in a meticulously braided ponytail which hung down his flannel-shirted back. He wore jeans, clean and well-pressed. The sun pouring in through the window glinted off the polish on his black cowboy boots.

Finally, after each had taken measure of the other, the old man said, "It embarrasses you to be your father's son."

"No." It wasn't embarrassment Roman felt, it was shame.

All right, maybe a little embarrassment, too. Over reaping the lifelong benefits of having a hero for a father, when in reality the man was nothing but a common murderer. If he had to sit through another long recitation of Hector Santangelo's bravery and invaluable contributions to the American Indian Movement he might just have to be sick.

Luckily, the Chairman seamlessly changed the subject. "About these artifacts." He leaned back in his buckskin-covered office chair and motioned at a stack of cardboard boxes piled neatly against the wall. "What's your interest in them?"

The old guy watched him like a hawk. His eyes were sharp as an eagle's, and his nose bent in an elegant hook, giving his face an air of authority and distinction. This was not a man to be trifled with.

"I have no personal interest in the artifacts," Roman said. "But I grew up with RaeAnne, and she would do nothing to disrespect our heritage. If she says these are not Indian remains, they are not Indian remains. I would think twice about letting a hotheaded boy turn this into a high-profile political battle. My opinion is that this is not the time to stand and fight.''

The Chairman inclined his head. ''I will consider what you say. In the meantime, I suggest you take your lady home. I doubt there will be a decision this afternoon. You can call later to find out when we'll be meeting.''

Roman thought briefly of breaking his cover and telling the Chairman of his affiliation with the FBI. He could easily claim jurisdiction and confiscate the boxes on FBI authority. But he'd rather not have that come out. His next quest would be difficult enough without everyone knowing he worked for what most Indian people felt was the enemy.

''I doubt there's a phone at the dig, but we'll drop by later to find out what's happening,'' he said, easing out of his chair.

As they exchanged final pleasantries, the older man captured his gaze. ''Sometimes people and situations are not what they appear to be, even to the firmest believer. The truth is always there for us to find, if we just open our eyes. But beware, the truth can be dangerous.''

Roman could only hope the Board would see the truth of this particular situation, and do the right thing to keep RaeAnne out of any more danger from reckless teenage boys.

But as they stepped into the outer room, a nagging feeling came over him, that the old man wasn't referring to RaeAnne and her artifacts at all. Still, what else could he possibly be talking about?

RaeAnne stopped pacing when she saw them emerge. He could tell she was burning up with curiosity, but again she said nothing.

''I will speak with you later, then.''

''Yes. Thanks again for your help.'' Roman shook the Chairman's hand, then casually put his arm around RaeAnne. She stiffened, but didn't protest. Not until he'd led her outside.

She slid out from under his arm. ''What was that for?''

"Show of solidarity, personal connection. United front and all that."

She eyed him warily. "And are we? A united front?"

"God, I hope so." He pushed out a breath. "I'm taking a leap of faith, here, Rae, that you're the same ethical, principled woman you were when I knew you."

She bristled. "Of course I am. If anything—"

He held up his hands. "I never doubted it, or I wouldn't just have put myself way out on a limb for you."

She halted before climbing into the Jeep. "You did? What did the Chairman want?"

Good question. "Let's drive."

"Okay, give," she shouted a few minutes later, undaunted by the noisy rush of the wind as the open Jeep sped along the highway.

He looked over at her and was simply mesmerized. Backdropped by a blurry green streak of roadside vegetation and a frame of faded red metal, her blond hair whipped around her face in a tangle of curls and strands. A small frown marred her forehead, but otherwise she was the picture of confidence. He'd always liked that about her—that she took life by the horns and dealt with it head-on. No artifice. No whining. Just pure competence wrapped in a bone-deep femininity that had nothing to do with batting eyelashes or ploys of helplessness. A femininity all the more seductive because of her strength.

"He knew my father," he shouted back.

The frown disappeared. "You're kidding! That's great! I mean, it is, isn't it? He'll cut us a break then, right?"

Roman shrugged, savoring the little spin of joy her use of the word 'us' set off in his heart. Trying hard not to let his ambivalence about his father ruin the moment. "I suppose."

"What's wrong?" Again, that instinctive knowing.

"A while back I found out some things about my father."

"What kind of things?"

"Things I wish I hadn't found out."

There was a pause while she digested that. His fateful discoveries had come well after she'd left Rincon. "You want to talk about it?"

It was just like her to ask, despite the strain between them. And he'd wanted to talk about it forever. The only ones who knew the truth were himself and the FBI. And his mother, of course, who'd been the one to tell him. She'd held the awful secret in her heart all that time since his father had had to disappear, back when Roman was just six. She'd told him his father was dead. Everyone thought he was dead. A dead hero.

Yeah, Roman had wanted to talk about it. Talk to Rae-Anne, whom he could tell everything and know she'd understand. Comfort him. Hold him in her arms and rock him until the hurt dulled and the betrayal didn't seem like it would kill him. But he'd driven her away from all she'd known and loved, and had no right to claim her comfort now.

"Maybe someday."

She nodded and fell silent for the rest of the trip back to Cleary Hot Springs. They approached the cabin, and he spotted the Harley lying on its side in the dirt, his black leather jacket draped over it like a cloth covering a dead victim.

"So," she said, following his gaze, "you'll be leaving now."

Something in the way she said it made him reply, "No."

He hadn't meant to say no. He'd realized in the first minute forgiveness wasn't in the cards. He should leave now, before he got even more drawn into this stupid artifact thing with the Chairman—a man who made him distinctly uncomfortable. And especially before he got more involved with RaeAnne.

"What do you mean, no?"

"I promised we'd both go back later to see what the Board decides. I'll stay till then."

The frown came back with a vengeance. "I don't think that's a good idea."

"Me, neither. But I'm doing it anyway."

"All right. Fine," she said, a muscle jumping in her cheek. "But don't expect me to entertain you. I've got work to do."

She disappeared into the cabin and he went to take care of the bike. He raised it and wheeled it to a spot in back of the cabin, hidden from view, where he lovingly checked it for bumps and bruises. After a long moment of indecision, he lifted his pack and bedroll from the back of the seat and headed round front. The Sierras were notorious for sudden afternoon squalls, and he'd just as soon keep his kit dry.

"Rae?"

He stuck his head in the cabin door, but the room was empty. He slipped in, set his things against a wall and looked around. It was ancient, but neat and as clean as a hundred-year-old stone cabin could get. One room served as kitchen, living room and bedroom. But before he could investigate further, his astonished gaze landed on the full-size bed taking up an entire corner. It was covered by a beautiful Navajo blanket. The one he'd bought for her.

He closed his eyes against the deluge of memories that flooded through him, seeing it there on her bed. Memories of the soft scratchy feel of the rough weave on his bare skin, of the musky scent of natural wool mixed with the sweet perfume of young love. Of the first time he'd peeled away her clothes, inch by torturous inch, to reveal a sight that had awed and humbled him, and filled him with a jumble of tumultuous, tender emotions that had completely undone his sham of youthful male worldliness.

Emotions he'd only experienced with her.

"What are you doing?"

Her suspicious demand tried to rock him out of the old feelings. Tried, and failed. He turned to look at her in the doorway, and all he could think of was that he wanted to kiss her. He wanted to kiss her so badly his whole body ached with it.

Unbidden, his feet started across the warped and uneven heart pine floor, toward her. Just once before he left, he had to touch her. Feel his lips on hers. Taste her.

Just one more time. Before he left her forever.

Chapter 3

Roman advanced on RaeAnne for the second time in as many hours. Blind panic seized her in its icy grip. *Ohlord-ohlord-ohlord.* He was going to kiss her.

She couldn't move, she couldn't think. Couldn't do anything at all except watch him get closer and closer, his intent written all over his handsome face.

If she could have found her voice she would have screamed loud and long against his impudence. But it eluded her. The best she could manage as his hands reached out and cradled her cheeks and his face lowered to hers was a mute whimper of protest. Or maybe of bliss.

His lips met hers as softly as a sigh. They hovered there, barely touching her, as the taste and feel of him whispered through her like the haunting of an old, familiar ghost. She wanted to press herself into him, relive every angle, every muscle, every secret hollow of his hard male flesh. But she didn't dare move.

Trembling, she breathed in the seductive smell of him, bubbles of yearning bursting in every cell of her body.

Bliss. Definitely bliss.

The pressure of his lips increased infinitesimally and his chest brushed against hers. Her nipples hardened in ardent recognition, and her heart beat wildly. Just as it had the first time he'd kissed her.

She'd been fourteen, her body blossoming, along with scary, exciting new feelings. They'd been at a football game, strolling under the bleachers toward the snack booth, when he'd looked down and stopped her with a dark, smoldering gaze. And suddenly she'd known. Her best friend, the remarkable boy who'd teased her and taught her how to fish, who'd taunted when she cried at Hallmark commercials and driven her crazy dating girls his own age, had known all along how she felt about him, and felt exactly the same way about her.

And then he'd kissed her. Right there, in front of Tanya and Cole and half the kids in their high school. He'd taken her face in his hands and kissed her, just as tenderly as he was doing now. And her heart had melted completely. She'd known then they were meant to be together. Known with the conviction and naiveté of the young and innocent that they were destined to go through life as best friends and faithful lovers.

That kiss had changed everything.

And this kiss was fast threatening to do the same.

It was crazy. She was being stupid and gullible. *And what about Philip?* But she couldn't pull away. Not just yet. It was the gentlest, most tender, poignant kiss she'd ever been gifted with. Roman's lips brushed over hers, back and forth, back and forth, softly rekindling fires that had lain dormant, deep inside, since the last time he'd swept over her like wildfire.

What was she doing? She had to stop. Not just because of Philip, but for her own sake. This had to stop!

As if he heard her inner plea for sanity, he stopped. He lifted his mouth, taking the warmth of the day with him.

Her soul cried out with loss, craving the heat and the love

this incredible man had once shown her. He gazed into her eyes, and in them she saw pain, confusion and hunger.

It was the hunger that finally stirred some sense back into her—a hunger she herself had been running from for such a long, long time.

She'd found him inside the cabin staring at her Navajo blanket, no doubt shocked to see she'd kept it. She almost hadn't. She'd gotten as far as accepting a hefty check from a Los Angeles collector before she'd realized there was no way in hell she could give it up. It had then taken years of purposefully lying beneath its heavy warmth to purge the memories it held. To be able to fall asleep without picturing some random adventure or milestone they'd shared together, with it spread beneath them. Or fingering the small, nearly invisible addition giving him her virginity had left upon its design.

She should have gotten rid of the accursed blanket when she'd had the chance.

"Cara—"

"I have to get back to work," she said past the lump in her throat and turned, making herself walk calmly down the cabin steps and across the meadow, toward the spot where she was currently digging. Away from him and that damned blanket.

Except he followed her. Hands in his pockets, he watched as she collected her tools and buckets from the giant plastic storage bin she kept at the works, and hopped two feet down into the pit of unit 27G.

To the untrained eye, 27G probably looked like just some hole in the ground—rather like an open grave, except perfectly square—its dirt bottom reluctantly yielding up its old debris. But to her, it was beautiful. With carefully scraped, plumb-to-the-millimeter sides and a bricklayer-level floor, 27G had already yielded up a gold mine of fascinating and useful finds and information. RaeAnne only hoped she'd get G's artifacts back soon, along with all the rest.

She tamped down a spurt of renewed anger at Toby for

his misguided cultural "rescue" and gingerly knelt down in the bottom of the square. Pointedly ignoring Roman, who was peering down at her from behind the taut guide string that marked the perimeter of the unit, she began working. She could easily take the floor down another five or ten centimeters in depth before they had to leave for Bishop again.

She hadn't gotten in more than a dozen careful strokes of her small mason's trowel when he remarked, "I'd never have guessed."

She supposed it was too much to ask that he be quiet. It was tough to stay mad at him, or afraid of him, when he was being so agreeable, trying so hard to be repentant.

She stifled a sigh and said, "Guessed what?"

"You as an archaeologist."

She scooped up a spadeful of dirt and carefully deposited it in a waiting bucket. "No?"

"Nope. The last thing I'd figure you to be doing was troweling in the dirt for old Indian artifacts."

"Is this a test?" she drawled. "I told you, Cleary isn't an Indian site, it's—"

"You know what I mean."

"Do I?" She added another scoop of dirt.

"Sure. You hated history class. You were always too full of life and anticipation over the future to be concerned with the past."

He was right. In the old days, there'd been plenty of living people and their artifacts around Rincon—things like books and suntan lotion and wedding dresses and strollers—that nobody'd felt the need to dig up dead ones. Least of all her. That didn't come till later.

"When did it change?"

She sat back on her haunches and looked up at him. His expression was casual, but his eyes peered out from behind all the mild curiosity, begging for absolution.

"Why don't you make yourself useful and sift this dirt," she suggested, and handed up the bucket she'd filled, rather than get into a discussion she'd prefer to avoid. He was leaving in a few hours and the whole thing would be pointless. How could she explain all that had happened to set her on the path she was now traveling down? Why would she even want to?

She was grateful when he didn't push it, the momentary flicker of bleak disappointment in his eyes disappearing at record speed beneath a chortled moue of distaste.

"Sift dirt? Me?" He held the bucket gingerly.

She grinned. "I thought you liked getting dirty."

"I seem to recall a slightly different definition," he retorted, eyeing the bucket. "Oh, all right. What do I do?"

She showed him how to work the simple but cranky wooden frame screen that sorted small artifacts and debris into three graduated sizes. After filling a few more buckets and sifting them, together they picked through the chunks of dirt, rocks and other things remaining in the screens, and she taught him what to look for—anything made of metal, bone, ceramic, glass, charcoal, flint, or other materials possibly utilized by the people living there in the past.

"Good grief, you're not really saving all this old garbage?" he asked, holding up a Ziploc filled with charred bone.

"Yep." She was used to people thinking all archaeologists did was hunt for valuable treasure or unearth burials. "Believe it or not, this so-called garbage is much more informative than a hoard of gold coins."

"Get out."

She laughed at his incredulous look. "Okay, so maybe it's not as exciting...."

"Now there's an understatement." He poured a handful of broken crockery into another bag and zipped it.

"But seriously. Even the tiniest thing can have a story to tell. The bones tell us what the people ate, whether they hunted or had domestic animals, even the season they occupied the site. A single button can date a whole layer or group of finds that are found with it. And that's not even counting the Indian artifacts which can be stylistically identified and dated. Lots of good stuff comes from garbage.''

''Huh. No kidding.'' He studied the growing pile of bags with new respect. She just loved it when she made a convert.

''That's why we don't throw anything away. It could turn out to be important. Everything is separated by category into zipper bags, carefully labeled as to where it was found, and placed in a cardboard box for later analysis in the lab.''

''I'm beginning to see why you're so upset about those boxes.''

He looked around at the dozen or so square units scattered over the meadow and hillside which she'd already excavated, and she could see him mentally assessing the potential amount of data which would be lost if she didn't get them back. She didn't have to say a word. She just smiled, relieved that he truly understood.

''The kid mentioned skeletons. What's the deal with them?''

She grimaced, her instinctive reflex at the subject. ''I like to avoid them, myself. Finding human remains always causes a whole lot of trouble, and I'm not really interested in them anyway. My main focus is settlement patterns and use. Most often graves are marked or recognizable, so it's not a problem. If I run into human bones by accident, though, I usually cover them right back up and pretend I never saw them.'' She glanced covertly over her shoulder and winked. ''But don't tell the cops. That's slightly illegal.''

He suddenly started coughing. ''Illegal?''

She slapped him on the back a couple of times and shrugged. ''Technically, I'm supposed to report it to the authorities.''

He was still wheezing, but choked out, ''Don't worry. You're secret's safe with me. So why did you excavate the skeleton this time?''

She puffed out her cheeks in a long breath. ''No choice. It's the way I got the grant to work this site. I'm supposed to finally solve…'' she dropped into a dramatic Vincent Price voice with gestures to match "…the mystery of Cleary Hot Springs. God, what a stroke of genius that was. *Not.*"

He held her hand as she lowered herself carefully back into G to finish up the last corner.

"The mystery of Cleary Hot Springs?" His brow hiked.

"I'm sure you've heard the old tale. Eighteen forty-eight. Two brothers, Jake and Crawford Edisto, come to California to find their fortune, and somehow make a wrong turn and end up lost with two mules and a floozy on the wrong side of the Sierra?"

He shook his head, so she went on, "Crawford winds up dead with a bullet in his back, in this very meadow, and Jake turns up a year later very much alive, very rich, and with a very ambitious but suspiciously flashy wife."

"So what's the mystery?"

"The mystery is that the mother, who comes to claim the body, insists to her dying day that the dead guy isn't her son. Of course, it took her months to get word and come west from the old homestead in South Carolina to identify him." She wrinkled her nose.

"No refrigeration in those days."

"Hell, there wasn't even a morgue in those days, not out here anyway. It was winter, though, thank goodness."

"Why was she so sure he was the wrong guy?"

Holding out her hand she demonstrated a decent facsimile of a Vulcan greeting, except using only her little finger. "Crawford had a cotton gin accident when he was a boy. Left his right pinkie sticking straight out. Course, who could tell, the state the body was in."

"Yikes. No dental records, I suppose."

"Uh-uh."

"And I'm guessing these philanthropists who are financing your excavation expect you to find the real son buried here somewhere, along with evidence as to who shot him."

She nodded, pulling at the collar of her T-shirt. "It sounded like a good idea at the time. I mean, who would have given me eight thousand dollars to dig up a few hundred pounds of bone, rock and broken pottery shards?''

''Nobody in their right mind, I expect.''

She glared at him. Then they both burst into laughter. ''No, I guess not.''

''So what happened to the floozy?''

''I suspect it's her great-great-granddaughter who signed my grant check. But of course the family records omit that little historical tidbit.''

He groaned. ''It's the *descendants* who are financing the dig?''

'''Fraid so.''

''And now the Owens Valley Paiute Board of Trustees has Great-great-granduncle Crawford in a cardboard box in their office.''

She tried not to giggle. She really did. But the whole situation was just too weird for words. And if she didn't laugh, she just might cry. ''An interesting twist, huh?''

He shook his head, chuckling. ''Only you, Rae. Only you.''

She grinned back. ''It's a gift.''

He took the final bucket from her, set it down and hauled her up out of the pit and into his arms. ''God, I've missed you.''

Over the past hours they had slipped back into their genial camaraderie so easily and quietly, she'd never even noticed when they'd become friends again. It was scary how right it felt to be held in his embrace, secure and protected. Cherished. Why was it never like this when Philip held her?

''Every day of every year,'' Roman's deep voice whispered in her ear, ''I've kicked myself over what I did. Over leaving you like that.''

She found herself leaning into him, soaking up the feelings she missed so much, wishing she could stay just like this until his soothing words made the past eighteen years fade away completely. Wishing like hell things had been different.

But they hadn't.

She pulled back. "I don't know what to say, Roman."

Yes, she did. She knew exactly what he wanted to hear. He'd run her to ground and come for her forgiveness, so he could move on with his life, guilt-free, without the weight of his thoughtless actions dragging him back to the past.

Well, she wasn't ready to forgive him. Not yet. How could she forgive him when she hadn't even forgiven herself? He didn't know the whole truth, but she wasn't about to blurt out something like that only to have him leave her again.

Perhaps if he were willing to stay, to really talk about it, help her through the misery, maybe then they'd both be able to heal... But he wasn't willing to take the time. He'd made that clear.

His somber face spoke volumes. "I understand. I do, *cara*. I just wish—"

She touched her fingertip to his lips, preventing the words from being spoken. Words that would only break both their hearts. "We both do. But that won't help. You can't just roar back into my life on your Harley, apologize and roar back out expecting everything to go back to the way it was before."

"I wasn't planning to roar back out," he refuted hotly.

"No?"

His guilty expression spoiled the denial. "Well, not permanently. I have things to do at the moment but—"

"You'll keep in touch, right?"

"This time I will."

"Uh-huh."

"I swear."

"I'm sure you do."

"You don't believe me." Hands on hips, he regarded her for a long moment. "All right. Do you want me to stay?"

She felt the hairs raise on her scalp and a stinging heat settle in her cheeks. *Be careful what you wish for....*

Oh, Lord, what should she say? That yes, ever since the day she'd woken up and found him gone, she'd dreamed he would seek her out and ask that very thing? Or no, no, no!

She'd finally gotten her life together—she'd landed a new job in a new city, and had a new man who seemed fond of her even if she didn't see stars when he walked into the room. There was no place in her life now for Roman Santangelo. No matter how confused he made her. There was simply no place for him.

"No, you can't stay," she said. "Even if you meant it, it's impossible."

"Why?"

She couldn't read him. His older, more street-wary face had learned to keep secrets, something he'd never done with her before. "Does it really matter why?"

"It matters. I screwed up once with you, RaeAnne, and I'm not about to do it again because I didn't stop to listen."

The thought of someone listening to what she had to say— really listening—was so novel, she gazed up at him, wondering if she was about to make the biggest mistake in her life by sidestepping the question.

"I'm involved," she said.

And that was that. Philip O'Donnaugh might not make her heart sing quite as loudly as Roman once had, but the local sheriff was kind and handsome—and a fourth generation Inyo County resident. His dad had been sheriff here for twenty years before him. Philip would never, ever pull up stakes and leave town in the middle of the night.

In all her years working as a gypsy dig-bum she'd come to realize that she missed the stability, security and roots having a real home gave a person. That's what she wanted now, and she aimed to get it. She didn't know yet if Philip was the right man, but she was determined to find out. To finally give herself a chance at happiness. And one thing was certain, the right man was *not* some motorcycle-riding outlaw who breezed in and out of her life on a whim.

"I see," Roman said, still standing there with his hands on his hips. "I see." Then his face shuttered down like venetian blinds snapping shut. "You should have said something."

"You were only staying for a few hours. It didn't come up and I didn't see the need to mention it."

"I wouldn't have kissed you."

Pain zinged through her heart. "Well, I'm glad you did," she quietly said, and began gathering up her tools and artifact bags.

"Rae, I only meant—"

"I know. You were being honorable." She tossed the buckets and trowels into the big plastic bin and thumped the lid closed with deliberate composure.

"There's something wrong with that?"

"Of course not."

What was wrong with *her?* Did she think she was so irresistible he'd risk censure and dishonor just to taste her lips again? Sweep her off her feet, try to change her mind, even knowing she was involved with someone else? *Get real, lady.* Roman might *look* like a pirate these days, but his kiss had hardly been wild passion demanding release. More of a peace offering.

Which was fine. Really.

"If we're going to make it to Bishop before the Board closes we'd better wash up," she said. "The hot springs are just up the hillside. I'll go first, then show you where they are."

Soaking in the volcanic springs for which Cleary had been named usually soothed RaeAnne, body and soul. But not today. She didn't worry about Roman walking in on her—a man who wouldn't kiss an involved woman would surely not risk seeing her naked. She was more worried about why she sat there wishing he would.

Scolding herself for being disloyal to Philip, she quickly washed and got dressed.

"You have to use this special biodegradable soap," she explained as she led him up the narrow path to the hidden granite basin. "So we don't wreck the ecology of the stream below." She handed him the bar in its case.

He accepted it, juggling the clean clothes he'd gotten out

of his pack. When they arrived at the steaming pool, surrounded by ferns and wildflowers, canopied by sweet-smelling Jeffrey Pine, he whistled appreciatively. "Wow."

"Pretty amazing, isn't it?"

"Can't wait." He set his belongings on a rock and began to strip off his T-shirt. "I feel like a dust magnet."

She chuckled. "One of the joys of archaeology. After a day at the sifter, you look more like a coal miner than a scientist."

Roman agreed, inspecting the distinct demarcations on his arms and neck where the T-shirt had shielded them from the dirt.

"It'll wash off," she assured him with a smile, her gaze lingering on his muscled biceps and broad, bare chest. His man's body was even more beautiful than the boy's had been. He'd filled out in all the right places, and had still managed to stay lean and trim. A tingle of attraction tightened her throat.

"No fair," he murmured.

"What?" she said, unable to tear her eyes from the rippling bronze geography of his chest. A curl of desire spun lazily through her breasts.

"I didn't get to watch you."

"Huh?" Her eyes shot to his and she gave a little gasp. "Oh! I'm sorry, I'll—"

"No, stay."

She shook her head vigorously and turned. "No, I should—"

"What's his name?" he asked, and she froze. She didn't have to ask who he meant.

"Philip. Philip O'Donnaugh."

She heard a splash and then a sigh. "And you're engaged?"

"No."

"Going steady?"

"Not exactly," she hedged. "It's complicated." Though no more complicated than that she and Philip had dated casually since meeting a few months back, and he was pressing for more. She'd resisted up until now, but Roman didn't need to know that. She liked Philip and didn't want to blow her chances with him.

"You sleeping with him?"

Outraged, she whirled. Big mistake.

He was naked. Immersed in bubbling water up to his neck, but still fully visible.

"Th-that's none of your business!" she stammered, and spun back around.

Unfortunately the damage was done. Ribbons of longing shimmered through her body, the familiar excitement his nakedness had always triggered within her.

"None of your damn business," she repeated and fled down the path to the cabin.

She had to get hold of herself. She paced the uneven cabin floor grasping for control. She couldn't, wouldn't, let him do this to her. She'd known letting him stay would lead to disaster. But it was far worse than she'd imagined. She'd never thought her own body would be her worst betrayer.

He had to go. Now.

"As soon as we speak to the Chairman, you'll be leaving," RaeAnne stated as they piled into the Jeep.

It had taken the entire half hour he'd spent bathing to get her wits back. But she'd marshaled every ounce of willpower and succeeded in banishing her momentary foolishness.

"Absolutely."

"It's best that way."

"No doubt."

And since she'd succeeded in banishing her foolishness she risked a glance at him. "You've changed your hair." Instead of a river of black flowing over his shoulders, it was now slicked back in a severe ponytail. Even the peculiar braid over his ear had disappeared.

"More businesslike."

She smiled inwardly at his definition. He'd always looked

the part of a rebel, though he'd been the farthest thing from defiant...gentle, almost philosophical in his manner, even as a young boy. After washing up he'd changed into well-worn jeans and a plain white T-shirt, but the innocuous clothing only emphasized the image of a hungry wolf trying to pass as a sheep.

"Yes, much more businesslike," she agreed, and tried to relax. Just a few more minutes and he'd be gone. She could manage a few more minutes.

They arrived at the Board's offices just before closing time and hurried in. She could hardly contain her nervousness.

"Ah, Miss Martin, Mr. Santangelo," the Chairman greeted them and ushered them into his office. "I have good news for you."

"Thank goodness," she said, whooshing out a breath of relief. "You're returning my artifacts?"

"Yes. Well, some of them at any rate."

"Some of them?"

He nodded and gestured to a stack of boxes that was sitting next to the door. "After some discussion the Board felt it would not be in our best interest to keep the artifacts. However, we've already gotten many calls from the Indian community expressing their concern about the skeletal remains."

"I assure you."

He held up a hand. "Yes, I know. But you must understand our position. We have to be certain. Therefore we will turn over all human remains to our expert to determine who we are dealing with before deciding their disposition."

"Your expert?"

"Professor Marie Claire Cooper, at UC Berkeley."

RaeAnne had heard of Dr. Cooper, and knew her impeccable reputation as a forensic anthropologist. An analysis had to be done anyway, and the eminent Dr. Cooper's name on the report could only be a plus. "Okay, I have no problem with that."

"As for the other material, I have been authorized to release these eight boxes to Mr. Santangelo today. In the morning, the Board members will examine the contents of the remaining four and make their decision regarding them.''

She stared at the Chairman in disbelief. ''I don't understand.''

''They are the ones that contain the real historical artifacts. The ceramics, buttons and shell casings, the Native arrowheads and such.''

''Yes, I realize that,'' she said, tossing a distracted glance at the four boxes of her most valuable finds. ''But you said something about releasing the others to Mr. Santangelo. What did you mean?''

The Chairman walked around his desk and looked from one to the other. ''The Board feels the best interest of the tribe will be served if the artifacts are under Native supervision. Mr. Santangelo is Paiute.''

A slow horror crept up her spine. He couldn't possibly mean… It just wasn't possible! ''What exactly are you saying?''

''Quite simple. We will release the artifacts, but only if they remain under the personal protection and custody of Mr. Santangelo.''

Chapter 4

"Whoa! Wait a minute," Roman said, whipping to attention. "What was that?"

The Chairman couldn't tie him to this artifact deal. He had nothing to do with it.

The old man handed him an official inventory list and a pen. "It was my understanding Miss Martin's project has your full support."

"Yes it does, but—"

"You haven't helped her at the excavation?"

"Just today, as a friend. I'm not really connected—"

"That's not important," the Chairman vowed. "The main thing we're concerned with is that Indian interests are being protected. I trust you to do that."

"This is *outrageous*," RaeAnne sputtered, finding her voice. "Mr. Santangelo is not on the excavation team and has no authority whatsoever to take charge of anything on my behalf."

Not exactly true, he thought, thankful she'd preempted the debate so he could consider this newest mess. He thought of the FBI credentials tucked in his jeans pocket. What would happen if he pulled them out now?

He'd still end up in charge of the artifacts, but his cover would be blown. What would he gain by revealing his special agent status? Nothing, except the Chairman's, along with every other reservation resident's, mistrust. How would RaeAnne feel to learn he wasn't just some motorcycle bum blowing through, but a bona fide federal agent? God only knew. But he wasn't planning on finding out anytime soon. When he started searching for information on his father, the last thing he needed was to be identified as FBI.

"—giving him the authority," the Chairman was saying. "But I assure you, it's just a formality."

Roman folded his arms over his chest, trying to read between the lines. Was the Chairman urging him to accept the artifacts for RaeAnne's sake and then bow out if he wanted to? Just to give everyone a way to save face?

"I don't care if it is just a formality," RaeAnne shot back. "I won't stand for—"

"You realize of course that we must notify Toby Benson of our decision," the Chairman calmly stated, bringing RaeAnne's tirade to an abrupt halt. "Since he brought them in."

Roman came to full alert. "What's that supposed to mean?"

"Just another formality," the Chairman said, giving him a level gaze. "You might want to take some extra precautions tonight at your site. The boy's heart is in the right place, but he has a tendency to act before thinking things through."

"Fine. I'll lock my door. But that still doesn't give—"

"We'll be sure to take precautions," Roman interrupted, grabbing RaeAnne's arm and pulling her to the stack of boxes. "Tell him to see me if he has a problem with your decision. I'll straighten the kid out."

He picked up a box and dumped it into RaeAnne's arms. "Come on, let's get these loaded."

"You'll have to sign the inventory list," the Chairman said, handing him the papers.

"Sure." He hurriedly scrawled his signature, tore the carbon from the back and stuck it under the lid of the box RaeAnne carried. "Go." Hefting two more boxes, he herded her outside.

"If you think I'm going to put up with this, you're mistaken," she hissed out.

"It's not what I had in mind, either, but let's talk about it at the site."

"The whole thing is completely unacceptable," she said as they brought out the second load.

"Would you rather leave these here?" he asked.

"No," she grudgingly admitted. "But—"

"Then let's get the artifacts safely back where they belong. We'll pick up the rest tomorrow, then hopefully the Board'll forget all about me."

That seemed to mollify her enough to drive back to Cleary with things still up in the air. But she was not done steaming even after they'd returned to the cabin and finished stacking the boxes neatly in one corner.

"I can't believe the audacity of the Board. Making you caretaker of what's legally my responsibility!"

He let her rant on for several minutes about the unfairness of the situation while he stoked up the woodstove and put on a kettle of water.

She always did have a hot temper. She might have looked like a bookworm in high school, but he recalled making tea many a time in her mother's kitchen, listening to Rae go on and on about some injustice or another that was being perpetrated on either some other kid, or the school, or the world in general. She'd always been big on doing the right thing, sticking up for the underdog. It was one of the characteristics he admired most about her.

He watched her pace back and forth, gesturing angrily, and almost smiled. Such a beautiful, passionate warrior, his RaeAnne.

"Where's the tea?" he asked, before his mind could take him down *that* road. What he *didn't* need to be thinking about at the moment was passion.

"Huh? Oh, in that cupboard." She pointed, then went on as if he hadn't interrupted.

Oh, yeah, his little bookworm had been passionate. So passionate in every way it made his toes curl just remembering. And made him break out in a sweat wondering if she still was.

Definitely should not be thinking about passion.

"And if you think you'll be spending the night here with me, you've got another think coming," she said and glared at him.

Suddenly the room went absolutely still. Well, except for the blood pounding in his ears. *Spend the night with her?*

A flash flood of goose bumps spilled over him at the very thought. *Lord have mercy.*

"Tea?" he croaked, and pushed an enamel mug of hot mint at her, scrambling to get his brain jump-started and his hormones beaten back into submission. The room seemed to shrink around them so he could hardly breathe.

Without looking at him, she accepted the mug. Their fingers touched, sending an electric shock through him powerful enough to nearly jolt the cup from his hand.

"Damn," he swore, and spun to escape her wide eyes and flaming cheeks. And bumped his shins right into the big, blanket-covered bed.

"Of course. Philip will be coming," he said, grasping for a reason—any reason—not to pull her onto it and kiss her to within an inch of her life. And more. He turned his back on the bed, unable to bear the thought of some other man in it.

She shook her head. "No. He won't." If possible, her cheeks grew even redder. "I mean—"

So that's how things stood. He didn't know whether to jump for joy or jump on his bike and keep riding until his teeth rattled out of his skull.

"I have a sleeping bag," he said, clearing his throat. "I'll sleep on the porch."

"How about a motel?" She blanched. "It's still freezing at night."

"I'm not leaving you out here all alone. Not tonight. I'll be fine on the porch."

She licked her lips but didn't argue, backing away instead, putting much-needed distance between them. She suddenly seemed to notice the mug in her hands and took a sip. Her hands trembled and for the second time that day he had to stop himself from reaching out to her.

"*Cara*, nothing's going to happen here that you don't want to happen."

"I know," she whispered. "That's what I'm afraid of."

The words were spoken so softly he wasn't sure he hadn't imagined them.

But before he could react, her back straightened and her eyes cleared. "In the meantime, we'd better have dinner. Keep up our strength in case we have to defend ourselves against Toby and the gang tonight."

"He wouldn't dare."

"Oh, wouldn't he?" Her lips turned down wryly. "Toby's nothing if not persistent."

Roman strolled to the kitchen area and looked around. "I'll cook," he said. "It's the least I can do to make up for…everything."

Cooking would work. He needed the distraction. He needed something in his hands. Besides her. Pots and pans and spoons and spatulas were a hell of a lot less complicated.

"There's not much here. I do a lot of cans." At his wrinkled nose she chuckled. "Still the gourmet snob, I see. Well, I'm afraid preparing real food on a woodstove stretches my culinary abilities past their already meager limits."

"Ah," he said, eyeing the solid black contraption as he started opening cupboards. "I hadn't thought about that."

"Backing out, Santangelo?"

"Not a chance. But I guess the chocolate soufflé will have to wait."

She moaned. "Beast! You know how much I love your chocolate soufflé."

Smiling wistfully, he pulled out flour and baking powder from the cupboard. "I remember. I haven't made it in…a long time."

RaeAnne opened a bottle of wine while he stirred up some biscuits and put them to cook in a large iron frying pan. Eggs and peppers seemed to be the only fresh foods in the larder, so he settled on a very primitive western omelet as the entrée.

"So, tell me," she said, chin in hand as she watched him. "What have you been up to all these years?"

The question had been inevitable so he figured he'd play it for maximum shock value. Dishing up her half of the omelet, he said straight-faced, "I'm a special agent for the FBI."

She almost spit out her wine with a bark of laughter. "Yeah, sure." Her mirth faded at the look on his face. "God, you're serious!"

"Yep."

"But…but the Harley, the leather, your *hair!*"

Grinning at her astonishment, he savored the moment. Earlier he'd let it out of the ponytail, so it hung loose in all its glory. "You don't like my hair?"

"Well, it's, um, it's…inventive."

"Funny…women usually go for my hair."

Strange, but true. A lot of women had a thing for bad boys, and his image was definitely bad. One of the many reasons he avoided bars. Being a sex object had never appealed to him—not since he'd left RaeAnne, anyway.

"No accounting for taste," she muttered. "And the FBI puts up with it?"

"It was their idea. Helps my undercover work."

"That's what you do? Undercover?"

He nodded. "But I'm breaking about twenty-seven regulations by telling you."

"You're secret's safe with me."

"Now we're even."

She smiled, and his heart squeezed at the trace of sadness still in her eyes. No, they'd never be even. It had been naive to think she'd ever be able to forgive him. Foolish to think he'd ever be able to lift the melancholy from her eyes and make her truly happy.

"Eat up," he said, and drained his wineglass. "Then we need to talk about Toby."

She sighed. "I don't know what to do about that boy. I met him at the local high school when I gave a presentation on the project last month. He seemed so interested. So smart. I guess all he was really interested in was making trouble."

"Not necessarily. Indian kids have a lot of pressures placed on them from both sides—their own culture wanting them to preserve their heritage, and society in general wanting them to throw aside the old ways and assimilate into the mainstream. This might be Toby's way of working those things out in his head."

"Great. And I'm caught in the middle."

"You can handle it." He gave her a smile of encouragement. "Growing up on the rez gave you special insight. Use it and you'll be fine."

"Like you do, you mean?" She lifted a brow. "I can't believe you're an FBI agent. Your father would roll over in his grave."

Her words hit him like an unexpected fist in the gut and he had to clutch the edge of the table to stave off a wave of sick torment.

"As it turns out, my father is not dead." He pushed his plate savagely aside. "And it would be more likely he'd run for the hills."

She frowned, pausing with her fork halfway to her mouth. "Not dead?"

"As in still alive."

Roman lurched to his feet and cleared his dishes with a clatter, then swung open the door and leaned a shoulder against the frame, gulping down a lungful of the crisp, calming air. Damn, this was not what he wanted to talk about.

"Have you seen him?"

"No." He turned and jerked his head toward the hills. "Come on. I need some space. Show me your thinking spot."

She blinked. "How do you know I have one?"

"You always have one."

He was grateful when she didn't hesitate, but rose and fetched a puffy down jacket. "You should take yours, too. We can watch the site from there. Maybe Toby'll show up before we freeze to death."

"I'll bring the blanket," he said without thinking, and had it halfway off the bed before he noticed her staring at him in consternation. *Damn.* Still, he continued to fold the blanket, perversely unwilling to break their tradition. "Old habits die hard, I guess."

He saw her throat work, but she didn't comment, just grabbed her purse and keys. "Should we make some coffee to bring?"

He shook his head. "I've got something better." Pulling a flask and an unmarked bottle of clear liquid from his pack, he filled the silver flask with it. "Slivovitz. A friend of mine makes it in his basement."

She rolled her eyes. "You always did have the most bizarre taste in liquor. Should I bring a fire extinguisher?"

He winked. "Nah. If we catch on fire, a good roll in the blanket should do the trick."

Their eyes met. Hers narrowed, but the telltale throb of a vein in her flushed throat gave her away. Hell, the idea aroused her just as much as it did him. Every cell of his body crowed in triumph before he subdued his reaction.

Careful, compadre. He was taking off in the morning, and she didn't deserve to be loved and left.

Again.

That particular thought really dampened his ardor. He was a cad even to consider making love to her. It wouldn't be right. Especially with ol' what's-his-name Dann-o waiting in the wings to make an honest woman of her. A *happy,* honest woman.

He ground his teeth together, unable to bear the thought of *that,* either.

"Coming?" she asked, and walked out the door.

"Yeah," he mumbled, ignoring the sharp desire that roiled through him. *He wished.*

Damn, he had to get out of here before he drove himself crazy. He couldn't hope to make her happy even if he wanted to. The wariness in her eyes every time she looked at him sent the message loud and clear.

But even if he could get past that barrier, what kind of life could he offer her? He traveled all the time, was always embroiled in dangerous situations, and his only home was a room in his mother and stepfather's house that held his collection of books and music, and a few clothes. He saw his best friends three, maybe four times in a good year.

True, he'd saved and invested enough to buy a small island and retire. But he liked his life and his job. He didn't want to retire.

Suddenly, as he climbed into the Jeep beside RaeAnne, the idea held a lot more appeal than it ever had before.

Like he said, driving himself crazy.

Her thinking spot was magnificent, as he'd known it would be. She'd always had a knack for discovering the perfect eagle's nest, no matter where they'd found themselves.

He'd never forget one in particular on their trip to the Grand Canyon with her mom. Perched high in the blazing orange sandstone cliffs, their private hideaway had overlooked miles of breathtaking canyon views, surrounded by fragrant piñions, filled with the cheerful chatter of chipmunks and blue jays. It had been the day after he'd bought her the Navajo blanket from a grizzled old man weaving by the side of a dirt highway. The place they'd first broken it in.

He swallowed hard on the memory and ventured out onto

the huge granite boulder she'd led him to, about a quarter-mile from the road above the cabin. The whole valley was laid out before them in panoramic Technicolor.

"Wow," he said with a low whistle. "What a view."

He could see the road leading over the hills down to US 395, a tiny black ribbon dotted with occasional moving bumps. Beyond the highway the Owens River glittered in the evening sun, which was already waning where they stood.

"If we were just a bit higher you could see Death Valley, behind those hills." She indicated the long, low range of mountains stretching across the horizon like a sleeping dragon.

"Pretty amazing," he said with admiration. Then turned his focus to the site and cabin. "And strategic. We can see the whole setup, including the road leading up the mountain. Good choice."

He watched a pair of headlights crest the hill, but the car didn't turn onto the path to the cabin, instead proceeding higher up into the sierra. "Where's that guy going?"

"There's a logging camp at the end of the road, about five miles up."

"Seems late for traffic."

"I hear cars all the time, morning to night. I guess the guys go down to the restaurants and bars."

He frowned. "They ever bother you?"

"Nope. Only Toby." She searched the road below. "Do you think he and the gang will show up?"

"Who knows. I'm not too worried, though."

"No?" She looked surprised. "But the Chairman said—"

"Toby and his cohorts aren't out to destroy anything."

"And you know this how?"

"If that's what they'd wanted, they'd have done so this morning. They took the artifacts, but turned them in to the authorities—the ones they respect. No, if they come, it'll just be to scare you."

"Scare me?" she said incredulously. "Need I remind you

last time they tied me up and left me helpless, at the mercy of a man who looked like an ax murderer?''

''A man who was clearly coming to your rescue,'' he corrected. ''The kids knew you'd be safe with me.''

Behind them, a faint echo of thunder rolled across the distant peaks of the High Sierra.

''Yeah, right,'' she muttered, but he could tell she saw his point. She relaxed visibly.

Until he unfurled the blanket and draped it over his back, sat down on the rock, and held out his arms to her. ''Sit with me like we used to.''

The air turned chilly. She shivered and slipped on her down jacket. ''I don't think so, Roman.''

Pushing out a sigh, he dropped his arms and lay back on the boulder, still warm from the heat of the day. The sun had already set and darkness was racing over the blue sky. It never failed to impress him how quickly dusk fell on the mountain.

Silhouetted against the sapphire horizon, RaeAnne stood, back to him, hands in the deep, snug pockets of her jacket, her collar turned up. Wisps of blond hair fluttered around her head in the breeze; long, denim-clad legs braced in a wide, confident stance. He felt his body stir. How could she turn him on just standing there?

''Tell me about your father,'' she said.

He lifted his gaze to the splash of stars that were beginning to twinkle overhead. ''He was a traitor,'' he said before he realized he'd spoken.

She turned to face him. ''I don't understand. Everyone thought he was a hero.''

''He killed two men, Rae.''

''Yes, but in self-defense.'' She ignored his snort and exclaimed, ''Those FBI agents were about to gun down innocent people over some meaningless protest about feathers!''

''Eagle feathers are not meaningless. You know that. You also know the protest wasn't just about feathers.''

"So you're saying the FBI was right to shoot people, regardless of the reason?"

"No. I'm saying that's not what really happened."

She was silent a moment, then said, "What really did happen?"

It took him a good long while to put what his father had done into words. As if not saying it aloud would somehow make the things they spoke of not real.

But in the end, he wanted her to know. To know the kind of man who had fathered him. To be properly horrified, so she wouldn't mind so much that he had left her those years ago. So she would understand why he couldn't stay, even now.

"About ten years ago, my mom got real sick. When I was finally called, she'd been in the hospital for weeks."

Roman remembered the frantic feeling of not being able to do anything to make her better. It had been far worse than when he'd thought he was dying of AIDS himself. And after she'd whispered her confession, he'd wished he had.

"She was convinced she wouldn't make it and didn't want to die with her secrets, so she told me everything. How my father had been involved in a drug ring somewhere around here. He was a supplier, a distributor for the ring. Had been ever since he'd come back from Vietnam. The FBI finally caught up with the ring, and was about to arrest them all. So he killed the agents during an AIM protest and then disappeared, making it look like he'd been wounded escaping. The Native Rights hero."

"Oh, Roman." Shock and sympathy radiated from her.

He wanted none of it. "Hector Santangelo was not a Red Road warrior who died in the mountains evading the mock justice of the dominant society. He was a drug dealer and a murderer who's still alive and out there somewhere. And I mean to find him and bring him in."

RaeAnne was speechless. She knew how much the memory of his father had meant to Roman growing up. As had the knowledge that even though he was dead, he'd died honorably, defending his people and the things he'd believed in. The respect in every Native American's eyes when they learned Roman was Hector Santangelo's son had given him a strength and confidence rare in a young boy. And somewhat made up for losing his father at a fragile age.

"I don't know what to say," she said, aching to lie down beside him and gather him in her arms, hold him until the hurt went away. "It's a hell of a thing to find out. Are you sure it's true?"

"You think my mom would lie about something like that?"

"No, of course not. It's just so...so unlike everything I've ever heard about him."

But it would explain why Roman had felt compelled to join the very organization that had been accused of killing his dad. Roman's sense of honor had always been his defining trait.

A sad sigh whispered from deep in his chest. "I know. It took me a long time to believe it. But there were too many little things that added up."

She sat down on the boulder next to him. "Like what?"

"Like how we'd always been short of money while he was in Nam, but just a few months after he got back suddenly we seemed to be rolling in it."

"Maybe he got a good job."

He shook his head. "He worked for the Tribal Council for next to nothing. And he was always traveling. He said on tribal business, but nobody else on the Council ever did. I remember him and my mom fighting about it. They fought a lot toward the end."

She reached out a finger and toyed with the fringe of the blanket where it lay on his arm. "What else?"

"Visits from strangers at all hours, phone calls, secret meetings. Sometimes he'd see a car drive by and get all paranoid. Like he was afraid."

"How did he explain these things?"

He lifted a shoulder. "It was the seventies. The American Indian Movement was gaining momentum, and he was right in the thick of it. I just assumed it all had to do with that. I was young. Never questioned."

Stroking the soft wool strands between her fingers, she said, "But if the FBI knew all that about him, why would they hire his son?"

She looked down into his eyes, and the breath stalled in her lungs at the desolation reflected in them.

"Because I'm the one who told them about his crimes."

Stunned horror shot through her. But before she could squeeze a word through her constricted throat, his head tipped up and his eyes snapped to the valley below.

"Looks like we've got company."

Chapter 5

RaeAnne leaped to her feet and spun to see what Roman had spotted. Sure enough, a pair of headlights blazed a bumpy path along the road leading to her cabin.

"Toby!" she exclaimed. "Let's go!" She turned to head for the Jeep, but Roman's hand gripped her arm before she realized he'd also risen.

"Wait. First let's see what they do."

"Are you nuts? They could wreck the site! The cabin!"

"As I said, I doubt they want to. And if you're not around, their plan to scare you won't have nearly the desired impact."

"What if they get to the artifacts?"

"Let's just see what happens."

There was that confidence again. She couldn't help but succumb to it, skeptical as she was. "If they so much as break a window—"

"I'll arrest them myself. This is National Forest land, federal jurisdiction."

She pushed out a breath, already annoyed with herself for

caving in. Reluctantly she turned to watch the shadowy shapes of the kids as they piled out of Toby's truck into a patch of moonlight in front of the cabin. Youthful voices rang through the valley.

"I can make out three of them. Not a very big raiding party."

"Hmm," she said, reserving judgment. Whoops and yells echoed off the hillsides. "Doesn't have to be big to be destructive. And there might be others coming—just slower drivers."

"Don't worry," his voice murmured in her ear, right before his arms closed around her middle. "Trust me."

The words ricocheted through her mind as her body sparked in acute awareness of his frame pressing into her back. *Trust me.* She'd made that mistake once, and she'd be a fool to repeat it.

"We wanna talk to you, Miz Archaeologist! Come on out of there!"

Mutely she watched the kids hoot and holler and bang their fists on the cabin door, daring her to show her face.

"We know you're in there! No use hidin'!"

When she didn't appear, they shone flashlights into the two windows, rapping on the glass so hard she thought surely it would shatter. Roman's arms tightened around her waist, as if he could sense she was about to bolt.

"Easy."

When the youths finally realized she wasn't there, they held a conference in the glow of the headlights, heads together, animatedly discussing the situation. Roman handed her his silver flask and she took an experimental sip. The slivovitz burned all the way down her throat.

"Jeez Louise," she gasped, wiping her eyes.

"Better?" he asked, and she could practically hear his grin.

"Are you kidding?" she choked out, but nevertheless took another sip before passing him back the flask.

This time it just felt hot as it glided into her stomach.

Almost as hot as his lower body against her backside. She caught herself leaning into him when he shifted his legs apart to take a swig from the flask—automatically adjusting herself to his contours, fitting their bodies together as seamlessly as she knew they would. It was agony to pull herself away, but she tried, only to find his arm an iron band around her waist, preventing her from moving.

"What are they doing?" she asked, to distract herself from acknowledging the thrill that hummed through her.

"Getting back in the truck, it seems."

She forced herself to focus and, sure enough, the boys were opening the truck's doors. But instead of climbing in, Toby reappeared carrying a box of some kind. It looked about the same size and shape as her artifact boxes.

"What the heck…?"

Roman took another slow swig, and they both watched as the boys deposited the box on the top step of the cabin porch. Then, after more discussion, they mustered into the truck and drove off.

Astonished, RaeAnne followed the red of their taillights disappear over the hill.

"Well. I guess you were right," she finally ventured. "What do you suppose is in the box?"

"Dead rat. Coyote droppings. Something clever like that."

She made a face and turned to him. "Oh, gross. Are you serious?"

"That would be the usual pattern." His fingers brushed along her jaw and slid into her hair. Her heart stalled. "I'll open it for you when we get back."

"Roman," she whispered, uncertain whether she was warning him or encouraging him in his folly.

"You feel like a marshmallow."

She blinked up at him. "Huh?" His arm adjusted around her, sinking into the soft down of her jacket. Pulling her close. "Oh."

"You know how I love marshmallows."

"I—"

"Toasted. All hot and sweet and melty."

She was beginning to feel a bit toasted herself. "Roman…"

He lowered his face to hers. She expected him to kiss her. But he didn't. He just held it there, nose to cheek, cheek to nose, barely touching. Brushing his skin over hers, up and down, light as a fairy wing.

"Were you really glad I kissed you?" he quietly asked.

Her pulse zinged. She knew she shouldn't. But she couldn't help herself. "Yes."

She could smell his scent, dark, musky, perfumed with a drop of some exotic oil. She could smell the soap he'd used this afternoon, and the leather of his black jacket, warm from his heat. She could smell her own arousal, unexpected, potent, unbidden.

But she couldn't pull away. It was as though some giant, invisible magnet kept her from stepping back, reestablishing the distance between them.

His fingers held her head, gently guiding it to tip and turn, to accommodate his tortuous journey of touch around her face. Yet, not once did his lips leave their print upon her skin. No, this was far worse.

She stifled a moan when he brushed down her throat and buried his face between her neck and her hair, pausing to breathe deeply. She did moan when his tongue painted over the sensitive spot at the base of her ear.

"*Cara,*" he murmured, and suddenly his mouth was on hers.

Somehow her arms had wound themselves around his neck. He tasted sweet, and burning hot like the slivovitz. His tongue was rough as the years that had separated them, and exciting as no man had been since him.

A yearning, needy sound tumbled from her throat, answered by a low growl from his. He crushed her to his body, covering her mouth completely, thrusting deep with demand. Her limbs turned to liquid and she grabbed his hair for balance. Their lips parted, panting, their eyes met, desperate.

"We can't do this," she said, gasping for breath.

"No," he agreed, and claimed her again.

Being in his arms was like coming home to a family she hadn't seen in eighteen long years. She missed him so, missed him to the roots of her hair and the soles of her feet. Missed him so much she let herself melt beneath his tongue as it dissolved her resistance like so much cotton candy. She missed him to the very core of her soul.

"We should stop."

"Yes."

His mouth was like velvet steel. Soft, sensual, immovable, overpowering. Helplessly she surrendered to his urging, joined in his feverish resurrection of the passion between them.

His hands pulled her tight, center to center, kneading her bottom, grinding her into the long, hard column of his arousal. She shivered uncontrollably.

"Woman, I want you," he breathed.

Coils of desire tightened through her whole body. She groaned. Somehow, she had to summon the will to stop. Knowing if this happened it would be the end of her. She wouldn't survive his leaving again.

"It can't work. This can't work," she said, and put her hands on his chest. She could feel his heartbeat, usually so steady and strong, pounding like an out of control freight train. And her own, just as wild.

"I know," he said, low, tormented. "But I want you." He wrapped her in his arms. "Lord, how I want you. Be my woman, Rae."

And suddenly she wasn't sure what he was really saying. Was it only now he was talking about? Was he just asking for a hot and frenzied roll in the blanket to celebrate old times? Or was there something more he wanted?

All at once she was scared witless. Scared witless that she would accept his offer—whatever it was.

This was exactly why she'd gone on the run and hidden from him for so many years. The fear that he would return and hold out his hand, and she would take it. Forgive him his sins and set herself up for an even greater heartbreak.

"It's not possible."

"It is. You still love me. I can feel it."

One last time, she savored the feel of his arms around her, the touch of his rough cheek against her skin, the tickle of his hair drifting across her face. And her heart broke with longing for what could never be.

Then she whispered the words she knew would keep them apart forever.

"I was pregnant when you left me."

It took several seconds for RaeAnne's softly spoken bombshell to penetrate the haze of Roman's confused mind, and even longer before he could unfreeze his body and react.

"What?" He grasped her arms and held her away from him, chaos exploding through his whole being. *"What?"*

He couldn't see her eyes clearly. It was too dark. The moon had disappeared behind the jumble of peaks crowding above them like a pack of prying relatives. He wanted to lash out at them, tell them to step back and give him room to breathe. For suddenly he couldn't seem to get any air.

"You were pregnant?" Bayonets of agony slashed through him. "With a baby? My baby?"

He was completely paralyzed. He felt his fingers digging into her flesh, but couldn't loosen them.

She nodded and his world fell apart.

"Oh, God. Oh, God."

His friend Cole had just had a baby a few months ago. He hadn't seen it, or even the mother, but at Christmas Cole had told him about it. He still remembered the incredible look of reverence and awe that had come over his friend's face as he'd spoken of becoming a father. Roman had been jealous. He'd thought of RaeAnne then, and how much he wished—

"Is it…? Did you…?" He couldn't choke out the rest.

Her head wobbled, then she stood very still. "I lost the baby. A few weeks after you left."

She didn't say it, probably didn't even intend it, but the implication was clear enough. "After your mom died?" he asked, desperately hoping for a shred of absolution.

"No."

No. So there it was. It was all his fault she'd lost the baby. His baby. By leaving her, he'd killed his own child.

Guilt descended, crushing him within its jaws. "I'm sorry. Oh, God, Rae, I'm so sorry. If I'd known—"

She looked up at him.

What then? Would anything on earth have been able to drag him from her side? Or would the mortal fear of infecting not only her with AIDS, but his own baby as well, have forced him away even more surely?

"Would you have stayed?"

Damned if he left, double damned if he stayed.

"I probably would have driven myself over a cliff."

The certain knowledge settled around him like the warm feeling of well-being just before you froze to death.

Her eyes glistened in the starlight, spilling twin rivulets of glittering tears down her cheeks. "Then I'm glad you didn't know," she whispered, the words catching on a single sob.

He couldn't take it, so he swept her up in his arms, wrapped her in the blanket, and somehow got her back to the cabin. She didn't protest when he undressed them both, her silent tears still falling as he laid her down on the bed and crept under the covers with her.

"Tell me," he quietly demanded.

He wanted to hear all of it—everything she wasn't saying about what she'd gone through. The very worst she could throw at him. He needed to wallow in his grief and know exactly the extent of his guilt. He wanted to take it all onto himself, so her burden would be lightened.

He held her close as she told him of her disbelief when she'd learned of his abandonment, then of her rage and fear, and of her sorrow. Of days in bed not eating, not caring whether she lived or died. He rocked her in his arms as she described how in her confusion she'd accidentally taken one too many of the sedatives the doctor had prescribed, the terrible cramps and the crushing remorse and horror at what she'd done. He silently comforted her as she spoke of the desperate loneliness and desolation over her mother's sudden death just short weeks later, and kissed her brow over and over as she told of her decision to change her name and start over, hoping for some kind of peace of mind in a new life in a new place.

He folded her in his arms and let her cry until she had no more tears left and fell into an exhausted sleep. And then he eased down her body, laid his cheek on her belly and all alone he wept.

Long before dawn, RaeAnne woke, strangely light-headed. Her eyes felt puffy, the skin of her face tight. There was an unfamiliar weight on her stomach. She reached down and touched a warm head and a large, masculine hand nestled against her bare skin.

Roman.

Everything came back to her in a rush, and for a moment she held her breath, dismayed by what had transpired last night.

For years, bitterness over his desertion had let her diminish her own responsibility for the miscarriage and heap the lion's share onto him. But last night she'd realized how cowardly that was. And how wrong.

She was to blame. She was the one who'd starved herself and taken the pills the doctor had given her, knowing deep down they couldn't be good for the baby no matter what assurances he'd made. To blame Roman was unfair. The baby's loss was her fault. Hers alone.

She stroked her hand over his hair, coarse and silky as it flowed over her abdomen. And slowly the knot of anger she'd carried in her heart for years dissolved, leaving an aching emptiness in its place.

She would have to forgive him. For everything.

I probably would have driven myself over a cliff.

Last night, she'd finally understood why he'd left. And now she understood that it had been the very best thing that could have happened. If he'd stayed under those circumstances, he would only have been caught in a dilemma for which there'd been no answer, other than the worst possible. She'd have lost both of them forever—the baby and her love. And that would have been unbearable.

Under her hand he stirred, then crept up from beneath the covers and gathered her to him. With a deep sigh, he slipped back into sleep.

It felt so right lying there next to him, their naked bodies tangled in comfortable disarray. It was ironic, really. For the two years they'd been lovers in high school, they'd never once spent the night together. And now when they finally did, it was as friends, not lovers.

Friends. She'd never thought the day would come when she could call Roman a friend again. Her lips curved into a smile and she gently placed a kiss on his chest. It had surely been a day for miracles.

Closing her eyes, she snuggled into his embrace, enjoying every muscle and masculine angle, from his broad shoulders to his athletic thighs—and everything in between.

But as she drifted off to sleep, she reminded herself that friends were all they could ever be. Though she yearned for love and a family of her own, she needed someone safe and secure to build her future with. Someone she could trust. And no matter how much she might care about Roman Santangelo, she knew she could never trust him.

Not again. Not with her heart.

When she awoke for the second time that morning, it was to bright sunshine and the sounds and smells of coffee brewing on the woodstove. Roman was padding around the kitchen area in wool socks, an open flannel shirt and unbuttoned jeans, looking very rusticated. And sexy as hell.

"Good morning."

His greeting started her out of her reverie, and she wondered how long she'd been staring at his chest.

"Hi," she answered, and tugged the blanket up a little over her breasts. They both tried to smile, and both failed miserably as memories of last night flared to life between them. He crossed the floor and sat next to her on the bed, handing her his mug of coffee to share.

"How are you doing?"

"Okay. Better." She took several deep sips from the mug. "Good."

His gaze fell to his hands and a desolate look clouded his eyes. "RaeAnne, I—"

"Roman, I know what you're going to say," she interrupted, setting down the coffee. "There's no need. Honestly." This time her tentative smile stuck. "It was just so good to get it all out. I needed that more than I realized."

"I'm glad," he said. "But I'm feeling kind of shell-shocked." She put her hand to his cheek and he grabbed it, held it there. "Why didn't you tell me you were pregnant?"

How she wished she had! Maybe if she'd told him on that perfect prom evening, he'd have broken his rule and spent the whole night with her. And never run across that accident...

"I was waiting until I knew for certain."

He nodded and shuddered out a sigh. "I just wish..."

"I know. Me, too."

His arms came around her, and she lifted hers around him. The flannel of his shirtsleeves felt soft on her back, and his skin against her bare breasts spread a soothing warmth through her whole being. It wasn't a sexual hug, but one between friends who desperately needed each other's nurturing.

She knew he was grieving the loss of the child he never knew he'd created, and so she just held him tight for a long, long while, as he'd done for her the night before.

As he struggled with his emotions, she kissed his temple, his eyes, his strong, square jaw. And when he finally looked up, she whispered, "I forgive you. I forgive you for everything."

Maybe saying the words he wanted to hear would make him get on his motorcycle and drive away. Because friends or no, she could feel herself falling faster by the minute for this powerful, sensitive, passionate man. And that was the last thing she wanted.

It didn't matter how much she wished things were different. It didn't matter how good his body felt next to hers. It didn't matter how much she hungered for just one more kiss. He was wrong for her. All wrong. She'd finally met a man who might be able to give her everything she was looking for, and it wasn't Roman. She had to think about Philip. She had to.

But when Roman's lips sought hers, tenderly, pleadingly, she couldn't resist giving him the comfort he so obviously needed. And steal one last, selfish taste of the man she knew she'd never completely get over.

So she pulled him closer and held him like she'd never give him up. She let herself be swept away by the sharp longing in her heart, and by his warm, persuasive mouth.

And barely noticed when the cabin door opened wide and a tall man dressed in a khaki uniform took one step into the room and halted.

"RaeAnne!"

She jerked away from Roman's embrace and gasped in dismay at the shocked intruder.

Disbelief, hurt, fury, flamed across his face before he silently turned and stalked out, slamming the door behind him.

"Oh, my God," she whispered, and jumped from the bed. "Wait! Philip!"

Jealousy ripped through Roman as RaeAnne leaped up and called after the man who'd walked in on them. *Philip.* The man she was involved with.

He should feel like a bastard about what he'd just done to some totally innocent guy, but all he could think about was that she was getting ready to run out the door after him. Naked.

"Rae!" he yelled, ripped off his flannel shirt and tossed it to her.

She caught it, glanced down at herself and he could see the blood drain from her face. "Oh, no." Slipping on his shirt, she disappeared through the door.

Hell.

He fell back onto the bed and shot his hands through his hair. *Damn, damn, damn.* Remorse and exultation battled it out in his mind, one side telling him he should go out there and explain to the guy that things weren't at all what they seemed, the other side urging him to declare himself the winner and collect the spoils. But he knew darn well RaeAnne would only resent his interference, just as she surely resented his renewed presence in her life.

She'd also take care of it.

And if Philip O'Donnaugh was worthy of her love, and half a man, he'd believe what she said, come in here, beat the crap out of him and toss him out on his butt.

Roman almost looked forward to the prospect. If anyone deserved a beating, it was him, and after the past twenty-four hours, a good, hard physical release was just what he needed. If this was the way to get it, that was just fine by him.

Rising to his feet, he braced them apart, planted his fists on his hips and waited for his rival to bust through the door.

The defeated look on RaeAnne's face when she walked back in was enough to tell him there would be no fight.

Anger swelled in his blood. "What happened?"

"He dumped me."

He scowled. "Just like that?"

"Hardly a surprise." She hugged the flannel shirt around her middle and shook her head dejectedly.

"Didn't you explain?"

She only sighed.

He took a step toward her. "The man's a certifiable idiot."

"Roman, he caught me naked in bed with another man. I got what I deserved."

"No. You deserved his trust." He closed the distance between them. "If the man really knew you, he'd know you were telling the truth when you said nothing happened in that bed."

She bit her lip and gazed at the floor. "It looked bad, Roman. Really bad."

"Appearances aren't always reliable. I know that for a fact. And anyone wearing a sheriff's uniform should know it, too."

She looked up, tears welling in her eyes. "I can't believe he's gone."

Now he did feel like a bastard. He never thought— "You love him that much?"

"No. Well, yes. Oh, I don't know." She swiped at the tears. "The point is, now I'll never get the chance to find out. And he was perfect. Everything I wanted."

Roman's heart twisted. "Everything?"

She nodded morosely. "He was nice. Had a steady job, good standing in the community. Roots. He was secure."

She had to be kidding. He lifted his brows.

"And fun."

Roman had a hard time picturing the somber sheriff as the life of a party, but then, he'd caught him at a bad moment. "Really?"

"He likes to dance. And go fishing."

"Fishing. That's your definition of perfect?"

"And he's handsome, of course." She started to look distinctly uncomfortable. "Very attractive."

"Then why haven't you slept with him?"

Her mouth dropped open, and he reached out with one finger and slowly started to push open the flannel shirt, baring her breast. The nipple peaked as the soft fabric brushed over it. Or was it his gaze that caused the reaction?

"He's not perfect."

"Oh?" Her arms were still crossed stiffly over her waist,

but she made no move to stop him when he exposed her other breast, too. The vein in her throat pulsed madly.

He drank in the sight of her, her beautiful body, her pale skin, her long, bare legs. And ached to see the treasure between them, concealed behind a short patch of plaid flannel.

"I'll tell you why you didn't ever sleep with him."

A blush had pinkened her skin from her chest to the tips of her cheekbones. "So tell me," she dared, her voice low and breathy. "Why didn't I sleep with him?"

He held her eyes as he slid his hands over her shoulders bringing the shirt with them, and down her arms, uncrossing them so it fell to the floor. The tips of her breasts tightened to two perfect rose-colored pebbles. A tremor passed through her body.

"Because," he said, putting his hands to her waist, pulling her up against him. "He doesn't make you feel like this."

Chapter 6

Roman crushed RaeAnne to him, covered her mouth with his, drove his tongue deep into her. She stiffened for a fraction of a second, then threw herself into his arms. He groaned, desire ripping through him like a .44 caliber bullet.

Yes, yes, yes.

He wanted this...wanted *her* more than he'd ever wanted anything in his life. More than when they'd been kids, more than redemption, more than air to breathe.

She melded into him, matching his fever, spurring his excitement. His hands sought her breasts and she whimpered, a sweet, throaty sound of pleasure. Pinching the crowns he turned with her, backed her to the bed. There was no doubt in either of their minds where this was leading, and there was nothing on earth that could stop him. He picked her up, tossed her onto the soft mattress and climbed on top of her. She reached for him, urging him down with a hand to the back of his neck.

Gladly he yielded, sliding between her legs, lowering himself onto her molten body. Greedily he ate at her mouth, her throat, her breasts. Her moans filled the air, and her hands were all over him, touching him, nails scraping over his back, fingers tugging at his jeans.

Want exploded into need. He was on fire.

He didn't give himself time to think, to consider what they were doing. He slid his pants off and in a single, fierce motion plunged into her.

She cried out, wrapping her legs around his waist, panting to the rhythm of his savage thrusts. He pounded into her again and again until, shuddering uncontrollably, she grabbed his hair, screamed his name and her body convulsed tightly around him. With a roar of pleasure, at the last possible second he withdrew. Sinking his teeth into the soft flesh of her shoulder instead, he marked her as his own, and release thundered through him.

"Again," she ordered breathlessly when the beating of his heart had slowed to the level of mild cardiac arrest.

"My pleasure," he answered with only a shade of smugness, and rolled them so she was on top. "Your turn."

"You remembered," she murmured, and proceeded to oblige him with an eagerness that thrilled him to the bone.

"Oh, yeah," he sighed as he lay prostrate beneath her a long time later, wrung-out as a dishrag. "That's not something a man ever forgets."

RaeAnne slowly regained consciousness, enjoying every nuance of the sensations she woke to. She'd dozed off where she lay, stretched out over Roman's body. Her feet hooked over his ankles, her face tucked under his chin. A sheen of sweat slicked their bodies, and the air was redolent with the scent of fulfillment.

So much for just friends.

He let her roll off him, and didn't move except to moan, "*Cara,* I think you've killed me."

She smiled ruefully at the ceiling. "No such luck."

His hand groped for hers, and he wove their fingers together, then tipped his head to look at her. "Mad?"

She met his gaze and smiled. "You show up, turn my life upside down, lose me my boyfriend and then remind me what I've been missing all these years. Any minute now you'll hop on that stupid bike of yours and ride off into the sunset. Why should I be mad?"

A little-boy grin crept onto his lips. "No reason I can see."

She grabbed the pillow and whacked him in the head. "Such a jerk."

But in truth, she wasn't the least bit angry. Who could be angry when she felt so incredible?

Terrified, yes. Panic-stricken, yes. Regretful, maybe. Angry, no.

Except maybe a little at herself. This was definitely not on her agenda. If she wasn't very careful, she could end up in a world of hurt.

Best play it cool, so he'd never guess how much making love to him again had affected her. Made her yearn for things that could never be. Made the old feelings in her heart burst into bloom just as fresh and sweet as the first day she'd fallen in love with him, so long ago.

But it would never work. He had his motorcycle, his undercover job and a life filled with change and excitement. She had her burning need to find a secure nest and settle down. He had his mission to find his father, and she had her quest to find a man she could trust with her heart.

She thought briefly of Philip and the shattered possibilities with him. But, no, Roman had been right. Philip wasn't the man for her. If he had been, she wouldn't have been able to resist him any more than she'd been able to resist Roman. Philip was a nice man, and would make some woman a fine husband. But not her.

"Where are you, *Cara?*" Roman asked as he slipped his arms around her and gazed into her eyes. "A million miles away?"

Not nearly far enough, she thought achingly.

"No regrets," he murmured. "I couldn't take regrets."

She mustered up a smile. "Did I act like a woman who'd regret what she was doing?"

"Good," he said, "Because I don't. Not for a second." He kissed her and mirrored her smile. "I guess we aren't so impossible after all."

She sighed and answered, "Yes. We are."

When he seemed about to reply, she slid from his arms and reached for his flannel shirt. "We should get up. The Chairman is expecting us at the Board this morning."

He watched her for a moment, then followed her out of bed. "Okay."

She wished with all her heart she was brave enough to hear what he'd been about to say. But either way would be disaster.

She knew the only sensible thing was to fetch the rest of the artifacts, and send him on his way. But she couldn't stand to hear about his plans to leave her.

And any plans to stay really would be impossible.

She had to play it cool. Very cool. And hope he didn't notice her heart had tumbled from her chest and right back into his hands.

It was difficult to keep up her facade of casual cheerfulness in the face of her inner turmoil, and especially under the onslaught of Roman's boundless affection. It had always been one of the things she loved best about him—his habit of touching her constantly.

As they ate and gathered fresh clothes, he brushed over her with a caress, a kiss, a nuzzle. Her whole body attuned to it, reveled in its sweet familiarity, made her yearn for the next soft touch of his fingers or lips. When they went together to the hot springs for a quick wash she was barely able to resist his overtures to make love again. But being that close even once more would surely break the heart that was fast becoming hopelessly lost to him.

"I'll just get my purse and we can go," she said to distract herself from watching him straighten the bed.

"Right." He went over and rooted through his pack, slipping a wallet into his pocket and a big silver gun into the back waistband of his jeans.

She gasped in surprise. "What's that for?"

He looked up, briefly puzzled, then answered, "I'm a federal agent. I always carry."

"You didn't yesterday."

"I did. You just didn't notice." He tied up his pack and straightened. "Too busy worrying about other things, no doubt."

"I suppose." She sighed. "The FBI is a far cry from becoming a veterinarian. I can't believe you actually carry a gun."

"Does it bother you?"

She pursed her lips. "You know how I feel about violence. I thought you felt the same way."

"I do."

"Then how can you do it?"

He closed his eyes briefly, then took her by the arms, as if compelling her to listen to an explanation she wouldn't buy.

"*Cara,* when I ratted out my father for murdering those agents, the FBI couldn't believe their luck—a Navy-trained son of a Native American hero turning traitor to his father and his people."

"You're no traitor," she interrupted, objecting strongly to his self-condemning words. "Your sense of honor made you do it. It had nothing to do with betrayal."

He gazed at her, his eyes shining with desolation. "Thank you for that. I should have known you'd understand. But they didn't. They offered me a job on the spot."

"You didn't have to take it."

He sighed and dropped her arms. "My father killed two of their men. I needed to restore the balance. For my own sake."

Okay, that she could buy. He'd always believed in harmony and honor above all.

"Even though the FBI thought he was dead."

"Yeah."

"Because your father had escaped justice and gotten away with murder by disappearing and making everyone think he'd died a hero."

He shrugged.

"All right. So you felt you owed the FBI two lives. How many have you repaid since then?"

The corner of his lip went up, and she knew instinctively there had been dozens. "The FBI aren't as dumb as they look. They always send me after the nasty *wasichu* criminals."

The white bad guys. She laughed softly and took his arm, heading for the front door. "Ah, poetic justice. And that's why you've stayed on, despite the violence."

"No," he said, pausing to let her go first. "I stayed on *because* of the violence—of all kinds and colors. Every day I've seen what it does to this country. My job lets me eliminate some of that suffering, but to do it I need to carry a gun."

Turning to lock the door behind them, she smiled at his circular reasoning. It didn't matter how far afield they went in a discussion, he'd always manage to get back to the original point. "Then you're a bigger hero than your father ever pretended to be."

"Sure I am." He snorted dismissively, and she was about to argue when he said, "Aw, hell," and clumped over to the window. She looked up and saw him bending over a cardboard box.

Toby's box.

"Damn, we forgot about that, didn't we?"

Their eyes met, and it seemed like a lifetime of memories washed between them instead of just twelve hours' worth.

"I guess we did. Want me to open it?"

She nodded. "May as well get it over with. Wouldn't want some disgusting thing sitting on the porch all day."

He fetched a fallen pine branch from the ground and used

it to lift the lid from a few feet away, just in case. A frown creased his forehead. "That's weird."

"What?" she asked, and took a step forward from where he'd shooed her. "What is it?"

"Clothes. Old clothes."

They both approached, and perused the contents of the box from above. Sure enough, several articles of clothing appeared to be neatly folded and deposited in the bottom.

"Stand back," he said, and gingerly moved the top layer aside with the twig. "It's gotta be a trick."

But nothing was hidden under it, or under the other articles, except two old tattered envelopes. He dropped to his knees to examine the things closer.

"What does it mean?" she asked, and that's when she noticed he had gone deathly pale. "Roman?"

He pulled the bottom-most garment from the box, some kind of beaded vest, and looked up, anguish shimmering in his face.

"My God," he whispered in a strangled voice, "It's my father's."

Stunning disbelief coursed through Roman's body. How could it be? After all these years, how could this stuff suddenly reappear? The FBI had searched the Big Pine reservation and surrounding areas thoroughly for any trace of his father, his disappearance and supposed death thirty years ago.

Of course, Roman knew the answer without even thinking. The people of Big Pine would never have betrayed his father by giving a single clue to the hated enemy. No matter the cost.

Only Roman himself had done that, turned Quisling to his dead hero father.

Focus. He had to focus. Fighting the torment razoring through his insides, he answered RaeAnne's unspoken questions.

"This vest was part of my father's regalia. And these—" he carefully picked up the shirt and jeans that had lain on top, now recognizing them from news footage taken the day of the Native Rights demonstration ''—they're the clothes he was wearing when he disappeared and supposedly died.''

The Western-style shirt had long sleeves and a decorative yoke across the back. Several long, thin ribbons were sewn to the corners of the yoke. As he unfolded it, they fluttered in the breeze like unanswered prayers, almost diverting him from the hole that pierced the left shoulder, and the dried blood that surrounded it.

''Oh, sweetheart,'' she murmured when he crushed the shirt in his fists.

She came down next to him, put her arms around him. He went rigid, resisting her comfort. He didn't deserve her sympathy.

''Toby must have found out who you are,'' she said. ''He's from Big Pine. Maybe somebody's been keeping the clothes all these years and wanted to return them to you?''

He shook his head. ''I don't think so. Why would they do it like this?''

''Then why? What could they mean?''

''I don't know. But one thing I think we can count on. This stuff isn't here out of kindness.''

He fished up the two envelopes, desperate for a clue. One appeared much fatter than the other. Carefully he opened the skinny one and peered in. He blinked, a wave of sweet-painful recognition crashing over him.

''Feathers?'' RaeAnne's soft voice whispered.

''Eagle feathers,'' he corrected in a rasp.

Each of the three feathers screamed out a dissonant chord of memories. Of the bravery his father had displayed to earn it. Of a young son, bursting with pride at the ceremony where it had been bestowed. Of the fervent hope that he, too, would someday be worthy of such an honor. Hope that had turned to ashes.

''My father's eagle feathers.''

She didn't question him. Roman realized she had lived among Indian people long enough to know that each feather would be recognized as easily as the man it had been presented to—especially when a photo of his father wearing them still graced the wall of his mother's home.

"But that's impossible," she said, putting voice to the confusion beginning to swirl through his own mind. She also knew a man's eagle feathers were sacred. A man would never, ever part with them, not while he was on this earth.

"I thought you said he's still alive?"

"That's what I believe."

Reverently he laid the envelope aside, heedful not to bump or jostle it, and reached for the other one. As soon as his fingers gripped its thick bulk, he knew what lay inside. He couldn't believe it. Lifting the flap open, he was confronted by a literal fortune. In eagle feathers.

Roman leaned back in the Jeep's bucket seat and listened to the wind rushing past as RaeAnne drove down the mountain. He hoped the long drive would help him think. They'd slid Toby's box and its precious contents in among the stack of similar artifact boxes stowed in the cabin. Plain sight was always the best hiding place.

The whole thing made no sense. Who had sent the box? And why? Obviously, Toby had just been the messenger. Although naturally Roman still planned to grill the boy. He must know something.

"Is it a message, or is it a warning?" RaeAnne asked, uncannily echoing his own thoughts. "Could it be someone trying to tell you your father really is dead?"

"A good possibility. I have a hard time believing he'd part with those feathers otherwise."

After considering for a moment, she asked, "Who told you he's still alive?"

"The FBI."

She shot him a surprised glance. "You're kidding."

He shook his head wearily. "I'd never brought myself to look up his file before, until a few months ago. I thought I was finally ready to read what was in it."

"And it said he was alive?"

"Not outright. But a few entries had been added back in '86, and again in '88. Entries I couldn't read because they were classified Need To Know. When I asked about them, I was given the runaround by the special agent in charge of the case. Made all sorts of excuses, and sounded mighty uncomfortable talking to me. The only explanation that fits is that he was alive back then and he's still alive today."

"But you're his son!" Outrage sizzled in her declaration. "You have a right to know if your own father is alive!"

He sighed. "It's complicated. I told them he murdered their men. Maybe they think—"

"You'll run out and shoot him? Come on. They must know you better than that."

He chuckled. "Not necessarily. The Bureau's always considered me a loose cannon. But if he's still involved in the drug trade and they're watching him, or closing in for an arrest, it's more likely they're afraid I'll mess things up."

"You think it's the FBI who sent the box? Trying to throw you off the trail?"

"Nah. Too subtle," he said. "They'd just haul me in and slap an order on me if they thought I was getting too close."

She was quiet for a few minutes as she drove off the dirt road and turned onto the highway heading north. The valley was warm and fragrant, the sky crystal clear, but Roman couldn't relax and enjoy the beautiful day. He glanced up at the mountains. Ever since he'd arrived, he'd felt them hovering, watching him.

"It has to be someone who knew him well," RaeAnne said.

Shaking off the completely ridiculous feeling, he lowered his gaze to her. "Why do you say that?"

"Why else would they separate your father's eagle feathers from the rest? If they put them in a different envelope it just makes sense they knew you'd recognize them. Only someone who knew him well would care enough, one way or another, to do that."

He stared at her, impressed. Of course, he'd already realized those facts, but it was his job.

"Archaeology isn't so different from police work," she said at the look on his face. "We just usually deal with cultural rather than personal motivation for why things are left the way they are."

"Still. That was some pretty good logic," he remarked. "All right, so we know they care about what happens to Hector Santangelo, and my involvement in it. But the real question remains, was this a message or was it a warning?"

Roman took the news that the Board had voted to return the rest of RaeAnne's artifacts with mixed feelings. On the one hand, her beaming face as the Chairman led them into his office showed just how elated she was to get them back. But on the other, there was now no credible reason to put off leaving her.

He'd gotten the forgiveness he came for. He'd momentarily be done with his duties as Native overseer of the artifacts. It was obvious she'd never been in any real danger from Toby. And as for Toby's box, Roman planned to go straight to Big Pine, get to the bottom of that mystery, and start working on the bigger task of finding his father. She'd just be in the way, even if she felt like going along.

The sight of her happy smile and laughing eyes as they loaded the artifact boxes into the Jeep made his heart do a little leap, and his body fill with a quiet craving.

Making love to her had not been the smartest move. Though he didn't regret a single touch or minute in her arms, it would make parting with her all the more difficult. And finding out about the baby had added a new layer to his guilt and reluctance to just ride away. Somehow, even though they'd talked and he was sure she'd told him everything, it still felt unfinished between them. Especially now.

Because after being with her again like that, holding her close, whispering endearments in her ear as she sighed his name, he couldn't kid himself any longer.

He was in love with her.

He'd always been in love with her. Had known from the start, way back in junior high, she would be the only woman for him, ever.

Unfortunately she didn't share his deep feelings. What he'd done in the past had hurt her too much. And the baby…oh, God, his baby! His own heart carried a new blistering wound so profound he didn't dare think of it. It was too painful to contemplate how badly the loss of their baby had affected RaeAnne.

Despite her words to the contrary, how could she possibly forgive him for all that, let alone want to build a future with him? She couldn't. She just couldn't.

So there was no excuse to stay and a million reasons to hit the road. To stick around would only prolong the agony, and make it that much harder on both of them.

"Now who's a million miles away?" she said, laying a hand on his shoulder.

"Sorry. I was just thinking about—" He halted, before he could say something they'd both regret. Glancing back at the tribal building, he said, "Stay put a minute. I want to ask the Chairman something."

He marched off, hoping she hadn't noticed he couldn't look her in the eye. Questioning the Chairman would get his mind back on track. Back to finding his father. Not how much he was going to miss RaeAnne Martin's warm companionship and loving touch.

"May I speak with you?" he asked the Chairman after flinging open the door and striding back into the building.

A fleeting wariness passed through the older man's eyes, but he inclined his head and led Roman into his office. "What can I do for you? If it's about the skeletal remains—"

"When was the last time you saw Hector Santangelo?" he interrupted.

There was no mistaking the Chairman's brief flash of shock, but he quickly recovered. "Why?"

Roman kept his mouth shut, staring at him expectantly.

Their gazes warred for a moment before the old man looked away and said, "Your father disappeared many years ago."

"Did he ever come back?"

The Chairman turned away, facing the window overlooking the mountains. "Hector Santangelo is gone," he said, as if speaking to the towering peaks. "He will not return." He pivoted and pinned his gaze on Roman. "Don't waste your time on phantoms, my son. There are other things you should be concerned about."

"Like what?" Roman asked in annoyance, just as the intercom on the desk buzzed loudly.

"Keep her safe," the Chairman said cryptically, then turned away and lifted the receiver, effectively dismissing him.

Roman tromped back to the parking lot, but was brought up short by the sight of a sheriff's cruiser parked next to the Jeep, and RaeAnne in conversation with a man. The same man who had walked into the cabin this morning.

Just great.

A surge of panic shot through Roman's chest. What did the sheriff want? Had he changed his mind about dumping RaeAnne?

He stifled the urge to stalk over there and flatten the guy. *No.* Hadn't he just decided he was leaving anyway? If his rival had reconsidered, he should be happy for RaeAnne, and not blow it for her. It's what she'd wanted.

Gritting his teeth, he compelled a strained smile to his face and sauntered up to them.

"What's going on?" The words came out sharper than he'd intended, so he forced himself to stick out his hand to the sheriff. "I'm Roman Santangelo."

The other man stared for a moment before giving it a perfunctory shake. "Philip O'Donnaugh. I can't say it's a pleasure to meet you, Santangelo."

There wasn't much he could say to that, so he remained silent.

''RaeAnne and I need to talk. You won't mind if I drive her back to the site, will you?''

O'Donnaugh's whole attitude dared him to mind. It seemed the sheriff was spoiling for a fight as badly as he'd been this morning.

Roman looked over to RaeAnne, who appeared a little pale. ''Rae?'' She gave him a weak smile, and lifted a shoulder almost imperceptibly.

All right, fine. So she wanted to talk to the guy.

''No problem,'' he said curtly to O'Donnaugh, and slid into the Jeep. ''She's all yours.''

He ignored the widening of her eyes, and gunned out of the lot. No way in hell was he going to stand there and make nice with Mr. Steady-Job-And-Fishing-On-The-Weekends. If she wanted to settle for that, it was her life. None of his damned business. She'd made that clear with her casual attitude since they'd made love.

He kept his hands on the wheel and his eyes on the road whipping past, forbidding himself to turn the Jeep around and snatch her away from O'Donnaugh.

This morning had been an accident. A fantasy. One last burst of passion for old time's sake. Nothing in RaeAnne's subsequent actions or conversation had indicated their love-making meant anything more to her than mutual comfort after a bad night. She wasn't in love with him. Hadn't been for years.

She'd been crushed when O'Donnaugh left her. Roman had to keep reminding himself of that. Regardless of how much it hurt. It was his own damned fault he'd lost her in the first place.

He was so wrapped up in his misery that it took him several moments to realize there was a cop car right behind him, lights flashing, sirens blaring.

What the hell?

He narrowed his eyes at the County Sheriff's emblem on the door of the vehicle as it stopped alongside the Jeep, penning him onto the shoulder of the highway. Three good-old-boy deputies disgorged from the cruiser and approached the Jeep, all of them sporting nightsticks and arrogant grins.

"Well, looky here, boys," the first silver-haired deputy taunted. "We've caught ourselves a car-stealin' redskin."

Roman's grip tightened on the steering wheel, disgust tensing his muscles. *Morons.*

"A car-stealin' *woman*-stealin' redskin," the second man, also with gray hair, corrected.

Aha. So that's what this was about. He marveled at his own naiveté, thinking the good sheriff would let him off so easily. The man just didn't have the guts to get his own hands dirty.

"What do you s'pose we otta do with the filthy scum?" the third, younger one asked no one in particular.

Roman flexed his fingers and unbuckled his seat belt.

It looked as if he was going to get that fight after all.

Chapter 7

"Roman?"

RaeAnne pushed open the door to the cabin and turned to give Philip a last wave. It had been an awkward couple of hours and she was glad to see the tail end of his cruiser.

He'd apologized for his behavior, and tried very hard to be understanding—if not exactly forgiving—of the situation this morning. And was more than surprised when she'd made it clear she didn't think a second chance would be a good idea, despite her earlier pleas and a flat-out denial that she and Roman were getting back together. Of course, having slept with her "old friend" in the meantime had pretty much squelched any further declarations of innocence.

Especially when a niggling voice told her how incredibly reckless they'd been this morning relying on the withdrawal method for protection. Stupid, stupid, stupid. They'd used it for the occasional emergency back in school, and it had been a plain miracle she hadn't gotten pregnant before she did back then. This morning, neither of them had been prepared for what had happened, and in their unstoppable passion they'd had no choice. Luckily it was a fairly safe time of month, but there was always a possibility...

No, she couldn't even *think* it. It wouldn't happen. It just couldn't.

"Roman?"

The room echoed back at her in the hollow way of deserted places. She knew without looking he wasn't here, even though the Jeep was parked out front in its usual spot. Maybe he'd walked up to the site.

That's when she noticed her keys sitting on the small kitchen table, holding down a piece of paper. Instantly her gaze darted in alarm to the spot where he'd kept his pack.

Gone.

She closed her eyes and took a deep breath, refusing to give in to the flood of emotions which clamored to be let loose.

She'd known all along this would happen. He'd never made any secret of his lifestyle. Or made any promises to change. Hell, she'd *wanted* him to leave. She didn't trust him, and even if she did, she couldn't be with someone who was always on the move. She'd told him to go, and apparently, he'd honored her request.

As RaeAnne reached for the note, she choked back a wave of bitterness that he'd never even tried to change her mind.

Not that she would have—but it might have made her feel better about so easily giving in to old feelings, and about the new ones that had been sewn through that surrender. Not to mention if she was carrying his child. Again.

Picking up the square of paper, she viewed it through eyes that swam out of focus. There was no writing. No message. Just a heart drawn in ink around the letter R.

Once again, she hadn't even deserved a goodbye.

Her heart hitched, and she ran out the door, dropping everything in her haste to get away, out to the trees and the flowers and the sky, and all the things that had carried her through a lifetime of disasters. They would carry her through this one, too, she knew, and heal the pain.

It only *felt* like she would die. Again.

* * *

Damn, he hurt.

Roman drifted in and out of a strange fog of unconsciousness, only aware of the passage of time because at one point he cracked open his swollen eyelids and it was dark. At least he thought it was dark. Or maybe it was just the blood that had dried over his eyes.

No matter. His whole body was a bundle of aches and pains, so he was content to float about in that twilight haze where dreams are real and the flesh somehow isn't so important. Funny, he didn't feel cold. He should have felt cold. Especially since it must have rained somewhere along the line. His clothes were soaked with rain. Or was it sweat? He tried to raise his hand to feel which, but couldn't manage. Hell, maybe it was just the blood again.

One thing was for certain, it wasn't that snow those shifty mountains had tried to cover his face with. Nope, he'd managed to shake all that off. Those lousy mountains definitely had it in for him. Oh, yeah, he'd seen them, bending over him, craggy faces creased with mock worry, whispering about him in their guttural granite language.

But he'd outsmarted them. Yessir. Played dead he did, while they'd spirited him to their windy lair and covered him in a layer of freezing white.

He moaned, wishing he'd thought to lick some of it into his parched mouth before casting it all off.

So tired. Gotta get some sleep. Cold now.

Rae? Where's the blanket? Never mind, the baby's wrapped in it.

He smiled, despite the sharp pain it caused.

"Sleep, baby," he whispered, and slipped back into unconsciousness.

For RaeAnne, the next two days flew by in a flurry of hard work at the site and late nights cataloging the day's finds.

She rose at the crack of dawn and didn't lay her head down until she dropped from exhaustion. That was the only way she could make herself sleep in the same bed where they'd—

No. She wasn't going to think about it. About him. She would just drive herself crazy and it wouldn't do any good anyhow. She knew that from firsthand experience.

She excavated like a woman possessed. She opened three new units and took them all down to sterile soil. New boxes of artifacts and site debris were stacked nearly to the cabin's low ceiling. She found more skeletal remains, of what appeared to be two individuals, and carefully packed them up to send to Dr. Cooper for examination.

She didn't even mind when Toby and the gang showed up twice to hassle her. She just glared at them and told them to buzz off. And they surprised her by doing just that. Who knew? Maybe the Chairman had had a word with them.

On the morning of the third day, she even started the preliminary work on her final excavation report. May as well, since her time at Cleary would soon be up. She was well ahead of schedule by now, and could easily head home a few days early.

Home.

As she dragged her bucket of tools across the meadow to the spot where she'd decided to sink one more unit before lunch, she thought about the bare, white-walled bungalow she currently called home. She'd scarcely had time to rent it and stow her few possessions there before she'd had to leave for the dig. It was important to her to have a place she could call her own. Even if there was nothing in it but a few suitcases and a floor full of junk mail.

Maybe this time she'd plant a garden. She was ruminating about whether to have flowers or vegetables, when her trowel struck something hard, buried in the dirt. She hadn't paid too much attention to the fact that the soil had been much easier to dig here than in the other units. But now she sat back, noticing a definite difference in the color of the soil and the types of plants which grew in the shallow depression she'd chosen to investigate—both sure signs of human disturbance.

"Huh," she muttered, hoping for a nice kitchen midden rather than another grave which she'd have to fill out paperwork on in triplicate.

Once again she rued the day she'd come up with the dumb idea to get her grant money by solving the mystery of Cleary Hot Springs. So far, the biggest mystery was how she'd placate the family when she couldn't come up with any evidence of what had become of their great-great-granduncle.

Heaving a sigh, she carefully stuck her trowel under the obstruction and lifted. Then let out a scream and jumped about seven feet in the air, scrambling away as fast as she could.

In horror, she stared down into the shallow pit. Sticking up from the dirt were the remains of a human hand.

But this one was no bleached archaeological find. There was still skin on it.

Something was poking him.

"Go 'way," Roman muttered and tried to move his hand to emphasize the point. It wouldn't budge. He seemed to be cocooned in something heavy and scratchy.

Annoyed, he concentrated on dragging his mind from the dense fog that gripped his whole body. What the hell was wrong with him? He felt like he'd been run over by a Sherman tank, and his mouth was glued shut and tasted like dirt.

"C'mon, man, wake up. I'm late for dinner."

Roman pondered that bit of absurd information. *Late for dinner.* Who did he know who might be late for dinner? That implied a family. He didn't know anyone who would be late for dinner. Except Tanya. Or Cole.

"Oh, for cryin' out loud. I know you're awake under that freakin' blanket!" The hot, scratchy weight was jerked from his face. "Snap out of it, man! I know I gave you too much of that stuff but this is ridiculous!"

Drugged.

The question was, by whom? And why?

Roman forced his eyelids up, and attempted to focus on the face that bobbed above him. A kid. An Indian kid. *Toby.*

''Why'd you drug me?'' he asked in a rasp, sifting through the flotsam of disjointed memories that were starting to drift through his brain.

Worried black eyes peered back at him. ''You got beat up. We needed to move you before they came back. You looked pretty bad.''

Ah, yes. The fight.

Well, okay, the beating. He groaned, choosing not to dwell on that humiliation. ''RaeAnne?''

''She's fine.''

Roman grunted. ''How long have I been out?''

There was a pause, then a guilty-sounding, ''A day. Well, two. Two and a half.''

''Two days?'' Instinctively he jerked to a sitting position, then ground out a curse at the resulting explosion of pain all over. ''What were you thinking?''

''Grandmother said you needed sleep to heal. She gave me some herbal tea for you to drink. When I saw how bad you looked, I doubled the dose.''

Lord spare him from meddling grandmothers and well-intentioned, clueless kids. ''Thanks loads.''

''I'm sorry—I thought you were dying. But Grandmother says it's not serious. Mostly bumps and bruises, once we washed the blood off.''

Roman scanned the area around him as best he could. It was dark, and they were sitting in some kind of shallow cave, flanked by a small campfire. Judging by the barren terrain and the scent of dust and sage, they were in the hills on the desert side of the river. He frowned. Where was the snow? He definitely remembered snow. And something about a baby.

Baby? *Ah hell.*

''I need to get back to RaeAnne. She probably thinks—'' He groaned again, and held his aching head in his hands. *Oh,*

God. He could just imagine. Idly he noted the blanket that covered him was bright white. So the snow had just been a delusion.

"She thinks you left," Toby said softly.

No damn kidding. He didn't even want to think about what terrible delusions she currently harbored about him.

"We found your Harley and pack dumped off a cliff half-way down the mountain from Cleary."

Could it get any worse?

"Not a high cliff, though. The Harley's a bit dented, but still runs. Your other stuff's fine." Toby pointed out into the darkness. "They're down at the end of the trail when you want them."

Roman stared at him in surprise. "Thanks, kid." Then added, "But I don't get it. Why are you helping me? We haven't exactly been on the same side."

The boy averted his gaze and stirred the fire with a stick. Something was going on here.

"Well?"

"I know who you are." At his questioning glance, the kid explained, "They'd tossed your ID and gun next to you in the ditch where they left you." So much for the locals not finding out he was FBI. "I figure they spooked when they realized you're FBI. After they thought about it they must have gotten scared and set it up to look like you'd died crashing your bike, and were coming back to kill you."

The skin on Roman's scalp crawled at the simple logic of Toby's reasoning. Which was right on target. "Looks like I owe you my life, *compadre.* Thanks."

Toby shrugged as though saving somebody's life were an everyday occurrence.

"But I still don't understand why. Especially if you know I work for the FBI...."

"They need to be stopped," the boy said, suddenly displaying as much vehemence as when he'd strung up Rae-Anne from a tree.

Roman's brain was just not functioning. "Who? The FBI?"

"No, not them. The poachers."

Now he was really confused. Maybe if his head wasn't pounding like a machine gun… "You've lost me."

"The poaching," the kid said, as if repeating it would make everything clear. "You're an FBI agent. I figure you're here because of what your father found out. And to finally put these guys behind bars. Here—" Roman stared in bewilderment as Toby produced yet another envelope from a pocket and handed it to him. "Here's all his notes. And mine, too."

Roman's head spun in a dull throb of perplexity. He was sure there was a simple explanation. It was just eluding him at the moment. "My father's notes?"

"Yeah. And mine."

"About poaching."

"Yeah."

"Which you think has something to do with the guys who beat me up?"

"Who want to kill you," the boy corrected.

"Tobe," he said, easing himself slowly back to lean his bruised body against the wall of the cave, "Kid, I think you'd better start at the beginning."

Cops were everywhere. In the cabin, in the meadow, down in all the units, and a ring of them surrounded the spot where RaeAnne had found the body. She was going nuts, worrying about what they were destroying in the process of preserving their precious crime scene.

"Where's Santangelo?" Philip asked.

"Who knows. Gone," she said, uneager to elaborate. "How long will this investigation take? I've got work to finish."

"Probably another day or two. When you're dealing with multiple jurisdictions things get complicated."

"Swell."

"When'd he leave?"

She tapped her foot. "Same day you met him." Philip seemed surprised, so she couldn't resist adding, "I did mention he wasn't sticking around. Or didn't you believe me?"

Philip looked away, watching the crime scene guys do their thing over the shallow grave. "So he left four days ago, and yesterday you discover a dead body on your site?"

She gave an incredulous snort. "Sheriff, the remains I deal with are generally a couple hundred years old, but even I know enough to tell that body's been dead for longer than four days. Besides—"

"Besides what? He'd never do such a thing?"

"That's right."

Philip sent her a cool look. "Even with friends, sometimes people aren't what you think they are."

She turned away, unable to disagree, unwilling to let him see how hurt she'd been by Roman's precipitous departure. She should have known better—she did know better—but knowing in advance didn't always prepare you for the pain.

She couldn't hide the bitterness in her voice when she replied, "And sometimes they're exactly what you think they are."

They were following him.

Roman could feel it in the back of his neck and the incessant hum in his brain. He'd picked them up somewhere on Highway 6, and hadn't lost them yet. He hadn't had but a glimpse of the car, but it was back there somewhere. He knew it as well as he knew what they were after.

The papers Toby had given him.

He still couldn't quite believe what the kid had told him. Law enforcement officials involved in illegal poaching and trafficking of endangered species. The thought was incredible. More so because apparently it had been going on so long his father had been involved in trying to stop it thirty years ago. It was hard to credit. Then again, his own body bore the bruising evidence of just how bad these so-called lawmen had gone.

He must look like death warmed over. His whole body was one big jumble of aches and pains. Angry cuts covered his arms and face, and half his skin had turned vivid shades of black and blue, but at least nothing was broken. He'd live. His motorcycle, on the other hand, had fared slightly worse from its trip over the cliff; it sputtered and leaped its way along the highway's pavement, each jolt a punishment on Roman's tender bruises.

A flash of sun on roof sirens glinted in his rearview mirror, and he did a hurried decision. The next town he came to, he made a quick stop and had two sets of copies made of all the notes he carried. One he mailed to his boss at the FBI, the other to himself care of general delivery, Big Pine. He kept the originals with him. There was only one man he trusted with those.

As he drove the rest of the way to Los Angeles, he pondered the possible implications of what he'd learned. The Chairman had said sometimes people and situations weren't what they appeared to be. But this was really throwing him for a loop.

He knew it was stupid to read anything into a few scribbled notes about poaching written by his father thirty years ago. Just because the man cared about porcupines and eagles didn't mean he wasn't a drug dealer and a murderer.

Still, it didn't quite fit and it bugged Roman.

Unfortunately, now was not the time to try and figure things out. After five hours on the road, it was all he could do to keep the Harley rattling at top speed and not fall off in a blaze of agony outrunning his pursuer. By the time he got to Cole's place in Pasadena he could barely stand. No doubt he still had some of Toby's grandmother's drugs in his system and that's why he was having a tough time keeping his mind focused. Or his eyes, for that matter.

He had just enough presence of mind left to draw his

weapon as he pounded on the front door. He was sure that car had followed him the entire way.

A pretty woman opened the door, and he lurched past, jostling her aside. What was a woman doing in Cole's house?

Clearly horrified, she gaped at him, staring at his gun, then inched backward. He caught her arm, slamming the door shut behind them, leaning his back against a wall to gain a last vestige of concentration.

"No!" she cried. "No!"

Who was she? He cast a harried gaze around the room. And suddenly noticed it was all wrong. The wall color, the pictures, all unfamiliar. Cole never had frilly curtains and throw pillows.

He had the wrong house.

What the hell would he do now? He looked back at the woman, and something cracked through his woozy subconscious to register her extraordinary blue eyes.

Thank God. It must be— What was it Cole had called her, the mother of his child?

"Fire eyes," he croaked, then slid down the door and everything went black.

"Hey, *compadre*." Roman smiled up from the couch at his best friend, never so relieved to see anyone in his life. "Hell of a woman you've got yourself."

"Stubborn as a mule," Cole's wife, Rini, muttered. She stood at one end of the sofa, holding a cup of tea and attempting to look stern. But she'd already blown her forbidding nurse image, treating him gentle as a baby as she applied the gauze bandages he was now sporting everywhere. Gentle as the baby sleeping in the next room. Gentle as the baby in his dream.

Roman winked at Cole. "Thanks for the hospitality. I'll be out of your hair by morning."

"He's in no shape to travel," Rini primly informed his friend. "I saw that contraption he's riding, and—"

Chuckling, Cole rose and gave her a kiss. "No use, darlin'.

He's rattled out any brains he ever had a long time ago. One trip more or less won't make any difference.''

Roman closed his eyes and grinned inwardly as he struggled to sit up on the couch. Cole had done real good nabbing this one. Just the sort of woman his friend needed to keep his fancy lawyer butt in line.

When he opened his eyes again, Rini had gone, and Cole was handing him the tea. ''Drink. Then you can tell me just what the hell is going on.''

He eyed the tea warily then slugged it down in a grateful gulp. He was feeling considerably better. Especially since he'd been able to call his boss at the field office and report the beating incident along with his suspicions regarding the Inyo County Sheriff's Office, and secure permission to pursue things in his own way for the time being. An official investigation at this point would probably just drive the culprits to ground. He preferred the bastards behind bars for a long stretch, over instant gratification and a slap on the hand.

''I found her,'' he said, then reached for his jacket, which was folded over the back of the couch. Cole knew him well enough to know without asking he meant RaeAnne. He'd been in on the search from the very beginning. ''Can you keep this safe?''

His friend accepted the envelope Roman handed him with a nod. ''Of course.''

''Good.''

Roman leaned back and sighed. He felt oddly unburdened, as though a great weight had been lifted from his back. He wondered how much of it was the mysterious papers making it into safe hands, and how much had to do with the decision he'd made on the trip down.

Coming close to death had a way of compelling a man to see things a lot more clearly. And although his thoughts since leaving Toby's care before dawn this morning had certainly included his father and what this newest information meant to Roman's search for him, mostly they'd centered on one thing, and one thing alone: RaeAnne and how to keep her.

He'd thought forgiveness for the past was what he wanted, what he needed. But he'd gotten it, and guess what? It wasn't enough. Not nearly enough.

He'd be damned if he'd leave RaeAnne to the likes of Philip O'Donnaugh.

He wanted her for himself.

He didn't know how he'd manage to regain her trust, but he intended to try his damnedest. And this time he wouldn't let her go without a fight.

"I want to see your baby boy," Roman said, pushing to his feet and sliding his arm gingerly around his best friend's shoulder.

Together they walked to the nursery and leaned over the crib. The scent of baby powder filled Roman's nose and his heart stalled at the sight of the sweetly sleeping infant.

"He's beautiful," he squeezed out the words in a hushed voice. "You're a lucky guy."

"Better believe it," Cole said, gazing lovingly at his son. He looked up. "What about you and RaeAnne?"

A painful longing stabbed through him at the images his friend's innocent question sent spinning through his head. Of him and RaeAnne together, her belly swelling with their child, of finally being the family they were meant to be.

But first he had to deal with the good sheriff. Get her away from him. There was no doubt in his mind that as soon as he'd disappeared, O'Donnaugh had wormed his way back into her life, making the most of Roman's sudden departure and her surefire anger over it.

"She's mixed up with some creep," he said when he found Cole staring at him brows creased. "If he hurts her, I'll kill the bastard."

"You'd do that?" Cole asked, regarding him closely.

"Yeah." The man was bad news, down to the tips of his tin star.

"Would she thank you?"

"She loves me."

Of that he was dead certain. She might deny it, might fight

it to the bitter end. But holding her in his arms that last morning, he'd known. At the time, he hadn't trusted his instincts, finding every excuse to deny what he knew in his heart was true. She'd tried her best, but she hadn't been able to hide her true feelings.

She still loved him.

Before he'd been beaten to a pulp and left for dead, drugged, and ridden 250 miles through a meat grinder, he'd been resigned to accept her repeated declarations that they'd never work. That any future between them would be impossible.

Not now.

Now he realized how much she meant to him. Had always meant to him. Learning about the baby she'd lost, what she'd gone through because he'd left her, had nearly torn his heart out. He was not about to make the same mistake again. Not when he'd been given another chance to set things right.

As an FBI agent, he faced death often, sometimes daily. But his life had never meant much to him. He'd never had anything to live for. That's what had made him such a good undercover agent. Now he realized that he had something incredibly special within his grasp, if he only had the courage to reach out and grab it.

So, as he spoke quietly with his friend, stroking his new godson's soft cheek and downy hair, he decided it was time to fight fire with fire, friendship with passion, excuses with unrelenting willpower.

And take back the only thing that would ever make his life complete.

The love of his woman, RaeAnne.

Chapter 8

She heard him before she saw him. The motorcycle gave him away before he'd even crested the hill overlooking the site.

"Damn," RaeAnne swore, and glanced up toward the road, instantly filled with a host of conflicting emotions.

Roman was back.

Sure enough, silhouetted against a robin's-egg sky, he appeared atop the hill in a puff of dust, a vision in outlaw black and chrome, with silver chains glinting in the sun. There he halted the bike and scanned the valley, looking just like an updated version of a Hollywood Indian scouting out a wagon train to ambush. RaeAnne might have laughed at the image, except she knew darn well what precious plunder was at stake. Her heart.

"What's the problem?" asked Bugs Delaney, the lanky crime scene investigator she was helping to excavate the area where the body had been found.

"Roman," she muttered, furiously cutting off a transfusion

of unwanted elation the sight of him was pumping into her bloodstream.

"Santangelo?" Bugs asked.

She tossed him a glance. "You know him?"

The agent's eyes lit up. "Sure. Worked with him a couple of times. Good guy."

"If you say so."

She returned her attention to her digging and pointedly ignored the sputtering of the Harley as it headed down the hill.

"What's he doing here? I thought Dawson was in charge of this case."

RaeAnne wondered what calamity had brought Roman back. Maybe he'd heard about the body and gotten nosy. Maybe it had dawned on him she could be pregnant.

"We're old friends," she said, unwilling to speculate further on his motives. She'd find out soon enough.

"Oh," Bugs said, openly curious. Then a grin spread over his handsome face. "Oh!" he repeated, and RaeAnne instantly wanted to bean the guy with her trowel. It was obvious what he thought.

"*Just* friends," she said forcefully.

And meant it. She'd slipped up once, but it wasn't going to happen again. Roman's disappearance after they'd made love had taught her a hard lesson. One she needed to remind herself of every minute he spent in her company, regardless of the results of the pregnancy test she planned to take, just in case.

He hadn't changed. He still wasn't someone she could trust with her heart. Or with a child.

It didn't matter how many times he came back. The fact remained, to come back he had to leave. She could not deal with a man who would disappear from her life with no notice, no explanation and no goodbye save a worthless scribbled drawing. And a child shouldn't have to.

"Hi," his voice rumbled above her and suddenly she felt like crying.

Steeling herself against that weakness, she glanced up. And gasped. His face was covered in bruises, cuts and small white bandages.

"My God, you're hurt!" she cried, jumping to her feet and coming out of the unit in a single motion. She grasped his arms, saw him wince, and dropped them immediately. "What happened?"

"A little accident," he said. "Are you okay?"

"I'm fine. What happened to—"

"Anyone try to hurt you?"

"No, but—"

"Thank God." He seemed like he was about to pull her into an embrace so she stepped back. After a second's hesitation he stuck his hands into his pockets and turned to the investigator behind her. "Hey, Bugs. You working this one for CSI?"

"Yup," the other man answered, giving RaeAnne a much-needed moment out from under Roman's probing gaze to gather herself.

"Talk to me, buddy."

What had happened to him? Seeing him battered and bruised like that shook her to the core.

Bugs didn't even appear to notice. "Homicide by gunshot. Standard twelve-gauge shotgun to the back, fairly close range."

Naturally, none of her scenarios for Roman's leaving had envisioned him being hurt and unable to contact her.

"Time factor?"

"Still doing tests but a preliminary estimate would be one to two years."

Of course, that was nonsense because even if there wasn't a phone at the site, he only had to get in touch with the sheriff's office and Philip would have gotten her a message.

"Any ID yet?"

"Nothing local's popped out yet. We're running a missing persons."

"Who's the SAC?"

"Dawson." Bugs pointed to the front porch of her cabin, where the special agent in charge sat on the top step looking through crime scene photos.

"Better have a word."

Roman took hold of her hand, and to Bugs' grand amusement towed her toward the cabin like a rag doll. Which she went along with only because of the large gauze bandage wrapped around the breadth of his palm.

"Roman, you can't just ignore me and my questions."

"I'm not ignoring you. I'm assessing the situation."

"Which situation?" she mumbled.

"Both. Are you pregnant?"

"It's only been four days. I want to know what happened."

"We didn't have any condoms."

She shut her mouth in exasperation. The man was impossible when he'd determined to be obtuse. But exasperation was not good. Exasperation meant the anger had diminished.

"Santangelo!" Dawson exclaimed from the porch. "Man, am I glad to see you!" He bounded down the stairs and met them, stopping short. "What the hell happened to your face?"

"You don't want to know." Roman waved off his wounds with a grimace and shook the other man's hand. "How's it going, Dawson?"

Dawson gave him a beseeching look. "You gotta help me out, friend. There's just me and Bugs working this one. No phone. No electricity. How can I work from here? I've got to go around to the locals and see what I can dig up. Take over for me here at the crime scene, would you?"

"I'm on leave."

"Then what are you doing here?"

That's when Dawson noticed them holding hands and his eyes widened. Immediately she pulled out of Roman's clasp, but it was too late.

"Ah. I see. So then you won't mind." He grinned.

Roman gave her a quick glance but said nothing.

''Great! You follow the leads from up here, and the physical evidence Bugs turns up at the lab. I'll work it from the other end, in Bishop.'' With that he pushed the pile of photos at Roman and grinned. ''What a break. I'll call in and let the boss know. I assume you still don't carry a cell phone?''

''Nowhere to plug it in,'' Roman confirmed wryly.

''No problem. Bugs has one. Okay, I'm outta here. Bugs can fill you in on all the details. I'm gonna head for the Bishop PD.''

''All right,'' Roman calmly agreed. ''Keep in touch, *compadre*.''

''Thanks. I owe you one, buddy. I'll check in with Bugs at his motel tonight.''

Before she could utter a single word of protest, Dawson was hurrying toward his nondescript blue sedan.

''Hey wait a minute,'' she called after the rat, ''You can't just—'' He slammed the door and with a spin of his tires was gone. ''Oh, for crying out loud.''

Wonderful. Now she was really in trouble. An FBI investigation could drag on forever. There was no way she could be around Roman Santangelo forever. Or even another day. Just look at what had happened the last day he'd spent with her.

''No,'' she said determinedly. ''You can't be a part of this investigation.''

''Says who?''

''Says me. You can't stay here. I won't have it. Get Dawson back.''

''I don't think so.'' Roman turned and climbed the steps. ''Look, I'm about to fall over. Let's lie down and talk about things.''

Lie down?

''What are you, nuts? There's no way I'm getting in that bed with you, ever again.''

With a sigh, he paused at the door and said, ''I was afraid of that. Mad, huh?''

"Who me? You disappear without a word for *four days.* I'm supposed to be happy?"

"Would it make a difference if I said I had a good excuse?"

"You had a good excuse last time, too." Firmly pushing aside a stab of guilt over his bruises, she looked around for his bike. "So why don't you just do us both a favor and hop back on your motorcycle and leave?"

He opened the cabin door. "Sorry, I can't do that. The only place I'm hopping right now is into the sack. If you feel like talking, that's where I'll be." With that he went inside.

She crossed her arms tightly and stared after him, melting only slightly when she heard a deep groan as he settled onto the mattress.

She scowled. She *wouldn't* feel sorry for him. She refused to give in to the sympathy that welled inside her, or to her mounting worry over how he'd come by his injuries.

It wasn't her concern. It had nothing to do with her, and she wouldn't let a few bandages shake her resolve to insist he leave.

But she couldn't help wondering what *had* happened to him. A little accident, he'd said. Shoot, if that was a "little" accident, then the corpse they'd found was just a "little" dead.

Maybe she should insist he leave after he'd gotten some rest.

How had she allowed this to happen again? One minute she was mad as hell at him, and the next she was going all soft and mushy, letting him sleep in her bed, feeling the sweet sting of longing steal through her body.

She was headed for a heartache, and that was the sad truth. If he pulled rank and persisted in helping Dawson on this case—which she knew very well he had every intention of doing—she had no legal recourse. She'd have to let him stay.

And if it turned out against all odds she was pregnant, she had a sinking feeling she wouldn't be able to blast him away from her with dynamite. At least not until the next case called to him. Or the next good excuse to ride away.

She pushed out a long breath, telling herself for the thousandth time since he'd left that the man was no good for her. He was not what she needed. He was all wrong.

And she wouldn't let herself fall for him again.

It just was not going to happen.

Roman awoke to a pleasant hum in his ears and an unpleasant one in his head. Immediately he recognized the pleasant sound as coming from RaeAnne. She was humming a mindless tune as she quietly worked at the kitchen table.

The soft rustle of artifact bags and the crinkle of pages turning in a ledger filled the room with a homey atmosphere. Even the slight ache vibrating through his skull couldn't diminish the joy and satisfaction Roman felt at finding himself in such a cozy setting.

Somehow he'd managed to ensconce himself in her cabin, in her very bed, wrapped in her blanket and surrounded by the light, arousing perfume of her woman's body. He must have slept for hours and was feeling a whole lot better. Smiling, he snuggled deeper under the covers and kept his eyes firmly closed. He never wanted to move. Surely after spending about a hundred years right here he'd stop hurting completely, body and soul.

"You needn't play possum. I know you're awake," came her pert statement. "It's about time. I'm waiting for some answers."

"I'm not awake," he insisted, half hoping he was still on the mountainside hallucinating. This would not be an easy conversation and he'd just as soon skip it in favor of more pleasurable circumstance. "What time is it, anyway?"

"Ten o'clock. Now tell me what's going on."

"Ten?" He glanced toward the window and frowned. Sunshine poured through the dusty panes. "Then why is it still so light out?"

"It's 10:00 *a.m.* You slept nearly twenty hours."

"No wonder I feel better."

Had she lain next to him during the night?

"Why did you leave?" she asked. "And who did this to you?"

"Why do you assume it's a 'who' and not a 'what'?" he said, resisting the impulse to check her side of the bed for residual warmth.

"Because Bugs told me those bruises on your ribs and chest were made by a boot and the ones on your face by knuckles."

"You let him look at me naked?" Roman tried to feel whether he was completely bare or just his chest. And feet, he mentally added, wiggling his toes against the blanket.

"I described them to him."

"You looked at me naked?" He grinned, absurdly pleased she'd bothered to assess his condition. She did care, at least a little.

"You're not naked," she gritted out.

Sure enough, he could feel the rasp of denim against his hips and legs. Too bad. Lord, he *must* be feeling better.

"I just pulled off your boots. You'd done the T-shirt yourself. I couldn't help but notice the distinctive triangle shape of the black and blue marks, so I asked Bugs. He was very enlightening."

"Insects are his field of expertise, but he can wax eloquent about bruising," Roman agreed. "And does a mean exit wound, too."

He didn't have to open his eyes to know she'd closed hers and was counting to ten. His grin widened. He did love her hot little temper. It had always led to such gratifying make-ups. Maybe if he really pushed her—

"Please, Roman. Tell me who did this to you. And why."

The bed dipped and he felt her hand gently rest on his chest. His eyes sprang open to see her gazing down at him, eyebrows pleated.

Hell. He was wrong, she wasn't angry; she was worried.

It was almost as if she somehow knew it was connected to her, and couldn't stand that.

He looked up at her face, so concerned, so trusting. He wished to God he didn't have to shatter a piece of that trust.

"I didn't leave. I couldn't come back. Three Inyo County sheriff's deputies gave me a tune-up and left me for dead. Toby found me and saved my life. But I was out for almost three days thanks to his grandmother's home remedy."

"Oh, my God!" Her expression melted into a portrait of stunned confusion. "But that can't be true! Why would sheriff's deputies beat you up?"

"They mentioned something about me stealing cars and women. And that I should leave Inyo County and not come back. They did their best to persuade me to their point of view."

"Stealing women?"

"Course, that was before they found my FBI credentials."

Her eyes narrowed. "What are you trying to imply?"

He sighed. "I'm implying nothing, *cara*. Just answering your questions."

She leaped off the bed, fury emanating from every pore. "I don't believe it. You're saying Philip had something to do with this!"

"O'Donnaugh wasn't there. He was with you."

"You think he gave the orders!"

"I didn't say that."

"But that's what you believe."

Disgusted, he tossed off the blanket and rolled to his feet. "The only thing I believe right now is, something is going on here that shouldn't be. And trust me, I'm going to get to the bottom of it."

She'd stalked from the cabin shortly after that, and was out at the site helping Bugs. Roman could see them, heads bent together over something or other that had shown up in the screen. He had to parry a stab of jealousy over the sight of them standing so close. Bugs was smart, good-looking, and single. True, examining dead bodies wasn't exactly a glamorous profession. But still, if Bugs made a move on RaeAnne, it would be over *his* dead body.

Roman wrestled his jealousy back and shook his head over how quickly the flames of possessiveness had swept over him. It would be pure torture giving her up if she really meant to send him away.

But he was determined that wouldn't happen anytime soon. Luckily she hadn't pressed the issue of wanting him to leave. He hated to be hard-nosed about it, but there was no chance in hell he was going anywhere until this murder case was solved. There were too many questions. Too many co-incidences. And too many *cosmic* connections—the kind that intersected around him and her and Cleary Hot Springs. As an FBI agent, if there was one thing he totally mistrusted, it was coincidence.

On top of which, Bugs was staying at a motel down the mountain, which meant she'd be at the site alone.

Not an ice cube's chance.

After breakfast, he strolled up to the hot springs for a long soak, hoping the minerals in the water would hurry his heal-ing. He peeled off all the small bandages Cole's wife had plastered over his face and arms and lay back in the steaming granite basin, counting butterflies and the steady stream of vehicles on the winding road to and from the lumber camp.

And came up with a plan.

''Coffee anyone?''

Roman had put together some sandwiches and brewed a pot of cowboy coffee, figuring RaeAnne would drop dead from hunger before coming back to the cabin for lunch.

''You're looking a lot better,'' Bugs commented as he ac-cepted an enameled mug. ''What the hell happened, any-way?''

''Long story,'' Roman evaded, pouring RaeAnne a cup and adding sugar. He tried to catch her eye as she took it, but she wouldn't look at him. *This was going well.*

"So, Bugs, got any theories about our dead guy?"

Bugs sipped his coffee with an ambrosial expression. "You always did make the best java. Well, it seems like a pretty straightforward case of murder by gunshot. Nothing struck me as too out of the ordinary."

"Other than the burial site," Roman said, taking a seat near the edge of the unit they were working in.

"Right. No blood in the grave and not a lot left in the body, so he was killed somewhere else and brought here for disposal."

"Why?" RaeAnne said, then looked up when they turned to her. "Why here?"

"That's the big question," Roman concurred, glad curiosity had prodded her from her silence.

"The lab is working on some plant fibers from the clothes. Might give us a clue," Bugs said.

"Did you get fingerprints?"

Bugs nodded. "Some partials. Dawson should be getting the ID this morning, if he's in the system."

Thoughtfully RaeAnne gazed at Roman. "And with any luck, knowing who he is will give you a motive for his death, and thereby the identity of the killer as well."

"Ideally," he agreed, "that's how it works."

Open-and-shut. That's what he wanted out of this case. That, and no connection between the murder and RaeAnne or her excavation, which thank God was impossible, due to the timing of the death.

"It has to be someone who knows the area," she said, tapping a finger against her lips. He was captured by the image, supple strength against moist softness, and wished he could become that small column so casually accepting her mouth's caress.

"Otherwise they wouldn't know about this site," she continued, snapping him out of his daydream. "Hide a body in an old cemetery. Pretty smart. They probably hoped the remains would just blend in with all the others."

He swiped up his mug to keep his hands occupied, once

again impressed with her deductions. He frowned as a thought occurred. "And if the killer is still around, he must have been damn nervous when you first started your dig. Did anyone give you a hard time, or try to stop you?"

RaeAnne shook her head slowly. "No. Just Toby."

They stared at each other as the implications settled in. Just one more reason to find Toby immediately and grill the kid. Roman had accumulated quite a list by now.

"Toby can't be involved. He's just a boy."

As he said, Roman didn't believe in coincidence, and there were too many of them concerning Toby. He was involved, all right. Roman just wasn't sure how.

"I don't think Toby's killed anyone," he said evasively. "What about the lumber camp?"

"Lumber camp?" Bugs interjected.

Roman jerked a chin toward the high country. "Up the mountain a few miles. Pretty active, judging from the traffic."

"Maybe a fight got out of hand?"

"Would make sense. And here would certainly be a convenient spot for one of them to dump the body. They must all know about the historical site." More often than not the simplest explanation solved the crime. He prayed it was the case this time, too.

"A twelve-gauge shotgun is as common as it gets. I'll bet the lumber camp is littered with them."

"Do you know how long the camp's been there?" he asked RaeAnne.

She shook her head. "A long time. But Philip would know more exactly. He goes up there all the time."

He whipped his gaze to her. "Is that so?"

"Don't start with me," she muttered through clenched teeth. "A cruiser comes through almost daily, checking on things. The sheriff likes knowing what's going on in his jurisdiction."

Roman wasn't about to remind her that the National Forest wasn't part of the sheriff's jurisdiction. If the man was guilty of something, proof would surface and Roman'd be spared playing the Big Bad Wolf to Mr. Perfect.

Instead he said, "Then O'Donnaugh should know if any of the loggers disappeared in the past year or two."

"I'm sure he would," she answered in clipped tones.

"And if anyone quit recently."

"You mean the killer?" She suddenly looked worried.

He nodded. "If the killer is one of the seasonal workers, I doubt he's stayed in the area. Especially after you started excavating."

Nervously she glanced around the site. "God, I hope not."

He rose, dusting off his pants. "Don't worry, you've got Bugs here to protect you."

"Hey!" Bugs said, "Where will you be?"

He gave the other man a wry smile. "Doing my job. Which I can't do sitting here drinking coffee, as much as I'd like to."

"Uh, listen." Bugs stood up and handed him a pile of evidence bags. "I was wondering…"

Roman placed the bags in the carton next to the unit. "Spit it out, *compadre.*"

"Miss Martin has been very cooperative, helping me gather my samples and evidence."

"Thank you," she said with a smile.

"But the thing is, I'm down to the area right under where the body was, and, well, I prefer to work that part alone. You know how oblivious I get while I'm working, so I feel Miss Martin would be safer if she went with you today."

Bugs gave him a grin worthy of the Cheshire Cat. The man was a regular nuisance. "You do, eh?"

"That won't be necessary," RaeAnne said primly. "I have things to take care of. I don't need a bodyguard."

From her lips, the term bodyguard took on a whole new meaning. Oh, yeah. He'd love to guard her body. Closely. The trouble was, at this point the main thing her body needed protection from was him. Still, Bugs had a point.

"Until we know what we're dealing with, Bugs is right. It's best we stick together."

"Oh, honestly. You desert me for four days, and now you're worried about my safety? Make up your mind, Roman."

He turned and took in the sight of her. Her proud stance and tilt of her chin, the arms crossed across her chest like armor, the vulnerable trace of hurt and heartache that still lingered in the depths of her eyes. The hint of uncertainty.

No, there was no need to make up his mind. It had been made up long ago. It had just taken him too many years to recognize.

"Please," he said, stretching out his free hand toward her. "I want you with me."

It didn't come out as the order he'd intended, but more of a plea. Just as well. It made her meet his gaze and hesitate.

Just long enough for him to add, "But first I need you to do me a big favor."

Chapter 9

"You want me to do *what?*"

Caught by complete surprise, RaeAnne laughed out loud. "Cut your hair? Are you serious?"

Roman tipped his head. The long raven strands flowed from his crown to his shoulders, the shorter sides and braid over his ear making him look like some kind of space pirate. Amusement suddenly twinkled in his eyes. "Well, if you like it this way so much, I guess I could keep it—"

"Oh, no," she said, taking in the wild hairdo. "A new style would be good." She wiggled a brow. "But are you sure you still trust me with scissors near your neck?"

"Funny."

She smiled, remembering all the times she'd trimmed his hair in high school. She'd apprenticed for a summer in a beauty salon to get out of Home Economics the next semester, and he'd been her guinea pig. Most of her experiments had turned out okay. He'd never complained. Especially when she'd shampooed his hair at home afterward in the bathtub. To this day she couldn't take a bubble bath without being assailed by visions of suds slipping over smooth bronze skin, or getting a shiver over the thought of what would always come next.

He met her glance, and she knew immediately he was also remembering those times in the tub. She pushed the memories aside and asked briskly, "Not that I think a haircut won't be an improvement, but what brought this on?"

"Since I'm going official on this case, I suppose I should give my undercover image a rest." He watched her steadily, heat still blazing in his eyes, despite his innocuous answer.

"Ah." She licked her lips, unable to stifle her body's instinctive reaction to his unspoken invitation, or even look away.

"Time for a change, anyhow," he added.

The low, intimate timbre of his words made her legs suddenly weak. It was a tone that said he was talking about more than getting a haircut.

I want you with me.

His earlier declaration continued to ring in her ears. She didn't know what to think. He kept saying stuff like that, and yet he disappeared when she needed him most. When he should want to be with her and nowhere else.

"Want to borrow my surgical scissors?" Bugs offered from down in the unit, breaking through her confusion. "They're pretty sharp. Just do me a favor and don't mess up my crime scene."

RaeAnne accepted the scissors and led Roman to a tree stump in the meadow, well away from the grave site. He pulled off his shirt and took a seat.

Bugs was right. The scissors were really sharp. She had to give the job her full attention as she snipped away Roman's hair, and not look down at the broad expanse of strong back, the thick ropes of his biceps and forearms, the knotted discs of his male nipples. Or the blue-green web of bruises scattered over his otherwise perfect body. To see all that would surely shatter her concentration and cause a disaster.

Somehow she was able to hold her hands steady as she

clipped away long locks of obsidian-black, leaving a civilized man in the pirate's place.

Well, almost civilized. She stood back for a good look at her handiwork, and her pulse skipped at the sheer, primitive male power he exuded, even at rest.

"What do you think?" he asked, brushing snippets of hair from his shoulders.

A wedge of air stuck in her throat and she forgot completely what she was supposed to be looking at. Her gaze slid down his body and snagged on his lean, trim waist, his low-slung black leather pants hugging his hips without an inch of surplus.

"Um…"

Under the bruises, his smooth skin glowed like polished copper, muscles rippling across a washboard torso. She was seized with an irrational urge to stroke her hands over his battered chest and ribs, horror at what he'd gone through all jumbled up inside together with a potent attraction that wouldn't be denied. She wanted to soothe his hurts, and assuage her own hunger to touch him at the same time.

Lord, she had to get hold of herself.

She snapped herself back to the subject of Roman's haircut. "A little short for my taste, but it'll do."

"Come here," he said, capturing her eyes with his, beckoning her back to him through the pure force of his will.

A bad idea. She shook her head.

"Brush me off." He handed her his shirt and waited expectantly.

A really bad idea. She didn't move.

"Scared?"

She lifted her chin. "Of course not." Gripping the shirt, she made herself step nonchalantly between his legs again, afraid to admit to either of them just how terrified she really was. "Don't be ridiculous."

With firm swipes of the shirt, she dusted the fallen hairs from his shoulders, careful to keep from actually touching him. "What would I be scared of?"

"Touching me." He just smiled when she jerked away and stared at him. "Because if you do, you'll have to admit to yourself how much you want me to touch you back. And that scares you even more."

She felt the heat rise in her face. How did he do it? How could he constantly read her mind like that?

"I saw how you looked at me, *cara*."

She gave herself a mental kick and replied, "You're a good-looking man. Who wouldn't?"

His lazy smile blazed through her like a torch on ice cream. "Not like you were looking."

"You're dreaming, Santangelo."

"Oh, yeah," he said. "I'm dreaming." His hands reached for her hips, pulled her closer into the V of his legs. "Dreaming of you and me together."

She subdued the jolt of electricity his touch sent through her and extracted herself from his grip, circling around to his back. "I told you I'm not going to bed with you again."

"Who said anything about bed?"

She rested her hands on his shoulders, oh, so tempted to slide them around to his chest, embracing the warmth of his body, filling her arms with the feel of him.

"I want you," he quietly said. "Anywhere I can have you."

It was no more than she already knew, but his words, spoken so simply and with such emotion, almost did her in.

Squeezing her eyes shut, she whispered, "Please, Roman, don't."

"Why not? It's the truth."

"It can't work. We both know it. There's too much past between us, and not enough future."

"What if you're pregnant?" He turned on the tree stump and tugged her onto his lap. Tenderly he took her face between his hands. "What if you're having my child?"

Then he kissed her. Long and sweet and warm and persuasive. In his kiss she tasted his hunger, his yearning for her, and the sincerity of his desire for their child. He wrapped his arms around her and she almost melted into him, wishing with all her heart she could just let herself go and be everything he wanted her to be.

But she knew he was only feeling guilty about the baby he hadn't known about, and blaming himself for her losing it. He was grasping at a straw of redemption by trying to turn their relationship into something it wasn't.

"I'm not pregnant," she murmured, trying to pull back. "We were careful. Besides, it's the wrong time of month."

"You can't be certain. Not until we do a test."

"We will. But I am sure," she said with a confidence she didn't come close to feeling. She couldn't even bear to contemplate the choices ahead if she was. But she wasn't. Withdrawal wasn't foolproof, but it generally worked.

He kissed her again, tearing away another brick from her crumbling defenses. "If you can't forgive the past," he whispered, "and won't give me your future, at least grant me now. Now, while we're together."

Her whole body trembled, crying out with a need to say, *Yes! Yes, let's be together, truly together, for these few precious days. Damn the cost to my heart!*

But he was right. She was scared to death. Not just of being pregnant, or reliving the horrors of eighteen years ago. But because if she let herself fall for him again, to the depths she had before, this time she'd never recover.

The sound of tires crunching and a door slamming across the meadow filtered into Roman's consciousness. He tore his eyes from RaeAnne's to look. Sheriff O'Donnaugh was walking through the grass toward them.

Roman muttered a vivid curse and tightened his hold on RaeAnne as she started to jump from his lap. "We aren't done with this conversation," he said, waiting for her reluctant nod before allowing her to escape.

Damn the sheriff and his meddling. The man could take his fake smile, his evil plots and his corrupt deputies and go to hell with them all.

Pausing for a deep breath, Roman banked the hot spike of anger and rose to his feet. He shook out his shirt and donned it, along with his best official expression. He was nothing if not a professional, and he had a job to do. O'Donnaugh held potentially important information about the case he was working, and getting in the man's face in any way, even under present circumstances, would not help solve it. The sheriff would pay dearly for having him beaten, but that would keep.

"I thought you left town, Santangelo," O'Donnaugh said as he strode over to where Roman stood waiting with RaeAnne.

"I'm not that easy to get rid of," he replied stonily.

"Where's Dawson?"

"Up in Bishop. I'm in charge of the crime scene now."

"You?"

Roman flipped open his FBI credentials and held them up like a dare.

The other man's brows flared, then beetled as he read them. "You're working this case?"

"Got a problem with that?"

O'Donnaugh shrugged. "Why should I?"

The man was cool, Roman had to give him that. Very cool.

The sheriff looked him over assessingly, a perusal that stopped briefly on his fresh haircut, then moved to RaeAnne. "Morning, RaeAnne. Are you all right?"

Her warm smile for his rival sliced right through Roman. He had to restrain himself from putting a protective arm around her and growling.

"I'm fine, Philip. Though I'll be glad when this investigation is over." Roman didn't care for the voice inside telling him she really meant she'd be glad when her time with *him* was over. "I don't suppose you've found out anything new?" she asked.

O'Donnaugh pulled a file from under his arm. "Well, as a matter of fact, I came to deliver this to Dawson." He reluctantly turned to Roman and handed it over. "It came in from AFIS this morning for him."

"The fingerprint ID?" Roman snapped open the jacket from the National Automated Fingerprint ID system and scanned it quickly.

"Yeah."

"What does it say?" RaeAnne asked, peering over his shoulder to read.

The sheriff bristled. "RaeAnne, I really don't think you should be—"

"Jason Danforth? Any idea who he was?"

Roman turned to the second page, a photocopy of the victim's driver's license. "Forty-eight years old. From Bishop."

"So he was fairly local," she said.

"Seems so." Ignoring O'Donnaugh's continuing protests, he leafed to the third page and whistled low as several coincidences clicked into place. "Fish and Game," he read, and swiveled to meet RaeAnne's gaze. "I'll be damned. Jason Danforth was a Fish and Game agent."

"Poaching. I just can't believe it."

Roman had spent the better part of the trip to Big Pine Reservation relating to RaeAnne the story Toby had told him at the cave. He described the contents of the notes the boy had given him, including all the sordid details about how the sheriff's office was the hub of a small but steady trade in illegal animal parts. Bear gall bladders for oriental herbalists, mountain cats for trophy seekers, exotic meats for pricey restaurants and hides, eagle feathers and porcupine quills for Native American regalia. Roman's father, and later Toby, had carefully recorded dates of suspected dealings, along with species, location and any other details, depending on the source of the information—usually elicited from a hunter or backpacker who'd come across what was left of the remains. Over the years they had built up quite a list by talking to everyone possible who came off the mountain, but unfortunately none of the notes contained any hard evidence.

"Why would they do it?"

"Poaching, even on a small scale, is a very lucrative business. When profits are big enough, some people don't care if the animals they kill are endangered."

"But murdering Danforth?"

"People are killed every day over a wallet with ten dollars in it. Here, we're talking thousands, maybe tens of thousands per year. The punishment for poaching is basically a slap on the wrist. They probably didn't want to lose their golden goose."

"But still, murdering someone... These people are law enforcement officials!"

Roman snorted, fingering his cheek. "Right."

She darted a somber glance at his bruises and grimaced. "Point taken. So you think this Fish and Game guy stumbled on their scheme and they eliminated him?"

"It's a theory."

She didn't speak for the short drive from the highway onto the Reservation and to Toby's house, but he could practically hear the cogs spinning in her head. She obviously didn't care for the conclusions she was reaching.

"I still refuse to believe Philip is involved in any of this," she said as they walked up the driveway.

"Time will tell," he answered, knocking on the door.

He wasn't going to get involved in that debate. Only real evidence would convict the man in her eyes. The fact that the initials *O'D* appeared in the notes written by his father wasn't proof. They could mean Old MacDonald for all they knew—not that he thought for a second the initials referred to anyone but the good sheriff.

Maybe Dawson would come up with some angle or connection between the sheriff's office and Danforth in his questioning. Since the Bishop Police Department had handled the initial investigation into Danforth's disappearance, Dawson had moved his base of operations to the Bishop Homicide squad, bringing himself up-to-speed on the missing person's file, reinterviewing everyone mentioned in it and following up on all the leads. That left Roman free to pursue things from this end—working from the physical evidence backward. Hopefully they'd meet somewhere in the middle, and he'd bet his last dollar that would be right on top of O'Donnaugh and his deputies.

"May I help you?" A middle-aged woman peered at them from behind Toby's screen door, bringing him back to the situation at hand. He assumed it was the kid's mother.

"Yes, ma'am."

Roman introduced RaeAnne and himself, once again inwardly flinching at the woman's warm reaction to his father's name. He also noted that she politely pretended not to notice his bruises but couldn't quite mask her curiosity. Interesting. Toby must have skipped Mom when he'd consulted Grandma about the herbal tea.

"We're looking for Toby. Is he home from school yet?"

"Is there a problem?" she asked, motherly concern clouding her eyes.

"No, not at all," he said, choosing not to make this an official visit. "He delivered a box to us up at Miss Martin's archaeological dig, and we just had a couple of questions about it, that's all." Roman smiled reassuringly.

"He won't be home until Sunday." She hesitated, then added, "He went up the mountain."

The way she said the words made it clear she believed the trip was some kind of spiritual quest or pilgrimage. Roman had his doubts. He figured the kid was either off investigating another wildlife kill report, or dodging Roman.

Whatever. The kid had picked a hell of a time to go walkabout. Roman glanced up at the mountains, and tried not to give in to frustration.

"Any idea where he was headed?" Toby's mom shook her head.

No. She wouldn't. Toby himself probably didn't know. That is, unless he'd heard something specific, which Roman gave about a-thousand-to-one odds, considering the microscope local law enforcement was currently under because of the FBI presence on the Danforth case. The kid was almost certainly avoiding being questioned.

"When he gets back can you have him come up to the site right away?" he asked the mom, uneager to go after him.

"Sure."

They thanked her and were heading back down the driveway when he came to an abrupt halt. Toby's truck was parked right there under a tree. Suspicion suddenly filled his gut and he called back to her, "What's he using for transportation?"

"Horseback," she answered and tipped her head toward the main road. "Medicine Wind Stables."

Horseback. He followed RaeAnne back to the Jeep.

*Horse*back. Good grief. It had been years since he'd sat a horse, and had no desire to renew the acquaintance. Roman Santangelo was strictly a Harley man. There were plenty of other leads to follow without having to chase after a teenager on horseback for answers.

His gaze landed on RaeAnne's shapely backside, all wrapped in tight jeans like a pretty package. On the other hand, a nice long ride might just have its compensations. Especially if it involved overnight camping.

"Where to next?" she asked.

He looked up and almost gave in. A blush rippled across her cheeks. She knew exactly what he was thinking. So he said it. "Feel like a ride?"

Her eyes flared and his lip curled up at the intended double entendre.

"No," she said and flounced around to the Jeep's driver's side.

He was suddenly aching with a desire to strip her naked and zip her into his sleeping bag. With him.

Battling back the unruly impulse, he gingerly slid into the passenger seat. "Me, neither," he lied, forcing himself to think of nasty-smelling horses and not the sweet warmth of her bare skin. "I hate riding horseback."

"I remember." A reluctant smile tugged at the corner of

her mouth as she glanced at him. "What was his name again? Jocko?"

She had to bring up that disagreeable beast. "Yes."

"Whatever happened to him?"

"Got sent to the glue factory for biting one too many riders." She gasped and he sent her a long-suffering look. "Just kidding. Unfortunately," he muttered, not really meaning it despite his dislike for the four-legged devil.

"You're horrible."

"No, *he* was horrible." Jocko, a sixteen-hand bay, had lived next door to Tanya's house at Rincon while they were growing up. Every once in a while they'd gotten it into their heads to go for a ride. Big mistake. "Foul-tempered creature. What you ever saw in him I'll never know."

"He only bit *you.*"

"You bribed him."

She grinned. "Can I help it you didn't bring him sugar cubes and I did?"

"Yes."

"What?" She darted him a surprised look.

"I was too busy thinking of you to remember anything else."

Her expression softened and she glanced away. "You were not."

"Yes. I was." He reached for her hand and brought it from the steering wheel to his lips. "I still am."

She didn't respond except for a little wobble of her chin, which she quickly lifted as she snatched her hand away. "Like hell. I know exactly what you're thinking of."

He couldn't deny it, so he laid a hand on her thigh and gave her a caress. "Only with you, *cara.*"

She harrumphed, but didn't swat away his hand. He took some comfort in that. And for the rest of the way to the turnoff he continued to rub her thigh. Which she pointedly ignored.

"Back to Cleary?" She swung off the highway onto the dirt road leading up to the site.

"No. Let's check out the lumber camp first. See if we can come up with a suspect in Danforth's murder up there, before we go accusing the sheriff's office of foul play on top of poaching."

Headquarters for the busy lumber operation was located about five miles up the road from the dig. On the drive, RaeAnne filled Roman in on the few facts she knew about Tecopa Logging Co.

"They got their permits from the Forest Service decades ago and everyone says they've run a clean, ecologically sound and profitable operation ever since."

"Hmm."

"Doesn't sound to me like a company that would be involved in murder or poaching," she admitted.

"Where'd you get your information?"

"Philip mostly."

"Before or after the body was discovered?"

She shot him a glance. "Does it matter?"

He grabbed the door to brace himself as they went over a deep pothole. "A man who doesn't want the FBI poking around the forest asking questions is a man who'd lie through his teeth to prevent it."

She ground her jaw. She didn't blame Roman for his avid dislike of the sheriff. He had every reason to suspect the worst of him. But he didn't know Philip like she did.

"Then why give Tecopa a glowing report?" she reasoned. "Wouldn't a guilty man try to deflect suspicion onto someone else?"

She could see his annoyance as he backed down. "All right, so there's a piece of the puzzle missing. Damn that Toby for disappearing and taking it with him."

RaeAnne pulled into a clearing which served as parking lot to the camp, and immediately a man strode out from a nearby log cabin to greet them. He was short, lithe and muscular, his iron-gray hair pulled back into a stubby ponytail.

"What can I do for you folks?" The tone was friendly but

the man's body language said he knew she and Roman didn't belong there and wasn't about to let them get a step farther until he found out why they'd come.

She stood back as Roman pulled out his credentials and explained who they were. Listening with one ear, she looked around the camp. Tidy rows of barrackslike log cabins lined the parking lot area, converging on a larger building which she assumed served as the mess hall or some other community function. Behind that was a massive barn surrounded by an orderly lineup of trucks, Caterpillars and other heavy equipment. The motor pool? Storage? Maybe a combination?

Since her research specialty was human settlement patterns, the way people organized their settlements always fascinated her, no matter how mundane. When she ran across an anomaly—a missing kitchen, an extra shed, or an out-of-place fire ring—she couldn't contain her curiosity to find out the reason behind it.

What struck her most about Tecopa Lumber's camp was that nothing was out of place. Not a single thing. Not a building, not a piece of paper, not even a pinecone on the ground.

Besides the man speaking with Roman, she spotted three others, older-looking men but fit and muscular. None of them were working, or even moving. They all just stood there, watching them. She shivered, a feeling of intense scrutiny crawling up her spine.

"I'd be happy to give you a list," the gray-haired man was saying in response to something Roman had asked him, "if you'll come with me to the office."

RaeAnne started when Roman turned and she realized she'd moved right up to him, practically leaning against his arm.

He gave her a puzzled smile. "Miss Martin?"

His formal manner threw her for a second, until she remembered they'd agreed it was best not to reveal their personal relationship to any of the suspects.

She rallied. "I'll just stay here, if—"

"I'd prefer you come along," the other man said, and led them toward the cabin.

"What's wrong?" Roman whispered as they followed.

She shook her head. "Later," she whispered back.

Inside the cabin, stark metal furniture gleamed under fluorescent lights. "You have electricity?" she asked the man, who stepped behind one of two desks the room held. On it was a triangular wooden name placket which said "Doug Pritchett" in plain block letters.

Pritchett nodded. "A couple generators in the barn. Couldn't run the operation without them."

"No, I guess not," she murmured, eyeing the generous array of computer equipment and electronics lining the two desks. "Quite a setup." One she'd give her eyeteeth to have available at the excavation.

It took Pritchett about two minutes at the keyboard to cull out the list of the names Roman had requested, print it and hand it to him.

"Is there anything else I can help you with?" Pritchett asked politely.

Roman slowly folded the paper. "How many guns do you have in camp?"

The man's brows narrowed. "Guns?"

"Shotguns."

"Several. I couldn't say exactly."

She could see Roman's jaw set. "Couldn't, or wouldn't?"

RaeAnne's eyes widened as the two subtly shifted positions, squaring off against each other. Despite the smiles that continued to be fixed on both men's faces, she could practically feel the testosterone flooding the small room.

A small thrill zinged through her insides watching Roman stare the other man down. She had to actively resist an instinct to step back and hide behind him, letting him protect her from some unseen danger.

Pritchett blinked first. "Couldn't." He folded his arms across his chest. "But I wouldn't if I could."

Roman nodded. "I understand. But I'll need to test ballistics on all the shotguns belonging to your men. To eliminate them as suspects. I'd like it to be voluntary.''

After a short hesitation, Pritchett said, "I'll pass on your request. Anything else?''

Roman held up the paper in his hand. "I'd like to talk to the men on this list who were here two years ago.''

"That can be arranged. When would you like to debrief them?''

"As soon as possible. How about tomorrow?''

"Tomorrow's Saturday. Most of the men won't be working. Be here at eleven hundred hours and I'll have them assembled.''

With that, Pritchett ushered them back to the Jeep. Again, RaeAnne got a prickling sensation in the back of her neck, and for the first time noticed the tall, razor-wire-topped link fence surrounding the entire encampment. The three other men hadn't moved a foot from their spots.

With deliberate composure, she maneuvered the Jeep through the wide gate and out of camp. All four men stood watching until they drove out of sight and down the track toward Cleary.

She couldn't get out of there fast enough. The whole place gave her the creeps. As soon as the last cabin disappeared from view, she gunned it, taking the narrow forest curves at high speed until they were safely back in known territory.

"*Cara*, what's wrong?''

At the last second she swerved off the road and onto the turnout at her thinking spot, coming to an abrupt halt. She wiped her palms on her jeans. "Damn, Roman, what was with that place?''

"How do you mean?''

"It was like…like a prison camp or something. Didn't you feel it?''

She closed her eyes and leaned back in her seat, letting the purr of the motor and the familiar tang of the sun-warmed vinyl upholstery soothe her jangled nerves. A moment later the engine sputtered to a halt and she felt Roman's strong fingers dust over her cheek. She smiled, opening her eyes to his concerned gaze. He'd gotten out and was opening her door.

"Come on, let's go sit for a while and talk."

Hand in hand they made the short hike to the spectacular overlook. As soon as her bottom settled on the giant granite slab she felt better.

"I'm not like this," she said, looking up at Roman, who had yet to sit. "I don't get all touchy-feely with vibes and stuff."

He chuckled. "I know. So what was it about the Tecopa Lumber camp that got to you?"

"Besides the six-foot razor-wire fence?" She gazed out over the valley below, trying to match words to feelings. The long grass waved in the meadow, the stream gurgled past her stone cabin.

"It was too perfect," she finally said. "Neat, clean, silent. Nobody was just goofing around, no loud music, no laughing men. Like you'd expect in a boisterous all-male colony."

"They were probably all out in the forest cutting trees," Roman suggested as he went down on his haunches next to her. "And how do you know there aren't any women working there?"

She snorted softly and cut him a look. "Check your list. I'll bet you a night in my bed there isn't a female on it."

His brows shot up. "You must be damn sure of yourself."

"I am." She grinned as he dug out the paper and meticulously went through the names. She knew what he'd find, but it was kinda fun seeing him sweat, hoping she was mistaken.

She didn't know what had possessed her to say something that reckless. Must have been nerves. It wasn't as if she'd ever honor that bet, if by some miracle she was proven wrong. But she wasn't, as evidenced by the word Roman said disgustedly as he stuffed the paper back into his pocket.

"Am I right?"

"What do you think?" He made a face at her as he

plopped onto the boulder and stretched out his legs. "You're a cruel woman, to give a man hope like that."

She chuckled. He heaved out a suffering sigh and studied the desert in the distance. "So, you think there's something going on at Tecopa, or do you just think they're taking camp discipline to an extreme?"

She considered for a second. "Hard to say. Those three men sure looked like guards to me. Why would a lumber operation need guards?"

"It's Friday. Maybe they're payroll guards."

"I hadn't thought of that." She was starting to feel silly. "You're right. It was probably all my imagination."

"I don't think so." He lay back on the rock and stacked his hands under his head. "I felt it, too. And I never disregard gut instinct."

She turned to look at him. "You did?"

"Yep. There is definitely something fishy going on at Tecopa Lumber. The problem is, I doubt it has to do with the poaching."

"Why do you say that?"

"Doesn't fit. Our poachers are small-time opportunists, striking only when they run across a random animal. They might organize an occasional hunting expedition, but that's the extent of their planning. This thing at the camp, whatever it is, it's very well-organized and meticulously planned."

"But is it something illegal?"

He shrugged. "Who knows. Could just be the payroll and they're being extra cautious."

"Still, what about the murder? One of them could be involved in killing Jason Danforth, couldn't they?"

"Yep." He turned to her. "That is one of my two big questions."

His serious, dark eyes drew her in with their power, and a thousand warning bells went off.

"What's your other big question?"

He reached out and circled her wrist with his fingers, then

slowly slid them up her arm. When he couldn't reach any farther he gave her a gentle tug.

"My other question is… Why did you offer me a night in your bed?"

Chapter 10

RaeAnne's pulse rocketed out of control as Roman continued to tug on her arm, bringing her closer and closer to his stretched-out body. If she didn't stop him, she'd end up spread on top of him like new-fallen snow.

"Well?"

"I didn't offer," she declared, resisting his pull.

"I distinctly remember—"

"It was a bet. One I knew I'd win."

"Did you really?"

"Of course I did. And so did you."

His brow went up and with a deliberate movement he withdrew the paper from his pocket. "As a matter of fact, there are a few disputable names on this list."

"Don't even think—"

"This one, for instance." Without letting her arm go, he maneuvered the paper around so she could see it. "Pat Campbell. Could be a woman."

"Oh, sure."

''And here.'' He moved his fingers down the list. ''Taylor Brooks. Or how about Caroll Smith?''

''You're grasping at straws, Roman.''

''I don't think so.''

In an instant the paper had disappeared into his pocket and his other hand was gripping her waist. A jolt of heat ripped through her. Suddenly her body was pressing into his. Her breasts sang with pleasure, her hips vibrated with delicious anticipation as they settled over his.

He let go of her arm and grasped her other side, his thumb resting perilously close to her breast.

''I say I won that bet.''

Gazing into her eyes, he just held her there above him, not doing the things with his hands they both knew he could. Her body yearned to feel them slide slowly over her, setting off sparks of ecstasy as they touched sensitive, hidden places.

She licked her dry lips. ''There's no way of knowing, is there?''

''Not until we talk to them. You still haven't answered my question.''

Her brain was totally paralyzed, trapped by his commanding presence under her as surely as her body was held captive by his powerful hands. ''What question?''

''You keep saying you aren't going to sleep with me. If that's true, why did you offer me a night in your bed?''

At the juncture of their thighs, she felt his excitement grow. Her legs turned to jelly, gradually slipping down the outside of his to rest on the smooth, cool rock.

''This isn't fair,'' she protested weakly. His arousal pressed into her, thick and hard, hopelessly tantalizing. And he knew damned well this was one of her favorite positions.

''All's fair in love and war,'' he murmured.

''This isn't love,'' she returned. ''This is sex.''

He was silent for a moment, his Adam's apple bobbing in his throat. ''I offered you love. You turned me down.''

''It wouldn't work.''

''But this does.'' He held her hips firmly and ground them

in a circle over him. Leaving no doubt what he meant. "Give me now, RaeAnne. We can figure out the future later. But right now I'll die if I don't have you."

He raised up to capture her lips and she thought surely she would tremble into tiny pieces. Goose bumps ripped over her as he lifted her T-shirt up and off, then rolled her to her back and gently laid her on the soft cotton.

His low moan matched hers. His seeking fingers captured her breast and squeezed seductively as he moved over her.

"Ah, *cara,* don't deny me."

"I—" She felt her jeans slide over her bottom and down her legs, and the words died on her lips. "Roman," she whispered, as yet unsure whether she was protesting or welcoming his brazenness.

"You are still the most beautiful woman in the world," he said, his voice low and rough with need.

Her heart swelled painfully. She loved him so much, regardless of how impossible it all was. She wound her arms around his neck and pulled him to her, lip to lip. "Kiss me," she softly ordered.

He kissed her. Long and hot and wet and thorough.

The warm breeze played over her bare skin along with his fingers, his touch searing her hotter than the late-afternoon sun. His mouth plundered as his hands claimed, and it was all she could do to keep from pulling him between her thighs and demanding an end to her enormous craving.

"Please, Roman," she moaned.

"I'm here, *cara.* I'm not going anywhere."

If only that were true.

She gasped in pleasure as his mouth sought her breasts. "Yes," she urged him. "Oh, yes."

It had been so long. Last time they'd come together so quickly, so explosively, there hadn't been time to enjoy the delicious skim of his tongue, the nip of his teeth, the scrape of his hair over her body. And out here in the open air, being surrounded by nothing but the robin's-egg sky and sheltering mountains, only heightened the freedom and forbidden delight of his sensual ministrations.

He pulled on the turgid tip of her breast and her nipple splintered with electric pleasure. "Harder," she gasped, and he obliged, suckling so deep and demandingly she felt it all the way to her very core.

With a growl he switched to the other breast. And she fell. Down into a whirlwind of sensation she plummeted. Without pausing he slid between her legs and spread them wide. Her breath caught. Suddenly his mouth was on her, at her most sensitive center. She cried out, the setting sun prisming into a thousand million sparkling rainbows all around her. Her back arched as a torrent of pleasure caught hold and tossed her into the churning abyss of rapture that was his mouth and tongue.

And then she shattered.

It went on and on, and when it was over he was inside her. Then it started all over again. Building and growing, hammering through her, finally delivering a burst of indescribable bliss, until at last the mountains stopped spinning and the skies were only blue.

He rolled off with a soft groan, cuddling her to his side.

"Your bruises," she murmured, kissing his shoulder.

"What bruises?" he asked and gathered her closer.

It felt so good, so right to be in his arms again. She'd given up ages ago trying to find a man who could make her feel anything close to this contented and thoroughly loved. Making love with Roman had always been perfect. From the first tender brush of his lips to the last powerful thrust of his manhood. And this was no exception.

Like a shipwrecked sailor she lay in his embrace, sated, pleasantly exhausted from their physical joining.

And then, it hit her.

"Oh, no," she whispered, panic squeezing at her heart. This time he hadn't withdrawn.

* * *

Roman didn't move. He hardly dared to breathe. He knew immediately what she meant.

Damn. How could this have happened?

Last time at least he'd had the presence of mind to pull out at the last moment. This time he'd been too far gone to remember, and apparently she'd been, too.

It was just crazy, almost as if both of them had a secret, unconscious wish to get RaeAnne pregnant.

He thought about that for about three seconds and realized it could well be true—on his part. But not hers. Having his baby was the last thing she wanted. She'd made that crystal clear at every opportunity. She may find him physically irresistible, but she didn't consider him husband material.

"It'll be all right," he said, hoping like hell he could make it so.

He felt a puff of air on his neck as she sighed. "That's easy for you to say."

"I'll take care of you. I swear."

"I don't need taking care of."

"I will anyway."

She looked up at him, eyes serious. "How?"

That stopped him.

At his hesitation, she slipped from his embrace. "Just as I thought."

"Wait." He grabbed her hand before she could stand. "I'll do anything you want." Instantly he knew that was the wrong thing to say.

She shook him off and reached for her clothes. "You'll quit your job?"

"What are you asking?"

"Sell your motorcycle and settle down in my town?"

His mouth dropped open as he struggled to understand what she wanted of him.

"Have you even once asked where I live?"

Almost desperately, he jumped to his feet and yanked up his pants to follow her quick stride toward the Jeep.

"RaeAnne!" He jogged after her, catching her by the

shoulders, swinging her around to face him. His heart blanched when he saw tears in her eyes. "*Cara,* baby, please. Don't cry. Yell, hit me, anything else, but don't cry. We'll work this out."

"How?" she demanded again, as one lone teardrop slipped onto her lashes. "Oh, why did you come back? For eighteen years I've been just fine hating your guts. And now— Oh! Never mind!"

She wrenched herself free and ran. He stared after her, wondering what the hell to do. He wanted to chase after her, grab her and compel her by any means necessary to drive to Vegas and marry him today.

He drilled a hand through his hair. So much for the liberal, New Age, sensitive guy he'd always thought he was. RaeAnne seemed to bring out something primitive, something primal in him that he didn't know how to deal with. Half of him wanted to throw her over his shoulder and drag her back to his cave while the other half just stood there, gaping in mortification at such uncivilized behavior.

Muttering a curse through gritted teeth, he ran after her, and found her waiting in the purring Jeep, back straight as a fence post and chin high.

"Honey—"

She held up one rigid hand. "I don't want to talk about it, okay? Let's just try to get through this investigation. By the time it's solved, hopefully we'll know if I'm—"

Her words halted, and her jaw clenched.

"*Cara—*"

"No, let me finish." She glanced over at him and her expression thawed a little. "I'm sorry about what I said back there. I want you to know I'm not angry at you. I'm angry at myself."

"And you think that makes it better for me?"

"I'd hoped. Look—"

This time he held up a hand. "No, it's my turn to talk. You asked if I'd quit my job, move to your town. Yes, I will. I'll marry you. I want to make this right any way I can."

She stared at him for so long he started thinking she'd gone into shock. Finally she let out a long breath. "Well. You certainly know how to sweep a girl off her feet. But I'm afraid I'll have to decline your generous sacrifice."

Sacrifice? "No, that's not what—"

"Would you be saying this—*any* of this—if you didn't think I could be pregnant?"

"Well," he hedged, "probably not at this exact moment. But—"

"I rest my case," she interrupted, and let the clutch out. "Being pregnant isn't a reason to get married these days. Not for me, anyway."

He bristled. "It is for me."

She glanced over and he could swear there was a glimmer of respect under all that mistrust in her eyes. "That's very noble. But we're not even sure if I am pregnant. Don't make any offers you'll regret when we find out I'm not. Which we will."

"I've already been regretting not marrying you for eighteen years. I doubt if anything I say now will change that."

The Jeep rolled up to the stone cabin, and she turned off the engine. "Marrying me now won't alter the past, Roman. Nothing will." Her eyes met his. "Let it go."

"I wish I could," he quietly said. "But I can't."

Bugs had already gone down the mountain by the time they got back to the cabin, so they were on their own. Despite that, dinner was surprisingly low-key. Roman wasn't exactly sure what kind of uneasy truce had been struck between them as they washed up and settled in for the evening, but a truce there was.

He built a river-cobble fire ring between the cabin and the creek, and over it grilled some chicken and corn on the cob they'd picked up at a store coming back from Toby's. RaeAnne popped the cork on a bottle of good Merlot, and together they bundled up against the growing chill. The mountains seemed to snuggle up around them, pulling their snow-blankets around their shoulders and surrounding them with an ambiance of peaceful quiet. Even the frogs and the insects in the meadow seemed mellower tonight, the soft chirping a muted score to their low conversation.

He and RaeAnne ended up stretching out in front of the fire until much too late, eating, drinking and sharing stories of their lives.

And maybe avoiding bedtime.

Roman had never been so torn in his life. He knew he wouldn't sleep a wink unless it was in her embrace. And yet, how could he possibly ask her to accept him into her bed after all that had been said this afternoon?

Damn.

He smiled as she related an incident going through Turkish customs for an archaeological survey team she'd been on one summer. Dang, and he'd thought his life had been exciting. Even six years in the Navy didn't compare to some of the stuff she was talking about.

"Don't you miss it?" he asked. "Having all those adventures?"

She shook her head. "No. It was great at the time, but I'm ready to settle down. House, dog, two and a half kids." She glanced up and quickly added, "Eventually."

He barely resisted taking her in his arms and making sure those two and a half kids were his.

"I take it you would?"

He licked his lips. "Um…"

"Miss the adventure, I mean. Being an undercover agent for the FBI must be pretty wild."

"Ah." He tried to pry his mind off the image of making babies with her.

"You know, the glitz and glamour. Riding around on your Harley with no one to answer to."

"Sure it's exciting," he said, hanging on to his wineglass for dear life. And launched into a description of his most interesting jobs and Navy gigs over the years, just to distract himself. Talking about his job was a lot safer than letting his imagination wander.

After the third story, she said with awe, "Boy, that's sure a long way from being a veterinarian."

He smiled nostalgically at the reminder of his long-held childhood dream. RaeAnne was going to be a music teacher, and he would become a vet. He loved animals, and had always had a house full of pets when he was young. He missed that.

"Maybe someday," he mused. "If I ever settle down."

"Do you have a place somewhere?" she asked, an odd note coloring her voice.

"No. Never been a reason to get a place of my own. My things are at my mom and stepdad's at Rincon. First the Navy and now the FBI keeps me on the road most of the time. I don't have a lot of ties."

She nodded, then after a moment asked about his parents and the other people she remembered from high school. Pretty soon they were laughing over memories of youthful antics perpetrated by themselves, Cole and Tanya on the unsuspecting citizens of northern San Diego County.

"So where *do* you live now?" he finally asked.

"Sonoma. Cotati, actually. I just got a teaching position at Cal State." She made a face. "But then, you knew that."

He chuckled. "Just the job part, because of the high school transcripts you requested for the application. Is it my fault the high school reunion committee is so efficient?"

She shook her head and said wryly, "What I want to know is how you found me at the dig. I'm pretty sure the reunion committee didn't know about that."

He leaned his chin in his cupped hand, staring thoughtfully into the fire. "You know, I was starting to wonder about that myself."

Her head came up, her brows furrowed. "You don't know?"

"Technically, yes." He shrugged. "When I learned you were going by the last name Martin, I put out feelers all over the state—cops, government employment, on the Internet, you know, the usual thing.''

''And?''

''And in the mail a few days later I received a photocopy of your site permit with the Forest Service. I recognized the handwriting immediately, and was so excited finally to have found you, I didn't put much thought into the paper itself, or where it came from. But now that I think about it, it did seem a bit…fortuitous.''

She looked surprised. ''You think someone had ulterior motives for reuniting us? For what possible reason?''

''Heaven only knows. But whoever it was couldn't know I was looking for you for personal reasons. I used my FBI credentials.''

Her eyebrows lifted.

He flashed a grin. ''But don't tell anyone. The point is, maybe when I put out those feelers the person thought you were in trouble with the FBI and this was a convenient way to get rid of you and the dig without having to show his hand.''

''Oh, my God! You think it was related to the murder? Doesn't that seem like a bit of a stretch?''

''Yeah,'' he admitted. ''It definitely does. But I can't think of any other explanation, and I really hate coincidences. Are you sure you never told anyone where you were? Ever?''

RaeAnne's expression turned decidedly guilty.

He relaxed considerably. ''Okay, spill.''

''I may have sent Tanya a postcard or two…''

''Aha. One mystery solved. It was probably just Tanya trying to be cute.'' He shook his head. ''I can't believe she knew about you all this time and never told me. The traitor.''

''I wouldn't let her.'' RaeAnne's mouth turned down. ''But she's hardly a traitor. Before I left, she always stuck up for you. Even when things were at their worst.''

''Funny, she always gave me hell when I saw her. Not in words, of course. Just with that Look she has. She never even hinted she knew where you were.

"After the first month or two I forbade her to even mention your name. Then I left and communication ever since has only been one-sided."

They fell silent for a few minutes, gazing up at the incredible night canopy twinkling in the heavens above them. A shooting star pirouetted across the sky and he automatically made a wish. *Let me have RaeAnne and the baby.* He prayed there was a baby. He stole a look at her, and their eyes collided. She quickly looked away—too quickly—and he wondered what she'd wished for.

Probably for him to disappear.

He sat up and started gathering plates and glasses. "We should get to bed. Bugs'll be here bright and early, and I need to run those names we got from Tecopa through the system first thing."

Even in the firelight, he could see her face go pale. "All right."

She picked up a shovel and began to douse the fire with creek sand. He left her to finish up and visit the facilities while he did the dishes and put things away in the cabin. When she came in, he headed outside to do his own ablutions.

"May I borrow your sleeping bag?" she said before he was out the door.

He halted and turned around. "Why?"

"I'll sleep on the floor, here by the fire. You have the bed."

"No way. I'll take the floor."

"But your bruises. It'll hurt to sleep on the hard, uneven floor. You won't get a bit of sleep."

He crossed his arms. "I'll live. Like hell am I sleeping on the bed while you're on the floor."

She *pshawed* and went for his sleeping bag. "Don't be such a macho man, Roman. You'd do it for me if I was hurt."

"That's different. Besides, I'm not hurt. Just a bit bruised." He strode across the room and firmly plucked the bag from her grip. "You're sleeping on the floor over my dead body."

"That could be arranged," she declared, hands on hips.

An unwilling smile tugged at his lips. "I'll just bet. Look, this is not happening, so get a different plan."

Behind her frustrated scowl she actually looked worried. He was incredibly touched that she was so concerned for his still battered state that she'd give up her own comfort.

"Share the bed with me," he said, determined to get it out in the open. "That's the only practical solution."

Her lips parted. Then she shook her head.

"The bed, Rae. Not your body."

"No. It won't work."

He was getting a little tired of hearing those words every time the subject of them being together came up. If he could defeat them just once, over this issue, maybe he had a chance at the big picture, too.

"How about if I'm in my sleeping bag on top of the blanket? You couldn't possibly be worried about me attacking you through all that."

She pushed out a breath. "And what if I attack you?"

He tried not to smile, recognizing the reluctant tone of a confession. But it was no use. "I'll put up a valiant struggle, but you're pretty strong. And I am a wounded man…"

"Just give me the damn sleeping bag and get out of here," she groused, snatching it from his grasp. "And I'm warning you, touch me and you'll be a *dead* man."

"Whatever you say, *cara.*" He was whistling as he opened the door to go out.

When he got back, she was already in bed. His sleeping bag was spread neatly over the bed on the side nearest the door, and she'd burrowed deep under the blanket on the wall side, so only her nose peeked out. A pool of moonlight streaming in from the window illuminated her watching eyes and the halo of blond hair spread around her face on the pillow.

Was she naked under that blanket? He wondered if he

should undress, and how far... Well, nothing ventured nothing gained.

After stoking up the woodstove, he turned out the lantern, took a deep breath, and reached for his belt buckle.

He could see her eyes get bigger and bigger as he stripped off his jeans and T-shirt, and went for the waistband of his BVDs.

"What are you doing?"

"Getting undressed."

She sprang up and grabbed for his sleeping bag. "That wasn't in the agreement."

He raised his hands in surrender. "All right, all right. I'll leave them on. Sheesh. It's not like you haven't seen what I've got. Fairly recently."

"I don't need a reminder sleeping less than a foot away," she said irritably.

"Okay. I'm covered," he said placatingly, sliding into the chilly bag. "*Brrr.* I could use some warming up."

"Roman," she warned.

"I'm cold all over. My lips, my fingers, my b—"

"*Roman.*"

Part of what had made them so good together was that, no matter what, they'd always had fun with each other. So he gave it a stab. "I think they're turning blue."

"More like green," she retorted.

"Huh?"

"From all that blarney."

He grinned. "You telling me I have an Irish skeleton in my closet?"

"Undoubtedly."

"Promise you won't tell anyone."

There. That was a definite chuckle.

He turned on his side to face her. "How about warming them up for me?" Her eyes whipped to his and narrowed. "My blue lips, that is."

"God, you're obnoxious."

He feigned a squawk of pain as her forefinger poked his

biceps through the pile of blankets and his sleeping bag, then his grin widened.

He inched the bag closer to her, crossing his fingers against the plush softness. "Just a good-night kiss."

"No."

But how did she really feel? "Come on. Just one."

"No."

Still, she didn't turn away. There was hope yet. *"Ohhh,"* he moaned. "I think my bruises are starting to hurt again."

Above the blanket, her eyes twinkled in the moonlight, and crinkled just a little at the corners. "You are the biggest faker. If you think I'm falling for that one…"

"No, huh?"

"Uh-uh."

He sighed. "I won't be able to sleep, you know. All I can think about is the taste of you. I'm not asking for more, Rae. Just a taste."

He could see the hesitation in her eyes and thought for sure he'd spend a sleepless night craving her. Then she sighed, too, and whispered, "Just lips. No hands."

"I swear."

"And you have to promise not to make love to me. Even if I beg you."

His jaw dropped in surprise. "That's a pretty tall order."

"Those are my terms, take them or leave them."

"Oh, I'll definitely take them."

"Say you promise."

"I promise."

"All right."

The blanket slowly lowered to reveal her whole face, beautiful and luminous in the silver moonlight. Usually so strong and self-assured, she looked somehow vulnerable and fragile as she waited for him to make a move. A sudden rush of protectiveness nearly knocked the breath from his lungs.

"I never wanted to hurt you," he whispered. "And I'll die before I do it again."

Her eyes pooled. "I know."

As his lips met hers, he lowered his lashes and thanked God he was already lying down. For if he'd been standing he would have been brought to his knees by the overwhelming love that rushed through his heart for this woman.

Her mouth was warm and tender. Everything he wanted in life was offered to him in the welcoming succor of her parting lips.

In this she trusted him, and he felt enormous awe at the act of faith she bestowed upon him by letting him kiss her. He knew she didn't want to. Knew she was certain he would only hurt her again. And yet she laid herself bare to him. Admitted that despite her fears, she cared enough about him to risk it all for...

For what? A kiss?

He sank into her, his tongue a pilgrim seeking haven in the sweet paradise of her devotion. She matched his ardor, moaning softly with each stroke, each probe, each sweep of moist, supple flesh against flesh. He canted up against her, blankets and sleeping bag keeping them apart like a pair of unyielding spinster chaperons. He groaned in protest, wanting to strip them away. To feel her in his arms again, naked and eager.

"I want you," he whispered into her mouth.

"I want you, too," she answered breathlessly, rolling to her back in the age-old sign of surrender.

Elated, he followed, wrestling with the thick tangle of fabric surrounding him to free his hands. And stopped just before he pulled the blanket from her body.

"But I can't," he said.

She looked up at him, trust radiating from her eyes in a heavy-lidded glow. "Why not?" she softly asked.

She still loved him, really and truly. That had to be it. Love was the only explanation.

If only he could make her see it.

"Because," he said, laying his forehead against hers, "I promised."

Chapter 11

Happiness.

Happiness and guilt.

Those were the feelings RaeAnne awoke to the next morning. Happiness because she could feel Roman stretching by her side, his distinctive scent filling her bed, the taste of him lingering in her mouth. Guilt because once again she had let herself be carried away by her unruly passion, instead of following the practical dictates of her mind.

How could she ever reconcile this enormous craving for his body with the certain knowledge that if she gave in to it she'd be heading for another heartache? Thank goodness he was made of stronger stuff than she.

She smiled, remembering how noble he'd been the night before, keeping his end of their bargain even at the price of great personal discomfort. It had been cruel of her to extract that promise, but she'd known she didn't stand a chance otherwise. One thing about possessing a well-developed self-awareness—of both her own strengths and weaknesses—it was impossible to lie to herself. Once their lips met, she knew

her surrender was inevitable. When it came to Roman Santangelo, she was as weak as dandelion fluff dancing in the
storm of their desire, helplessly caught in the winds of his
will.

"Morning," he said, and traced his lips over her cheek to
her mouth.

She sighed, accepting his lingering greeting. After he'd
thoroughly stirred her hungry hormones—again—she smiled
languidly up at him. "Hi."

They had kissed all night. Neither of them had been able
to sleep much. Not with the other so close yet so unobtain-
able. But Roman had refused to be absolved of his promise.
And protected by the safety net of his word, she'd given free
reign to her lust for him. She had taken shameless advantage
of his kissing skills, indulging in a long, liquid exploration
of his mouth and face and throat, the memory of which still
left her dizzy and thrumming with unfulfilled need.

But humbled with a new respect for the man.

How could he be so calm and serene after spending a night
like that? The smile on his face was worthy of a saint, not a
man dying of sexual frustration. Like she was.

"What have you been doing in that sleeping bag?" she
asked suspiciously. "You look way too happy."

"I *am* happy."

"I knew it. Cheater. That's not fair."

He laughed out loud, his deep baritone reverberating
through the cabin. He peeled away his sleeping bag and slid
out of it, rolling his feet to the floor.

"No, I'm happy because I spent the whole night kissing
the sexiest woman in the universe." He stretched, showing
off his broad back and rippling muscles. Her mouth went
dry. "Why? Anything wrong?"

He quirked a brow as he rose and, whistling, padded to
the woodstove to add a few sticks.

She sat up. "You aren't a bit...oh, say, frustrated?"

He dumped some coffee grounds into the coffeepot and

added boiling water from the kettle that was always simmering on the back burner. "Nah. Should I be?"

She fell onto the mattress and rolled her eyes heavenward. "Must be some Native American thing," she muttered.

"What's that?"

Could he really be so obtuse? "Not being completely, utterly—"

He turned back to the bed carrying a steaming cup of coffee.

Oh, dear...

"Aroused?" he completed, since the word seemed to have gotten stuck in her throat.

She nodded.

He offered her the coffee with a grin. "You should get up, too, *cara*."

She shook her head. This was too much to bear.

God knew she shouldn't, but damn, she wanted him like crazy. After the night they'd shared she had completely lost her capacity to be rational. Hell, they'd already made love twice in the past few days. What harm could once more do? Or even twice, or three times?

He'd been right all along. They should enjoy each other while they had the chance. Because she knew so well the damage had already been done. She'd hurt just as badly regardless of what happened or didn't happen in this bed for the time he had left with her. The only difference would be how much she'd regret after he'd gone. And she suddenly knew without a shred of doubt, if she didn't let him make love to her ever again, she'd regret that most of all.

"Please. Come back to bed," she whispered, almost desperate in her need to feel him close.

Surprise furrowed through her when his grin melted into a wistful smile and he shook his head. "No."

"But why?" She blinked back the bleak knowledge that it wasn't going to happen.

He sat on the bed and pulled her into his arms. "Because you were right. It wouldn't work. Not like it is."

"What are you saying? I don't understand." *She wouldn't cry.*

His fingers combed through her hair, his thumb tenderly traced the outline of her kiss-bruised lips. "Last night, I realized I'd gotten things backward. I'd thought if we made love, you would start to trust me again."

"But I do trust you."

His smile turned sad. "With your body, yes. But not with your heart. And until I've earned the confidence of your heart, I have no right to the treasures of your body."

Her chin trembled. "But I want you."

"I want you, too." He gave a strangled laugh. "God, can't you see how I want you?"

She nodded miserably. She saw. With her eyes she saw his handsome face, shadowed with torment. With her fingers she saw his body, straining with need. With her heart she saw the man she loved, now more than ever, struggling under the weight of his honor. "Yes, I see."

"Will you ever trust me again?" he asked, his voice haunted with doubts.

And with the heartache of eighteen long years she saw how much he was asking of her. But did he?

At her silence, he sighed, and kissed her fingertips. "It's okay. You don't have to answer."

And then he stood, handed her the coffee, and walked out the cabin door.

She made him breakfast. It was the least she could do. French toast wasn't that hard to prepare, even on a wood-stove, and she needed something to keep her from running after him in desperation.

He'd be back. She hoped.

No. She *trusted*.

But did she really? As she dipped and turned bread in the big iron frying pan, she thought about it. Yes, she trusted he'd be back this morning, if only because of the investigation he was conducting. But what about after the investigation was over?

Last night he'd talked about his vagabond life on the road, going undercover for the FBI on case after interesting case. Would he really give it all up for her? Did she want him to? Despite his earlier ambitions to become a vet, it was plain to see he had a real calling for law enforcement. She didn't want to be the one to put an end to a career he so obviously loved. If he quit, eventually he'd resent her for it, and she'd be hurt. Again.

Seemed no matter what she chose to do—trust him or not trust him—she'd be the one to get hurt.

No, that wasn't fair. If she was honest, she'd have to admit he'd been hurt plenty by what had happened in their past. And even more by what she'd told him about their baby. He was trying hard, in his own way, to make it up to her. And she recognized that her constant rejection up until this morning had also hurt him. Too bad it had taken her so long to realize how much she really wanted him. Now it was too late.

The door swung open and he walked in, looking freshly washed and combed and handsome as ever she'd seen him. She smiled, her heart melting into a puddle in her chest.

"Breakfast is ready."

Ignoring his mildly shocked expression, she piled thick slices of French toast on his plate and motioned for him to sit down at the table she'd set, complete with wildflowers.

"Why'd you do that?"

"What?"

"Cook for me."

She paused to cock a hip at him. "I figure a woman takes ruthless advantage of a man in bed, she owes him breakfast."

"Did I hear the words *bed and breakfast*?" Bugs's voice wafted in from the front door, cutting off any reply Roman might have been contemplating.

He gave her an incredibly tender smile before calling back,

"Sure did, *compadre*. Come on in. But I gotta warn you," he added, "bed's taken."

Bugs grinned as he trooped in, bearing a short stack of file folders. "Never doubted it. So guess what, kids? We got results."

RaeAnne tore her gaze from the afterglow of Roman's smile and looked at Bugs. "You know who the killer is?"

One hour and four pans of French toast later, the three of them leaned back in their chairs and contemplated the scatter of papers before them on the table.

"So," RaeAnne said, hugely disappointed in both Bugs's forensic findings and the reinterviews Dawson had sent along with him. "The only new fact is, we now know our upstanding Fish and Game warden Jason Danforth was a pothead."

Roman chuckled. "Not necessarily. Finding marijuana traces on his clothes and a handful of leaves in his pocket could have any number of explanations."

"The guy described in this report didn't really strike me as the pothead type," Bugs said, a forefinger tapping the copies of Danforth's Homicide and Missing Person files.

"You never know," RaeAnne protested. "It's probably not something he'd advertise."

"True. To his work buddies. Though you'd think some of his personal friends would be aware of habits like that." Roman extracted the lab report on the marijuana from the pile of papers. "But one thing bothers me about this analysis of the pocket contents."

"What's that?"

"They were whole leaves," he said. "Like they'd been pulled right off a stem—flowers, seeds and all. It says here they were hardly even crushed."

"So?"

"Marijuana that's sold usually looks more like dried oregano flakes than intact whole leaves," Bugs explained. "And generally the seeds are removed. The growers don't want you starting your own garden with their product."

"Ah," she said, enlightenment beginning to dawn. "So you're saying Danforth found this marijuana on the hoof, so to speak."

"Bingo."

"Which means we might have found a motive for his murder."

"Exactly. Or at least a hell of a good imitation," Roman said, looking well pleased.

"A motive that has nothing to do with poaching," she mused, trying to get it straight in her mind. This whole thing was getting more complicated by the minute. "Or Tecopa Lumber Company."

"Looks that way. Maybe all those coincidences really are just that."

She frowned skeptically. "I suppose."

"I'm betting if we find that field of grass, we find the murderer."

"I'm sorry I have to make you do this," Roman said to RaeAnne as they prepared to keep their appointment up at Tecopa Lumber at eleven o'clock. "But I'm not letting you out of my sight."

RaeAnne didn't know whether to be glad for his concern or irritated by it. The idea of going back to the creepy lumber camp held zero appeal, especially now that they'd moved way down on the list of murder suspects. But Bugs had packed up and left after their meeting, to report for another case down in San Bernardino. And Roman was being stubborn.

"I'm not a baby. I'll be fine by myself."

He took her into his arms and kissed her. "You're my baby, and I'm not leaving you here alone."

How could she argue with that? "Prove it," she murmured, cupping his head and pulling him closer, deepening the kiss.

Gently he extracted himself. But he was grinning. "You're very naughty, you know that?"

She tipped her head coyly. "And?"

He winked. "And I like that in a woman."

She pouted. "Then why do you keep running away from me?"

He drew his fingertips over her lips, his expression hungry but oh-so-determined. "We have to get going if we're to be on time for Mr. Pritchett's eleven-hundred debriefing." He grabbed the keys. "I'll drive."

As they jounced up to the camp she pondered their bizarre role reversal. Suddenly she was the one drooling over Roman and he was holding her at arm's length.

Maybe he was already pulling away, preparing them both for when he'd have to leave. Unable to help herself, she leaned over and kissed him on the cheek. The intimate smile he flashed her as he parked the Jeep said no, he wasn't planning on leaving her anytime soon.

Should she trust him? Put her heart in his hands and just take the leap and trust him? She wished she knew the answer. If she made the wrong decision, how would she ever go on living?

The meeting at Tecopa went as well as could be expected, Roman figured. Many of the men admitted to owning shotguns. Most had no objections to them being tested for ballistics. All expressed shock over the murder.

Nobody confessed. Big surprise.

"Whew, I'm glad that's over," RaeAnne remarked as they drove away from the camp, Pritchett again watching them until they were out of sight.

"Still give you the creeps?"

"Not as much as last time. Just Pritchett and his henchmen."

The same three older men who'd displayed such light-heartedness last time had stood at the back of the big room Roman had held the interviews in, looking ready to pounce. He'd been annoyed, but had been unable to convince the guards to leave. He'd done his best to conduct things quietly, to keep the men's statements confidential. Not that there'd been much worth hiding.

"Yeah. I got the feeling the men would have been a lot more forthcoming without being observed by management. But at this stage there's no evidence of wrongdoing by anyone at Tecopa. No sense antagonizing Pritchett without good reason."

"Tecopa could be growing marijuana on the side," she suggested.

"A distinct possibility. Perfect cover. Remote, plenty of forest to hide the fields, lots of equipment and outbuildings to cover the operation."

And his instincts had been going crazy the entire time in the camp. Things he'd noticed last time, such as the elaborate locks on a few of the buildings, and a couple of sleek, black luxury cars parked in the lot, had fallen into place in light of their suspicions.

"But unfortunately no evidence."

"It would be tough to keep so many employees from talking."

"If we're right, I don't think the men are in on it."

RaeAnne glanced over at him. "You mean Pritchett and those other three have their own marijuana operation going on the side?"

The idea made a lot of sense, and fit what little evidence they did have. "That would explain their watchfulness, and the fact that none of the grunts even hinted they knew anything strange was going on. It would be a bit tricky to keep secret, but not impossible."

"I get the feeling you know something I don't."

He grinned. "Being the superior agent I am, I did manage to find out something interesting."

RaeAnne looked over at him expectantly.

"There's a stand of supposed old-growth trees nobody's ever allowed to enter. Completely fenced, gated and off-limits."

"Perfect for hiding an illegal marijuana field."

"Precisely what I thought."

"Ooh, you're good," she said, matching triumphant grins. "I think you deserve a reward."

"Do you, now?" He glanced her way as he downshifted. "And what would that be?"

She tipped her head and angled back against the door, twirling a lock of her long blond hair. "Guess."

He took in the sight of her, all heated looks, warm smiles and delicious seduction, and almost lost his resolve. "You're being naughty again. I can tell."

She batted her eyelashes. "Doing my best. What do you say?"

"I say I'm in big trouble."

She laughed, the sound tinkling like a wind chime through the open Jeep. She sat up and watched the turnoff to the site whiz by. "Hey! Where are you going?"

Roman jerked his chin at the pile of carefully bagged and tagged shotguns they were carrying in the back of the Jeep. "Gotta take these to Dawson in Bishop."

"All the way to Bishop?"

There was nothing in the world he'd rather do than collect her "reward." But he'd made a firm resolution. Until she trusted him completely, he wouldn't compound the complications by making love again.

"He made arrangements with the police lab there to do the ballistics testing."

RaeAnne sighed. "You have to go right this minute?"

"Yep. So there's no question on the chain of evidence."

"Oh." She glanced out at the trees bouncing past. "Do I have to come along?"

"Yes."

She checked her watch. "I'd really like to get back to work. I still have a few days' digging to finish before I can wrap up the project."

Roman chewed over that last statement as he slowed to a stop at the highway intersection. She'd said it so casually, he almost hadn't caught the implications.

"Wrap it up?" He turned to face her. "Does that mean you'll be leaving soon?"

"I promised the investors the report in less than two weeks," she said, looking at the road, the mountains, the cars speeding by—everywhere but at him. "I need my computer to do the statistics and write it up. Computer's at home."

He didn't know what to say, so he remained silent.

She shrugged. "Besides, once this case is solved, you'll be leaving, too." She shot him a challenging glance, and he could almost hear her daring him to deny it.

"Only if you want me to," he said, tossing the challenge right back at her.

She puffed out a breath. "Roman, don't say things you don't mean. This is hard enough."

"But I do."

She shook her head, the breeze catching the ends of her hair and lifting them in a sunny halo. "You were right. We should forget about the past and the future and just enjoy the days we have left."

"No." He devoutly wished he'd never said those words. "I want more. And I'm betting you do, too, if you'd listen to your heart."

"No," she quietly said. "I can't."

He set the brake and reached for her. Pulled her gently into his arms and stroked her hair. "Trust me," he murmured. "Please trust me. I swear I won't hurt you again."

He felt her shudder, and lay her cheek against his shoulder. Her hands crept around his waist and held him. Expanding in a sigh, her soft breasts pressed into his chest.

"I'll try," she whispered.

It was all he could ask. He couldn't compel her to trust him, or shake her until her doubts clattered onto the ground like so much loose change. Not after everything he'd put her through.

By the time they'd driven to Bishop and dropped off the

shotguns at the police lab, he'd convinced himself that for now it was enough.

"Let's go back to the cabin and make love until morning," he suggested with a roguish grin when they were coming out of a grocery store laden with dinner fixings.

She gasped in surprise, avoiding the amused glances of nearby people who'd overheard his bold proposition. Beet-red, she shushed him, muttering, "It's not even three-thirty. Besides, you had your chance this morning, Santangelo. I'm going to get some work done before dinner," and then she marched to the Jeep with chin high.

God, she was cute. And he knew it was just for show. They had an understanding now.

Didn't they?

Apparently not.

True to her word, she helped him carry groceries into the cabin, grabbed her camera, then headed out to the storage bin for her shovels and pails. Well, hell. Guess he might as well lend a hand while he tried to figure out what to do next on the case.

He found her in the meadow, at the unit they'd dug to-gether on that first day—G, she'd called it, or was it E?

"This where you're going to be working?"

She glanced up from taking a photo of a wildflower grow-ing next to the precisely dug unit wall. "No. Unfortunately I can't afford the time to take G down any farther than I already have. At least not until I finish the total sample I have mapped out."

"Sample?"

"I have to do a certain number of random test units, or the statistics won't be meaningful."

He stared at her blankly. "If you say so. Well, if not here, where will we be digging?" At her questioning glance he added, "Thought I'd help out."

He ignored the annoyed look in her eyes and took the tools, leaving her with the camera bag. "Lead on, McDuff."

He could almost see her spine straighten. "All right. I guess I could use the help."

Together they trudged across the meadow and up onto the bottom slope of the canyon, where she stopped at a low, grass-covered rise.

"Here?"

"Yep," she answered. "I've been avoiding this spot for weeks, but I guess I can't put it off any longer."

"Why? What's the deal?"

"I figure there's another burial under there." She pointed to a barely noticeable oblong of dirt, disguised by a patch of thistles and brambles.

His gaze took in the innocuous-looking mound. "Seriously?"

"I just pray the guy's a hundred and fifty years old," she commented wryly. "And Caucasian."

"Still hoping to find Great-great-granduncle Crawford?"

"You've been reading my mail."

After RaeAnne had photographed and staked out the new unit, and taken the painstaking measurements needed to place it exactly on the site map, they began working the neat square, her digging and him sifting. It didn't take them more than fifteen minutes to find the skeleton.

"Damn, I'll never get used to this," he muttered as he watched her carefully remove a spadeful of dirt from around the skull.

"What's that?"

"Just digging up a body like this, with no Crime Scene Unit or anything."

"I'm a professional archaeologist, Roman. It's pretty much the same thing as being a CSI."

"I suppose. But how do you know this isn't some homicide victim, too?"

She gave him a long-suffering glance. "I'm trained to know. But if I don't catch it, the lab will. Damn. Looks like there's been some rodent activity."

"As in rats and mice?" He grimaced as she nodded. "Delightful. How can you tell?"

"See the disturbance in the soil?" She pointed out an area around one of the shoulder bones, which to him looked exactly the same as the rest of the dirt.

"Is that bad?"

"Maybe, maybe not. Rats've been known to completely mix up the bones in a burial, import foreign objects, destroy valuable artifacts. Sometimes they just build their nest in the rib cage and don't touch a thing. I guess we'll find out. Looks like it happened a while ago, though."

"Thank goodness." He had visions of sifting through rat droppings, and made a face. It was bad enough digging up people.

"Hmm. That's strange," she murmured, staring at a lump of soft blue stuff that had been exposed.

"What is it?" he asked, reluctantly bending in closer.

"Don't worry, just a bit of fabric. Could be a remnant of the buried person's clothes."

"Is that unusual?"

"Depends on the situation. Down in the meadow it's so wet, cloth disintegrates fairly quickly. But up here the soil stays much drier." She glanced up, grinning. "This is terrific. That fabric could tell us lots of good stuff, assuming it's not something the rats dragged in. Hopefully we'll find more around the bones which could nail it down as historical."

He watched as she packed the stuff meticulously in an artifact bag and labeled it with the exact coordinates and a description, along with a reference to the photos she'd taken of it in situ. Jeez, no wonder archaeological excavations could take years.

"Want to learn how to do this?" she asked.

"Sure," he answered willingly, and after that he was in charge of bagging the finds. Not that they unearthed many other things besides bones—which they left in place—and she always kept an eye on what he was doing. But by the time she'd removed a ten centimeter layer of dirt from around the skull, ribs and part of an arm, he was feeling comfortable with his duties.

"Piece of cake," he said with a wink, basking under her warm return smile.

The sun was creeping toward the horizon, and his thoughts turned to dinner and the interesting things that might follow, when suddenly his attention was grabbed by what RaeAnne's trowel revealed at that moment. It was a well-articulated skeleton of a hand and wrist. And wrapped around the wrist bone was—

"My God!" they exclaimed in unison.

"It's my father!"

"It's Crawford Edisto!"

Chapter 12

"What?" they chorused, darting each other astonished glances, then both did double takes at the skeleton.

RaeAnne was sure she was looking at the remains of Crawford Edisto, the ill-fated brother who had disappeared under mysterious circumstances in 1859—supposedly shot in the back.

"Impossible. This is an historical burial. No way are these bones fresh."

"My father was supposedly killed thirty years ago. That's hardly fresh," Roman countered.

"You said he was still alive."

"And then we got that box with his regalia and eagle feathers, and decided he could be dead."

She huffed. "But look at that little finger!"

The bones of the hand were arrayed in perfect order, undisturbed by rats or anything else since they'd been laid to rest—at least as far as she could tell. The little finger bones were poised at an acutely unnatural angle, pointing straight out to the side, presumably due to the man's childhood cotton gin accident.

"This has to be Edisto. What makes you think it's your father?"

"The bracelet. It's the one my mom gave him."

That put a whole different light on things. The Native-style bracelet was a wide circlet of engraved silver, a slip-on type not unknown in the historic southwest. Still, it would be somewhat unusual for a white man to have worn it back in 1859.

"Maybe it just looks a lot like his."

"Anything's possible," Roman said, but his expression showed how little he thought of that theory.

"Unbelievable." RaeAnne sat back on her heels and let out a long sigh. "Damn, damn, damn. How could this be?"

He looked more and more shell-shocked as he sat there, rubbing his free hand up and down over his mouth and chin in a nervous, shaky motion. "God knows. Jeez, first he's dead, then he's alive, then dead again. What the hell do I do now?" he murmured.

She wasn't sure exactly on what level he was speaking— as a law enforcement official, a crime scene investigator or as the victim's son.

"Do you want me to drive down the mountain and make some phone calls? Get Bugs back? Or call Philip?"

That snapped him out of his paralysis. "No! Not O'Donnaugh. But Bugs might be a good idea." Gazing at the remains, he appeared to think for a moment, raking his hand through his hair. "Except... There's something not quite right here. I just can't put my finger—" he blanched and jerked his eyes from the bones— "Hell, I need a drink."

RaeAnne took that as her cue. Rising, she tugged on his hand. "Come on, what you need is a cup of tea."

Though he didn't budge, that earned her a lopsided smile. "No problem too great for a cup of tea to solve, right?"

"You know it."

He shook his head, scrutinizing the skeleton and what was

left of the mound that surrounded it. "No, there's definitely something wrong." Pulling his hand from hers, he reached for the skull. "If only I could—"

"What are you doing!" she exclaimed as he gingerly grasped the lower jaw and tried to move it. "Stop that! You're destroying evidence! Of all the—"

"I need to know."

"Know what? Roman!"

He pushed out a breath and fixed his eyes on hers in an intense expression. "Before I said anything about the bracelet, you were positive this burial was a hundred and forty years old?"

"Well, yeah. But I—"

"Then I'm going with your instincts. Let's check his teeth. They didn't have fillings back in those days, did they?"

"Well, no. Of course not." She pried her eyes from his and glanced at the skull. "But I'm guessing your dad did."

"Exactly. In fact, I remember him having a root canal. We should be able to spot that, right?"

"Oh, yeah. But what if I'm wrong about the age?"

"I'll take that chance. I trust you, Rae."

How could a heart take flight and sink so low at the same time? He trusted her. With something this important, he trusted her. Why couldn't she do the same for him?

Maybe it was time she set aside her final doubts and took the plunge.

"All right," she said, and met his gaze. "Let's go for it."

He smiled, a tender, relieved smile, and for a second she thought maybe he was reading her mind again.

"Good. You do it. I'm not thrilled about touching dead people."

"Baby," she softly teased and accepted a kiss on her palm before she reached for the lower jawbone and gently wiggled it loose. They put their heads together and peered at the teeth.

"Not a filling in sight."

Roman let out a long breath. "Thank God. You were right."

She slipped the mandible back in place and let herself fall backward onto the grass beside the grave. "Jeez Louise, Roman, give me a damn heart attack."

"That was a close one," he agreed, lying down next to her. "Strange about the bracelet, though. It really is a dead ringer for my father's."

"It's not an uncommon type." She reached for his hand and laced her fingers through his. "And it's pretty encrusted with dirt and corrosion. Once it gets cleaned up, I'm certain you'll see it's not the same piece."

"I guess." But he was staring up at the mountain peaks with a weird, contemplative expression on his face, as though still trying to figure something out.

"You're not disappointed, are you?"

"I want to find my father, but I need him alive, to answer my questions."

"You're still planning to track him down?"

"If it's the last thing I do."

Her heart squeezed painfully.

There it was, then. Another reason she shouldn't trust him. Until he'd gotten this obsession with his father out of his system, he'd never be content to stay. He needed answers, and she'd just be in the way of finding them.

She slid her hand from his and rose to her feet. "It's getting late. I'm going to secure things for the night."

He blinked twice, looking up at her. "Sure. I'll—"

Suddenly the air was split by a loud bang, and a thin buzzing noise zipped past her ear. All was silent for a nanosecond, then Roman shouted, *"Get down!"* and all hell broke loose.

In an instant she'd been knocked off her feet, and pressed into the dirt, with Roman's weight on top of her. His arm was tight around her, his other hand holding up his gun. Where had that come from?

"Hang on," he whispered, and rolled their entwined bodies off the exposed hillock into a small ravine.

She barely had time to realize she was terrified. "What's going on?" she asked, spitting out grass and pine needles.

"Someone's shooting at us."

Another shot rang out, taking a chunk out of a granite boulder just above them. Roman swore and shielded her from the resulting shower of sparks and loosened shards.

"For crying out loud, Roman! Shoot back!"

"I can't see him, and don't want to waste bullets. Come on, we need cover."

He grasped her by the upper arm and practically hauled her along the ravine to a stand of trees, protecting her back the whole time with his body. By the time he flung her behind a large fallen log and landed on top of her again, her breath was coming in big gulps. But more from crushing fear than exertion.

"Are they trying to kill us?" she asked, shaking like a ninny despite his reassuring presence over her.

"That, or a damn good imitation."

She looked up at him. "But who…?"

Her stomach plummeted when he deliberately avoided her gaze. She suspected who he thought it was.

He had to be wrong! Philip would never try to kill her. Or him—despite what Roman believed. He had no motive.

"Maybe we hit a nerve with Pritchett and his gang this morning," she whispered into an eerie stillness. All the birds had flown off. Even the insects had gone silent.

"Maybe. Yeah, probably," he quietly conceded, and she could tell he actually gave credence to the suggestion. "Well, I'll never find out by hiding in the trees. Stay here."

"Wait! You don't intend to—!" She grabbed him as he started to lift off her. "Don't you dare leave me here alone!"

"I have to, *cara*. I've got to get that bastard."

"But—!"

"Don't move. Don't even breathe."

And with that he was gone. Vanished into the trees.

Great. A homicidal maniac was out to kill her and her protector had just left her there, her only cover a rotting log. She'd have no trouble with his last order. Her chest was so tight she didn't think she could breathe even if she wanted to.

Sweating, she lay quietly in the prickly moss for endless minutes, stretching into what seemed like hours. The sun crept lower and lower, the shadows of the pines lengthening into the menacing shapes of fanged beasts and gun-toting murderers. Ants crawled over her—and probably worse—but the only time she dared move was when she heard a noise and couldn't help jumping.

The sudden echo of gunfire blasted through the valley. *Roman!* Her heart leaped to her throat as she counted shots. *Two, three.*

No! He wasn't hurt. He couldn't be!

Four. She forbade the tears welling up to fall. She absolutely would not cry. And she would not move. *Five. Six.*

No way. She wasn't one of those silly women who crept down into a dark, dank basement to investigate a mysterious noise, only to end up dead. No, siree. Not this lady. Roman was a professional. An FBI agent. He was fine, and he'd told her to stay put. Stay put was what she intended to do. No matter how many shots she heard.

Seven. eight.

Ah, hell.

She scrambled to her feet just as something big crashed down the hillside, landing right beside her. She screamed. And spun around just in time to see a hulking shadow reach for her.

Roman clenched his teeth together as he ducked through the underbrush, running quickly away from RaeAnne's hiding place. He was determined to catch whoever was shooting at them—or more correctly at RaeAnne.

The man was history. No one tried to kill the woman he loved and lived to tell about it.

He headed toward the dirt track to the cabin, circling around in a wide arch. Cleary was too far from anywhere to hike in, even from Tecopa; the guy had to have a vehicle.

Roman figured it must be hidden somewhere along the road. If he could spot the car, the shooter was as good as his.

But who was it? Pritchett's henchman or O'Donnaugh's? Whoever it was, if they'd started to shoot at RaeAnne, they must be mighty worried about something—something even bigger than the murder of Jason Danforth.

It took Roman a quarter hour to circle around and meet the primitive road, working his way under cover of the trees along the canyon slopes. By that time it was nearly dark. A branch suddenly snapped a few yards away and he froze, hitting the ground just before bullets scattered bark from the tree behind him. He rolled and came up shooting.

He exchanged three more shots, then wheeled behind a tree trunk, listening intently. Light footsteps sped away, muffled by the forest. He darted after them, keeping behind trees and boulders, but the sound vanished. *Damn.* He sprinted along the darkened road, ignoring caution, his only thought to catch the man who'd tried to hurt RaeAnne.

The sound of an engine revving and tires crunching into the distance told him he'd been too slow. Roman swore vividly.

And that's when he noticed the last glimmer of the setting sun glint off the rack of a sheriff's cruiser parked behind the cabin.

"Philip! Oh, thank God!" RaeAnne exclaimed and launched herself at the dark figure that had stopped its headlong dash down the hillside at the sight of her. His gun was drawn, but she ignored it as she hugged him in terror.

"RaeAnne? What the hell's going on here? I was driving down from Tecopa and thought I heard shots."

"You did!" She hung on to him, but pulled back enough to peer up into his shadowed face. "They were shooting at us!"

"Who?"

"I don't know. Roman went after them and left me here all alone. I thought I'd die of fright."

"Calm down, I'm here now," he said, peering through the gloom around them. "Tell me exactly what happened."

The sun had gone down and within seconds a curtain of black descended on the valley. As he led her toward the cabin—at least she thought that's where he was leading her—she clung to his arm to keep from tripping and in a shaky voice told him about the shooting.

"It was awful. And the worst is that I don't know if Roman is lying out there somewhere bleeding to death."

"I should be so lucky," Philip muttered under his breath, and RaeAnne cut him a sharp glance. "Sorry, that was inappropriate," he said stiffly, then came to a halt. His cruiser was right in front of them and he quickly opened the door. "Get in. I'll take you—"

"You aren't taking her anywhere," Roman's voice hissed out of the darkness. "RaeAnne, step away from the car."

The overwhelming joy at seeing him unharmed was immediately tempered by the sight of a gun in his hand, pointing straight at Philip. "Roman—"

"Get away from her, O'Donnaugh. And keep your hands where I can see them."

"Don't be an ass, Santangelo. I'll admit I hate your guts, but why would I want to harm RaeAnne?"

Roman emerged from the shadows, her avenging angel in torn blue jeans, covered with dirt from sifting artifacts, willing to die to protect her if need be.

She didn't think she'd ever loved him more than in just that moment. She loved him so much she thought her heart would burst. Even if he was wrong about Philip.

"Suppose you tell me, Sheriff." He motioned with his gun for Philip to raise his hands in the air. "Let's see. The usual motives for murder are power, greed, and, gee, how about love?"

"Oh, yeah. That makes sense. I love her so I have to kill her." Philip rolled his eyes. "Oh, you mean because she prefers you? Sorry to disappoint you, Agent Santangelo, but even RaeAnne isn't worth spending the rest of my life in jail for.''

''Thanks a lot,'' she mumbled, but couldn't help smiling. Philip was being a snot, but under the circumstances she couldn't blame him. With his hands raised above his head, the man looked like he was about to blow a gasket.

''And as for power, I'm already one of the most powerful men in Inyo County. Why risk all that? For what?''

She could see Roman's jaw tighten. ''My guess would be for greed.''

''Give me a break,'' Philip said, lowering a hand to swipe it over his forehead. ''What would I possibly have to gain by doing something as stupid as murder? I can't believe I'm standing here arguing with an FBI agent while we both let the real bad guy get away.''

Something in his irritated, weary tone must have gotten through to Roman, because he narrowed his eyes at the sheriff and she could almost hear the gears turning in his head.

Still, his gun didn't as much as waver. ''That's right. I almost forgot. You have your deputies do the dirty work for you.''

''What are you talking about?''

''Don't play innocent with me, O'Donnaugh. I'm the one they beat up and left for dead, and were on their way back to finish off for good. Too bad for you and your little poaching scheme they didn't succeed. You know what? You're under arrest—''

Uh-oh. They were back to that. She'd almost forgotten about Toby's accusations of the sheriff's office's involvement in illegal poaching. After the murder, its importance had somehow diminished. Apparently not to Roman, though.

''What the hell?'' Philip shouted. ''Poaching scheme? Hey, you can't arrest me!''

Roman grasped the other man's shoulder and turned him around. ''Just watch me. You have the right to remain silent—''

Lord, she had to do something. Regardless if what Toby

said was true or not, Philip was not involved. He couldn't be. "Roman—"

Philip grunted as he was pushed roughly against his own cruiser door. "Stop it! You're a lunatic, you know that?"

"Yep."

She tried again. "Um, Roman?"

He ignored her and patted his own pockets, irritation filling his expression when he didn't find what he was looking for. Handcuffs, no doubt. "Anything you say can and will be used against you—"

"Roman!"

"Then I'll say this once and you'd better listen up good. I did not kill Jason Danforth or shoot at you or RaeAnne. I did not order my deputies to beat you up or kill you, and I have no knowledge of any damn poaching scheme. Now will you please explain to me what's going on?"

"Roman!"

"What?" he snapped, finally acknowledging her. "I'm trying to make an arrest here."

"Can I ask you a question?"

"What?" he repeated, his black eyes flashing impatiently in the rising moonlight.

She nodded toward Philip's revolver, resting safely in its holster on his hip. "Why don't you check his gun? Wouldn't it still be warm, or bullets missing, or something?"

Roman's lips thinned as he stared at the weapon for a moment. "You're a real pain in the butt sometimes," he finally said.

She shrugged, doing her best not to look smug. At least she'd gotten him to calm down and listen to reason.

"You think he's innocent, don't you."

She nodded.

With a jerk, he holstered his own gun. "I still have boot prints on my ribs, RaeAnne. And if that bullet had been two inches closer, you'd be dead right now."

"It wasn't Philip."

He blew out a breath. "You're that sure?"

"I dated the man for three months. I trust him."

"You dated me for seven years," he shot back.

And you don't trust me.

She felt as though she'd been struck. The words couldn't have been clearer if they'd been spoken aloud. "That's different."

"Yeah." Roman slashed a hand up at Philip. "Get the hell out of my sight, O'Donnaugh, before I actually check that gun." He started to stalk away, toward the cabin.

"Roman, wait." She rushed after him, determined to show him things were different now. That she did trust him. Which she did.

"No."

Philip's belligerent answer brought them both to a halt.

Roman spun, his features angular and ghostlike in the patchy moonlight. "You *want* to be arrested?"

"No. But if it's true what you say, and my men are doing something illegal, I need to know about it."

The silence stretched until she could hear the rustle of seedpods in the meadow and the whistle of wind in the peaks high above them. She held her breath for Roman's reply.

"All right," he said at last. "I'll go along with this charade. But not here. I want to get RaeAnne somewhere safe."

"A fine idea," she said, filling her starving lungs. "But first I have to take care of the skeleton."

"Forget it, Rae. It'll be fine for one night."

"But—"

"I'm not giving you a choice."

"I agree, RaeAnne. You're in danger here until we figure out what's going on," Phillip said.

"We?" Roman eyed him suspiciously.

"I'm still Inyo County Sheriff, Santangelo. Like it or not, we're working together."

Terrific. She needed this like she needed more complications in her life. Not. "How about if you two work together and leave me out of it?"

"No," they said in unison.

Well, would wonders never cease? They actually agreed on something. Too bad it was about telling her what to do.

Unfortunately, just then she remembered how terrified she was. "Okay, okay." She gave a gesture of surrender. "But at least let me cover the bones with plastic so they aren't damaged if it rains."

Fifteen minutes later they'd done that, thrown some overnight things into the Jeep and were following the sheriff's cruiser down the mountain.

"Where are we going?" she asked, peering nervously into the black void surrounding them. The Jeep's headlights didn't make a dent in the penetrating darkness. Even the moon had gone into hiding behind one of the massive, looming peaks.

While she'd carefully tucked a tarp around the skeleton, Roman and Philip had stood guard over her like a couple of junkyard dogs—snarling at each other the entire time. They'd argued in intense whispers after Roman told Philip about the possible marijuana cultivation at Tecopa, about Philip's deputies beating him up, about the evidence of long-term illegal poaching activity by someone in the sheriff's office, along with Roman's growing suspicions that they were all somehow connected, which was news to her. What could the sheriff's office's poaching possibly have to do with Pritchett selling marijuana and killing Danforth? And hadn't his beating been the deputies' pathetically misguided attempt to fix their boss' faltering love life?

There was a moment she'd thought they'd actually come to blows when Roman mentioned Philip's own initials being in his father's notes about the poaching. But then Philip had gone dead quiet, set his jaw and just stalked off to his cruiser.

"We're going for a ride," Roman answered, bringing her back to the question of where they were headed.

"No kidding," she remarked, grabbing the Jeep's door frame as he took the turn onto the highway too fast. "But where?"

"No, I really mean for a ride. How far is it to Medicine Wind Stables?"

She stared. "Stables? You're taking me horseback riding?" He nodded. *"Now?"*

He nodded again. "Got a better idea?"

She gaped at him, then glanced around at the dark forest. "Yeah! How about a hotel?"

He flashed her a grin. "Attractive as that sounds, we need to find Toby."

"It's pitch-black out! We'll be lucky to find the trail!"

"You forget, this tracking stuff is in my blood. I'm an Indian."

"You're a nutcase!" she exclaimed. "And this is crazy. Toby will be back tomorrow."

"Unless they get to him first."

Sudden alarm for the boy rocketed through her. "They? You mean whoever shot at us is after him, too?" That was something she hadn't considered. This was getting downright terrifying.

"Toby's the key, he has to be. I can't take the chance they realize that and try to keep him from talking."

"Who?"

"I wish I knew."

"Does Philip know where we're going?"

Roman shook his head. "O'Donnaugh seemed convincing, that he didn't know about his deputies or the poaching, and that he isn't involved in the marijuana. But I'm not willing to risk the kid's life on any of that."

She fell silent as she contemplated the danger Toby might be facing at this very moment, regardless of who was after them. They had to help him, before it was too late.

It was truly amazing how completely a life could change in virtually a split second.

Not a week ago, she had been living a safe, unexciting existence, digging up her rocks and arrowheads and casually dating a man who was nice if not exactly heart-pounding. Practically in the blink of an eye her life had become a roller coaster. She'd had her artifacts stolen then confiscated, lost her boyfriend, slept with the high school sweetheart she'd vowed never to speak to again, discovered a murder victim, possibly gotten herself pregnant, been shot at and fallen in love with the one man on earth she knew with certainty would break her heart into a million pieces.

How had all this happened in the course of a few short days?

Roman looked over at her, his eyes searching, and asked softly, "You up for it?"

Was she? On any level? Was she brave enough to face the bullets of the present, the heartaches of the past and a future filled with pain and uncertainty?

"I don't know," she answered truthfully, and though trembling inside, gave him her bravest smile. "But I guess we're about to find out."

Chapter 13

They'd raised a few brows at the Medicine Wind Stables when they'd shown up asking for horses at an hour most people were settling down with their families in front of the TV. But in the end they'd convinced the owners to rent them a couple of mounts by saying it was urgent they find Toby. Roman hadn't even had to flash his FBI credentials—once again his father's reputation had preceded him.

He swallowed the ever-present distaste the mention of his father produced, and listened carefully as the young cowboy who was saddling up for them mentioned some places they might run into Toby.

Roman didn't let himself think about what they were doing as he and RaeAnne urged their horses onto a narrow mountain trail in the dead of night with nothing to guide them but an old U.S. Geological Survey map and a drugstore compass. Thank goodness she was an archaeologist and knew which end was up among the dotted lines and squiggly contour markings on the puke-green map. Not that they could see anything, either map or landscape, even with a flashlight.

They were largely relying on their horses to know where the trail was or wasn't.

He fisted the reins and prayed they'd make it in one piece to the small lake the cowboy had recommended they camp at for the night. The lake was a hub for several side trails, on any one of which they might find Toby.

"I can't believe you talked me into this," RaeAnne grumbled from atop her horse, trodding along behind his.

"I thought you loved to ride," he said in a deliberately cheery voice. No way was he going to let on how uncomfortable he was feeling.

Okay, downright nervous. Yeah, Mr. Tough Guy Undercover Agent, who had nerves of steel and ice in his veins, able to outlast and outwit the nastiest criminal the FBI could throw at him. Lord. Ever since that fateful day he'd found RaeAnne tied to a tree he'd had a case of nerves big enough to last him a lifetime. And this Gordian knot of suspicious crimes and coincidences they found themselves in the middle of exponentially increased his worry.

Of course, straddling a thousand pounds of ornery horseflesh didn't help his peace of mind, either.

"I do love to ride," she retorted. "But not in the middle of the night with some maniac out there just itching to use me for target practice."

Roman shifted in his saddle and turned to look at her. "Dammit, RaeAnne, that's not funny."

"Tell me about it."

"Baby, there's no way they can know where we're going."

"Then why are we doing this now and not waiting until morning?"

He turned frontways again and cursed silently. The woman was too smart for her own good. "Because I wanted a good excuse to get you in my sleeping bag, that's why."

She didn't reply and he wondered if she was still frightened or if he'd managed to make her smile. He also wondered what she'd say when she found out he'd only brought one sleeping bag.

"I see you only brought one sleeping bag," she said, managing to make *him* smile, despite the fear gnawing in his gut.

"Yep," he allowed, and thought about how they'd have to spoon together to fit into it. It had been a long time since he'd made love in a sleeping bag. Over eighteen years, to be exact. The memory of a long-ago, sweet afternoon sifted through him and he felt himself grow hard.

Her saddle creaked. "So, where are you going to sleep?"

"Inside you," he answered before he knew what he was saying.

His horse's hooves plodded to the hard throb of his heart, each hammering beat more powerful than the last.

"I'd like that," she said at last, and he had to stop himself from jumping off the wretched beast and sweeping her into his arms right then and there.

Instead he simply turned and looked at her. He didn't say anything—couldn't say anything that would adequately convey his feelings at hearing those words spoken from her lips with such seriousness. The profound joy, the pure exhilaration, the agonizing desire.

The awful fear that something terrible would once again prevent him from being with her for the rest of his days.

Above him, the wind soughed through the trees, creating an eerie, lonely sound. He tipped his head up, seeking a glimpse of the high country into which they were headed. The crouching mountains yawned around them like a black, forbidding gullet preparing to swallow the two insignificant humans foolish enough to be on the trail at night. He suppressed a shiver. Even bundled up in his leather jacket he was cold, but he knew it wasn't the temperature that was making his spine crawl.

They rode for another two hours before spotting a shimmer of moonlight on water between the trees of a small valley below. *The lake.* Thank God, they'd made it.

Fifteen minutes later they'd reached the primitive camp on

its shore and he'd lit a fire in the iron grill box thoughtfully provided by the Forest Service. An old, blackened coffee can sat atop the grill, so he filled it with lake water and set it to heat for wash water, as no doubt dozens of campers had done before him, and then filled their cook pot with fresh water for tea. By the time RaeAnne had finished taking care of the horses, he had the welcome brew waiting.

"They okay?" he asked, nodding at the two brown giants, freshly brushed and tethered securely to a rail.

"Fine," she said and plopped down next to him on the sleeping bag. "The trick will be getting the saddles back on them tomorrow."

He chuckled, and stretched out his tired legs. "Ever ride bareback?"

"Not horses," she answered, grabbing her tin cup of tea from his hand.

He whipped his eyes to hers, and saw a million stars twinkling in their depths. Slowly he smiled, feeling the weariness in his body magically evaporate. "Long day tomorrow. We should turn in soon."

"Couldn't agree more," she said on a sigh, and leaned her head on his shoulder.

He put his arm around her and held her close as they sipped their tea. The fire crackled and flickered off the canopy of sheltering pines, enveloping them in a cozy, smoke-scented glow.

"It all seems so unreal," she murmured. "Jason Danforth, the poaching, Pritchett and the marijuana, being shot at... It's so peaceful here. How could all that be going on just a few miles down the hill?"

"Mmm-hmm. Hard to believe." How he wished he could snap his fingers and make all the unpleasantness go away. Come to think of it, there were a lot of things he'd like to make go away. Things from the past. Things that were keeping him from the future he wanted—with RaeAnne. *"Cara—"*

Before he could complete the thought her lips were gently

pressing onto his. "Then we'll have to enjoy tonight, before it all catches up to us again." Her mouth was warm and welcoming, until she pulled away. "But first I need to wash my face."

As they got ready for bed he watched her. How beautiful she was! Doing simple things like brushing her teeth in the moonlight, scrubbing her cheeks with soapy fingers, giggling like a teenager when she slipped out of her clothes and huddled shivering in the sleeping bag, waiting for him to join her.

The overwhelming need to rip off his jeans and plunge into her had him sparking with frustration, his body a hot bundle of anticipation. He forced himself to slow down.

With deliberate calm he cleaned up, refilled the coffee can with water for the morning, stoked the fire, rolled her down jacket into a pillow, and removed his clothing, folding each piece neatly and setting them all in a pile on the plastic ground cover.

All the while her eyes were on him, peeking out from the sleeping bag where she lay cocooned. Her body naked. Waiting for his touch. Was she trembling as badly as he was?

When finally, finally, he slid into the sleeping bag with her and zipped it to the top, she gasped. "You're freezing!"

"You're nice and hot," he countered with a kiss, slipping a knee between her kicking legs. "Hot and sexy and— Damn."

He didn't fit. The sleeping bag wouldn't allow her legs to part far enough to let him between them.

She giggled. "Serves you right, ice cube."

He groaned. "This didn't happen to us last time. Must be a smaller sleeping bag."

She wriggled under him. "Or a bigger you."

"I don't recall you complaining about my size back then," he said flipping them over, bag and all. Maybe if he was on the bottom…

"Bigger's good," she assured him, eyebrows waggling,

and he felt her fingers slide around him, along with her legs. But not far enough. He still couldn't—

He pulled her hand away. "I want to be in you," he said, low and rough.

Her movements stopped. Even in the darkness he could see the arousal in her eyes, the flush in her cheeks, her lips parted with desire. "I want you in me, too. All night. Like you promised."

This was hell. Like being in a straitjacket. He rolled back on top of her. He would not let this stupid bag defeat him. Lifting onto an elbow, he put his hand between them and touched her body. She whimpered, pressing into him, sliding her arms around his neck.

By now the sleeping bag was an inferno. He could feel her nipples, small and hard, poking into his chest. He seized one between his fingers and gently rolled.

She sucked in a breath, her body bucking under his. "Please, you've got to find a way."

He was beginning to enjoy this sweet torture. Being denied the ultimate joining had made his whole body vibrate with acute sensitivity. He'd never been more attuned to RaeAnne's every touch, every hair, every brush of her lips or her fingers on his skin.

He covered her mouth with his and kissed her deeply, letting his tongue roam and explore, until her throat sang a low, constant moan. She urged and reacted to every nuance, enflaming him even more with her heated response.

His fingers drifted over her body, lower, lower, until they met the hot, slick junction of her legs. "Yes," she whispered when he slid them between her honeyed folds, caressing, probing, encouraging.

He was hard and thick and throbbing with need as his fingers stroked over her, back and forth, around in circles. His arousal ached for completion, but he concentrated instead on hers. The smells of campfire and lake mingled in his nostrils with the scent of male and female and a hint of horse sweat. Never again would he be able to sit at a campfire or be near a horse without thinking of this moment.

Her moans increased in demand. "I want you," she whispered.

"I want you, too," he answered. In every way. He filled his hands with her flesh, filled his mouth with her taste, filled his soul with her love. And beneath him she started to quiver, and quake, then called his name so it echoed through the night.

Before the sound had died, he canted and turned her on her side, brought his torso hard up against her back. Pushing her knees up with his as high as they could go in the bag, he entered her from behind. Two voices, one high and one low, wove together in a duet of pleasure and completion.

"I knew you'd find a way," she sighed breathlessly, moving with him as he thrust deep into her.

The sleeping bag twisted around them like a shroud, but he didn't care. All that mattered was that they were one at last.

His breath came quick and shallow, between the altitude and the frustrating wait. His hands sought her breasts, her mouth, the place of their union. She reached down and grasped his thigh, holding firm, her fingers digging into his muscles as he plunged deeper and deeper into her. He wanted to shout her name over and over, declare his love before God and the watching mountains, claim her as his for all eternity whether they liked it or not.

But he didn't dare. He knew it would break the spell if he spoke of anything deeper than the feel of his body buried in hers. So he contented himself with that. Reveled in his body's mastery of hers, and vowed to have all of her, trust included—even if it took him the next hundred and eighteen years to prove he was worthy of it.

Roman awoke to the unmistakable sounds and smells of trout grilling over an open fire and the even more unmistakable feel of a woman tangled in his arms. He must have died and gone to heaven.

He cracked an eyelid and was assaulted by a punky grin beaming down at him.

"About time you two lovebirds woke up. It's almost noon."

An exaggeration. Even from where he lay he could see the sun had barely broken the horizon.

"Hello, Toby." Roman briefly mourned the demise of his own breakfast plans—something hot involving RaeAnne and not trout—but managed a smile nonetheless. The kid had no doubt saved his backside hours of unpleasant saddle-pounding by turning up on his own. "You okay?"

"Sure. Out for a nice Sunday ride?"

Roman grabbed hold of the edge of the sleeping bag when RaeAnne started to wake with a stretch. "Cut the BS, Tobe. You know very well why we're here."

An "uh-oh" look crossed the kid's face but was quickly scattered by an eager smile. "You're here to help catch those poachers?"

"Among other things." Roman was distracted by the feel of RaeAnne's bottom rubbing against his—

"RaeAnne. Baby, wake up. We've got—" his words choked off as she turned in his arms and planted a sleepy kiss in the vicinity of his mouth, and her hand traced over— "Company."

Her eyes slowly opened and focused on his lips, then rose to Toby's vermilion face. Her cheeks went nearly the same shade. "Oh, hi, Toby."

"Hi, Miss Martin. I uh, just remembered something I have to do back at camp. I'll just—"

"Don't you dare go anywhere," she said as she flailed an arm out and groped the ground sheet for her clothes. "Just turn your back for a minute."

Roman made sure Toby had obliged before stopping RaeAnne's movements with a hug. He wanted to whisper things in her ear—how much he'd enjoyed sleeping with his arms wrapped around her, how much he still wanted her…how much he loved her. All the things that should be said after the night they'd shared. But for that he needed privacy. So instead he quickly pulled her close, caressing her breast as he gave her a deep, silent kiss.

"Good morning," he whispered, pouring every feeling he could into those two words before letting her go.

"Are you sure you don't want me to get lost?" Toby mumbled from his stump by the fire.

"No," they answered in unison, then smiled at each other as they hurried to get dressed.

Toby told them he'd spotted their horses while fishing the lake early that morning, and since he'd had good luck, decided to share his catch.

"Delicious," RaeAnne said appreciatively, driving Roman nuts by deliberately licking her fingers after polishing off her portion.

"Listen, Toby, we need to talk," he said, forcing his attention to more pressing matters than his still-ravenous hunger for her. "I think you know more than you realize about this poaching stuff. And maybe even about the murder. I'm beginning to think they have to be connected somehow, and I believe you can fill in some of the blanks."

The boy's face drained of color. "I was afraid of that."

"You'd better tell us everything, son," Roman suggested, handing the kid a cup of coffee from the pan that had just boiled. "You could be in danger. And RaeAnne, too."

"I knew it." Toby gave her an apologetic look. "I tried to get you to leave so they wouldn't hurt you."

"Huh?"

"Stealing your artifacts."

RaeAnne gazed at him in amazement. "You mean all that was just a ploy to get rid of me?"

The youngster lifted a shoulder, pushing a sneaker toe into the dirt. "Sort of." He looked up. "I believe what I said, about not messing with our burials. But… Well, after hearing you talk at the high school that time, I kinda figured you were on our side. I didn't want you to get caught in the middle of something bad."

"You knew about the body buried at Cleary?" Roman asked, incredulous that the boy would have kept that a secret.

"No, not exactly," he hedged. "I suspected something had happened...something nasty. The Fish and Wildlife guy—Jason—was missing. I'd talked to him about the poaching and he believed me. That's why he'd gone up into the mountains that day. But I had no idea if he was really dead."

So now they were back to the poachers killing Danforth instead of Pritchett and his marijuana gang. Roman was beginning to get mental whiplash. He shook his head to clear it.

"What made you think RaeAnne was in danger?"

"Someone—the guys who did it—they must have seen me when I spoke to her at the site after her presentation at the high school. I asked some pretty pointed questions, and maybe they thought... Anyway, I got a phone call at home, a few days later. A guy said he'd give me a hundred bucks to chase her off the site, any way I could."

Now they were getting somewhere. "Who was it?"

Toby shook his head. "No idea."

Maybe not. "Why on earth didn't you report all this?"

"To who? The sheriff?" He snorted. "They're the ones who're doing the poaching. When I found out Miss Martin was dating Sheriff O'Donnaugh—" He halted midsentence, studying his feet.

"You thought I was part of it," she finished.

Roman gave her a grateful smile. "She was never involved in any poaching or anything else illegal," he assured Toby. "And don't worry, she's not dating the sheriff anymore."

A tide of red inched up the boy's throat to his ears. "Cool."

"So this phone call...?" Roman prompted.

"It made me think. Why would someone want her gone from a dumb archaeological site? Unless—"

"Unless there was something buried at Cleary that wasn't supposed to be."

"Exactly!"

"Stands to reason whoever was trying to scare off RaeAnne knew what that was. In this case, a dead body."

Toby got up and started pacing around the camp. "I figured if I did what they said, and could get a glimpse of whoever gave me the money, I'd know exactly who was behind that guy's disappearance and the poaching."

Roman winced. Dumb idea. "So what happened?"

Toby made a disgusted sound. "She dug in her heels. No matter what I tried she wouldn't leave. So I didn't get the money. And then you showed up."

He gave a wry chuckle. "Spoiled your plans, eh?"

"Scared the snot out of us when you showed up on your dang Harley like some kind of badass outlaw. Thought for sure Miss Martin was a goner."

RaeAnne rolled her eyes. "Gee, thanks for sticking around."

"We did. Doubled back and sneaked around to check on you. You seemed, uh…fine."

The kid's grin was vintage smart aleck. Roman stifled a smile and said soberly, "We're old friends."

"You guys getting married, or what?"

RaeAnne sprayed a mouthful of coffee over the fire. Roman chose to avoid the question. "What I want to know is, why did they start shooting at us last night, and not before?"

Toby spun to them, obviously horrified. "For real?"

"Unfortunately, yes. Therefore, we have to ask, what changed yesterday?"

"We found Crawford Edisto's remains," RaeAnne offered.

Roman thought about it, then shook his head. "They couldn't have known that in advance. Plus, it's an historical burial. Where's the motive?"

"Then it has to be our visit to Tecopa."

Toby's eyes widened excitedly. "Dang! I knew it!"

"What?" Roman and RaeAnne chorused.

"I've always thought there was some connection between Tecopa and the poaching, and you just said you thought so, too."

Toby went on to explain how he'd noticed after every poaching incident, the sheriff or a deputy would drive up and talk to someone at the lumber camp. "At first I thought they were investigating the poaching. But nothing ever seemed to be solved, and the animal carcass always disappeared right away. That's when I started suspecting both the sheriff's office and Tecopa, and writing things down." He looked up. "Afterward I realized the initials in your father's notes mostly matched men who had worked at the sheriff's office, too, in his day."

Roman's stomach clenched painfully. *His father.* He felt RaeAnne's gentle fingers pry his apart and realized he'd clamped his hands around the scalding cook pot handle. She took the pan from him and refilled his coffee mug with the muddy liquid, as he'd meant to do.

"Toby, there's something we need to ask you," she said, relieving him of the task. He ordered himself not to betray his roiling emotions to the boy, who didn't need to know what was involved. "About that box of regalia you left on the porch at my cabin," she added.

Toby suddenly turned his back, stirring the fire with a stick. "What about it?"

"We need to know where it came from."

"I can't tell you that."

"It's important, Toby."

The kid crouched silently by the fire, pushing burning embers back and forth between the spokes of the grill. "Why?" he finally asked.

Roman sighed. Why were things always so complicated? Just once he'd like to get a straight answer the first time out. Maybe he was in the wrong damn profession. Dogs wouldn't ask questions when you offered to fix the pain.

"I was only six when I was told my father had died," he began.

"I heard about him," Toby interrupted, looking up respectfully. "You were born around here, weren't you?"

"Big Pine," he confirmed.

"And your father was a real hero," the boy said wide-eyed with admiration. "He was shot during that AIM protest, back in '73—" admiration turned to doubt as he searched Roman's face "—by the FBI."

"After he'd killed two agents," Roman gently reproved. "There were no heroes that day. None. Do you understand?"

"No," Toby answered with the heat of youth.

"Me, neither," Roman wearily agreed. "And that's why I need to know where that box came from. I think my father may still be alive."

Toby's head jerked up. "Alive? But how?"

"His body was never found, and I've had…indications… from the Bureau that his file is still active. I've got to know, Toby. Surely you see that?"

"I guess." Reluctantly the boy nodded. "Okay. The Chairman. I got it from the Chairman. He asked me to deliver it to you, anonymously. Please don't say I told. I swore on my honor."

Roman's brain spun in his skull. *The Chairman.* What did *he* have to do with all this?

Lord almighty. He should have known. The old man had said from the beginning he knew Hector Santangelo back when. And he'd also said outright things weren't always what they seemed. Why had Roman been so dense, thinking the tribal elder was referring to RaeAnne and her artifacts?

He looked up to see RaeAnne watching him, empathy radiating from her tender expression. He had to look away. He couldn't take her kindness when it concerned this subject. It was too raw. Too furious. Too open a wound.

And all at once he wondered if this was how *she'd* felt about *him,* until he'd come back into her life just a few short

days ago. That raw, blistering fury over life-altering injustices
that you couldn't control.

Suddenly he couldn't breathe. Huge injustices, like his betrayal, their baby's death, the eighteen years of abandonment
she'd lived through, the plans for love he'd dashed, the new
life he may have selfishly created in her womb this week.
Painful insight burned like acid in the bloody wreckage of
his heart. He grabbed his chest, and the tin mug tumbled from
his hands onto the dirt, splashing hot coffee everywhere.

Jeezus, no wonder she couldn't trust him. It was amazing
she could even look at him!

And this woman had made love to him last night. Had let
him touch her and bring her pleasure, and given him more
in a few hours than a dozen others had done in half a lifetime.

"Roman?" her sweet voice wafted through the red mists
of his tortured mind. His eyes burned and he choked back a
torrent of blackness, reaching for her. Then he was on his
knees and so was she, clutching him, holding him so he
didn't surrender to the oblivion of his guilt.

"Roman, please, you're scaring me." He felt her gently
shake him. "Tell me what's wrong."

"I'm sorry," he said, pulling her into a tight embrace.

He never, ever, wanted to let her go. Yet he must, for how
could such an overwhelming fury ever find peace and forgiveness? She would never trust him. Never. He saw that
now. Saw it with the whole, huge, gaping hole that had once
been his heart, until he'd ripped it from his chest and placed
it at her feet.

All around them, shadows lifted as the sun rose high above
the surrounding mountains. The granite of the peaks shone
in the bright morning light, sparkling like teeth in a false
pearly smile.

He looked into RaeAnne's eyes and they looked back at
him, concern and alarm blazing in their depths. He felt utterly
hopeless. He would lose her. No, he'd never had her back
and he never would. He'd seen to that eighteen years ago.

"I'm so sorry," he whispered, and knew his life had
turned to dust.

Chapter 14

"The coffee's burned you," RaeAnne said, easing an ashen Roman back onto the log where he'd been sitting. He was definitely scaring her. But for Toby's sake, she didn't let herself panic. "Stay here and I'll get some cool water."

"No!" Roman grabbed her wrist, his expression just shy of desperation. "No. It's not necessary. I was just..." She waited anxiously for some clue to his distress. "...surprised."

"Whew!" Toby hovered above them, wiping his hands on his jeans. "Man, I thought you'd had a stroke or something."

"Are you all right?" RaeAnne prodded, immediately recognizing that Roman's stalwart regroup was just a show for her and the boy.

"I'm fine," he promised, a reassuring smile leaping to his face. "No heart attack. The subject of my father...still upsets me. I can't believe I sat right there in the Chairman's office and he didn't say anything to me."

"Maybe he doesn't know anything," she suggested, brushing a hand over her lover's cheek. She needed to touch

him. To make sure he was really okay. No, he didn't feel
clammy. Maybe a bit chilled. "Let me get your jacket," she
said, determined to bring back the healthy, happy man she'd
awoken with this morning, and banish this haunted-eyed
ghost.

"Why don't you put your arms around me instead?"

He drew her onto his lap and, though surprised, she went
without protest, despite Toby's presence. She smiled into her
man's worried eyes, wanting so much to ease the pain in
them. She'd had no idea he felt quite this strongly about his
father. No wonder he was obsessed with putting the specter
of his father's accused treachery to rest.

She wrapped her arms around him and for the first time
believed she understood this wonderfully, incredibly complicated man. He said he wanted her trust—and he truly thought
that's what was wrong between them. But the truth was, he
didn't trust *himself*. And he wouldn't. Not until he'd come
to terms with his father's betrayals.

It all came down to honor. Roman's whole life had been
lived as one long expression of his sense of honor. His father
was an extension of that honor—as was she. As a boy he'd
always done the right thing; later he'd left her because it was
the only thing his honor would allow, he'd joined the FBI to
balance the scales after what his father had done. Roman's
honor meant everything to him. Everything.

And that's why she had to let him go, to let him do what
he needed to do. And why when she took it, no matter what
color the stick turned, she must tell him the pregnancy test
was negative.

A feeling of great peace descended over her. True, she may
lose him to his quest. Might watch him walk out of her life
and never return. But this time she would be all right. This
time she would know why he'd done it. And that would help
her to survive the pain.

"If you two are going to start smooching," came Toby's
embarrassed voice from behind them, "I'm outta here."

RaeAnne smiled over her shoulder and eased out from Roman's arms. "Not a chance, bucko."

Roman seemed to gather himself, and followed her cue. "You should never be too busy to give your woman a hug," he said with a wink as he rose to his feet after her. "Remember that."

"Yeah, whatever," Toby said, making a face.

"So, what do we do now?" RaeAnne asked, trying to get her thoughts back to the information they'd pooled, and a logical course of action. "Shouldn't you report all this to someone?"

Roman nodded thoughtfully. "Absolutely. But first... Toby, do you know where that stand of old growth is on the Tecopa lease? The one they don't let anyone enter?"

"Sure. But it's completely fenced off with barbed wire. I've even seen guards patrolling the perimeter. They really don't want people to go in there."

Roman gave a lopsided grin. "Let's take a look anyway."

After breaking camp and saddling up, RaeAnne took one last, longing glance back at the lake before they rode off, knowing she'd have to wait for the hot springs for what she had in mind. And Roman, too, judging by the wink he gave her. Ah, hell.

It was a beautiful day, and if it weren't for her all-too-real fear of being shot out of her saddle, she would have enjoyed the almost three hour ride to Tecopa's old-growth enclosure. As it was, she was constantly reminded of the danger they were in. All around them lay Tecopa's leased timberlands, and the possibility of running into Pritchett's men.

Early on, they unfolded the map and discussed the best way to avoid the current areas of lumber operations, which Toby pointed out. They stuck to the least-traveled trails, kept their voices down, and didn't stop until they'd reached their destination, deep inside Tecopa territory.

By the time they spotted the barbed-wire fence, RaeAnne's heart was in permanent high-gear. "And why are we doing this, again?" she asked.

"I'd at least like to know if we're on the right track about the marijuana growing before requesting a search warrant. I still can't figure out how growing weed is connected to the poaching, but I intend to find out. Maybe we'll get lucky and find something to link them. But probable cause would certainly help the warrant, if nothing else."

Roman had gone into official FBI Agent Mode as soon as they'd mounted their horses this morning, taking charge, issuing orders, keeping a vigilant watch all around. She could tell it bothered him big-time that he was putting two civilians in potential danger. Under the circumstances he had no choice, but that didn't mean he was going to take any unnecessary chances.

So, she was expecting it when, checking the tension in the fence wire, he said, "I want you two to stay here. Find someplace to hide yourselves and the horses while I go in and nose around."

Toby, however, was not. "No way, man! I'm coming, too!"

"Not possible. I need to get in and out quickly."

"What about your probable cause?"

Roman scowled at the boy. "What about it?"

"How are you going to explain just accidentally climbing through barbed wire and finding whatever's in there? You need an informant and a witness." He darted RaeAnne a glance. "An *impartial* witness."

The hair on her arms stood up. "Oh, no." She held up a hand. "Uh-uh. You are *not* leaving me alone again. No way." She shook her head vigorously. "Just look what happened last time."

Roman scowled at *her*.

"Well, then it appears we're all going in," Toby said.

Roman's gaze lifted to the mountain peaks and searched them, seemingly for some kind of sign. Apparently he didn't find one. "All right, fine. But you both do exactly as I say. No exceptions."

She nodded obediently, along with Toby.

After secreting the horses behind a tangle of bushes, they

approached the fence. Naturally they hadn't brought wire cutters. Using their riding gloves, they each took turns holding the strands of razor-sharp wire apart so the others could slip between them and into the forbidden territory.

Once in, Roman took stock of their surroundings and whispered, "Stick together."

No problem there. RaeAnne wanted to grab his hand and hang on for dear life. She restrained herself, but stayed so close she smacked into his back when he suddenly stopped.

"Damn!" he muttered. "I can't believe this."

"What?"

"A trip wire!"

She looked at him blankly. "In the middle of a forest?"

"We must be getting warm," Toby said, gingerly stepping over the nearly invisible obstacle.

"Wait," Roman said. "I want to see what it's attached to."

She didn't like the sound of that. She had visions of spears flying out of nowhere and skewering them like shish kebabs. She sighed with relief when they found nothing more sinister than the wire's end tied to the trunk of a sapling.

"Still, keep your eyes open," Roman said. "This could just be a warning."

Sure enough, the next thing they spotted was a bear trap, sitting in a small open area, jaws open and ready to snap off an unsuspecting limb. Nasty...

"This is getting spooky," Toby murmured, visibly shaken.

"I'll say," she agreed. "What do you all say we turn around?"

"I don't think so." Roman peered at a cleared path ahead of them. "We're almost there. Can you smell it?"

"What?" She and Toby eyeballed each other, lifting their noses to the wind. Okay, there was something unusual about the way the forest smelled here. A trace of spiciness in the air...

"Grass?"

"Cannabis. Whoa!" Roman grabbed her around the waist and Toby by the shoulder. "Don't move!"

She didn't. She didn't even breathe. She was too petrified. Roman was definitely serious about not moving. His arm was a band of steel around her and she could see Toby wince from the grip of his fingers. Suddenly she realized what Roman had seen.

They were surrounded.

By transparent strands of fishing line hanging from the trees all around them. Suspended from the lines were clusters of viciously barbed fish hooks, which blended nearly invisibly into the forest scenery. Her pulse went into hyperspace. She felt like she was in one of those World War II movies where the unsuspecting star suddenly found himself in the middle of a field of land mines.

"What do we do?" she squeaked.

"Stand very, very still. We're okay as long as we don't get hooked."

The whole thing was surreal. Hundreds of tiny, shimmering filaments filled the air in every possible direction except straight back, and even there they blew back and forth across the path they'd just taken.

"My guess is they've been dipped in some kind of poison."

Oh, great.

The silvery lines drifted in the breeze, some as low as ground level. It would be a pretty sight, if it didn't spell instant death. Or maybe a slow, lingering death. Neither sounded appealing.

"Next time leave me behind," she muttered. "No matter how much I complain."

"Gloves," Roman prompted with a wry smile, and they all obeyed instantly. He glanced around, then peered ahead into the forest in the direction they were headed.

"You can't be serious," she said, reading his intent.

"Will this help?" Toby asked, offering up a Swiss army knife from his pocket just as Roman carefully stooped down to produce a blade that had been tucked inside his boot.

She wanted to kiss them both.

"Cut the ones beside us," Roman directed Toby. "I'll get the ones in front."

Just as he was about to take a step forward, she noticed something strange in the dirt ahead of them. A subtle shift on the ground. A shadow, or... Whatever it was, a small cluster of pine needles simply disappeared into thin air.

"*Stop!*"

Everyone froze.

"The ground. There's something weird with it." She pointed to where the needles had vanished. "There."

Roman studied the area she'd indicated. Then, being careful to avoid the fish hooks, he plucked up a nearby branch. With it, he poked the ground in front of them. Suddenly there was a rustle and a whoosh of dirt, and a large, gaping hole opened up at their feet.

At the bottom of the pit, arranged in neat rows, stood an army of sharpened bamboo spikes.

She was going to faint. The blood drained from her head so quickly she had to grab Roman's arm before she toppled into the hole.

"Damn," he swore. "I should be at the bottom of that." Instinctively she pulled him closer, away from the horrible pitfall. "I should—for bringing you two into this place."

"How were you to know?" she whispered. "This is sick. Crazy. Nobody could have predicted we'd run into stuff like this."

"You're wrong," he murmured. "It was right there in front of my face the whole time. I should have realized."

"I don't understand. Realized what?"

"Vietnam."

It was a satisfying sight that greeted the trio after they'd cut and worked themselves around the fish hooks and pitfall. Roman grimaced, taking in the freshly tilled rows of black earth, the foot-high green seedlings waving in the breeze, the smudge pots, and the brown camouflage netting suspended over the whole field like some giant prop left over from the set of *M.A.S.H.*

He'd recognized the setup immediately from old reports out of Mendocino County. Numbers of ex-Vietnam vets who'd gone slightly over the edge had taken to the woods stateside after the war, making money in a way that suited their war-ravaged minds. The booby traps were a dead give-away. And hadn't he noticed how everyone involved in this case had long, gray hair? Well, everyone except O'Don-naugh.

"Paydirt," Roman muttered, surveying the orderly, com-pact field tucked in amidst a disguising ring of pines. "Now we've got you, you bastards."

"Not exactly," a familiar voice said from among the trees. "Now *we've* got *you*."

Pritchett. Slowly Roman turned, pushing RaeAnne and Toby behind his back.

"How touching," Pritchett said, watching the maneuver as he emerged from the foliage, a Mossberg automatic resting in the crook of his arm. "Too bad your noble gesture won't do your friends any good."

Pritchett's three henchmen stepped out also, carrying au-tomatic weapons, all predictably aimed. Roman decided not to go for the Colt Python, tucked safely in his waistband as usual.

"But I must say, I'm impressed. Nobody has made it this far in a long time."

"Two years isn't so long," Roman answered, the final piece of the puzzle falling neatly into place.

"What are you talking about?" Pritchett asked, suspicious curiosity making his weapon tip downward a fraction.

Just as he'd thought. "Jason Danforth. He had a pocket full of your harvest when he died." Roman started to inch his hand toward the Python.

The automatic jerked up angrily. "I told you, we had noth-ing to do with his death."

He halted the movement. "I know. I expect we'll find the murder weapon among the duty shotguns at the sheriff's of-fice." Roman slowly folded his arms across his chest and cocked a hip, ignoring RaeAnne's gasp. "Even so, it looks bad for you."

The man snorted and motioned the others in closer, wordlessly directing them to aim their guns at RaeAnne and Toby. "You think it's a coincidence this operation's survived for over three decades?"

Roman shook his head amiably, striving for a calm mien under his cold sweat. "No. You're pros, I'll give you that much. But you aren't dealing with some corrupt hicksville sheriff's deputies anymore. This time it's the FBI. If three people involved with the case mysteriously disappear on your land, trust me, you're as good as fried."

The henchmen shifted nervously on their feet, looking to Pritchett for a denial. None came.

So, Tecopa hadn't been responsible for Danforth's murder. Or shooting at RaeAnne and him at the site, he'd wager. As soon as he'd seen the booby traps, he'd figured that one out—and should have done so sooner. These guys were far too organized to bury a dead man in the manner Danforth had been, and the same went for RaeAnne. If Pritchett and his cadre of Vietnam vets had wanted her dead—or killed the Fish and Game warden—their bodies would never have been found.

He sidled sideways to block RaeAnne and Toby from their gun sights. "Give it up, Pritchett," he fished. "So far you've only killed animals. Nobody gets the chair for poaching."

"We aren't part of the poaching," Pritchett said, bolstering Roman's theory. "That is the sheriff's office's gig. We deal strictly in weed." But Roman could see the man was seriously weighing his options.

"There must be a tidy fortune sitting in some offshore account, just waiting for you to escape the country. But that ain't gonna happen if you start killing women, kids and FBI agents." For RaeAnne and Toby's sake, he prayed he could pull this off.

"What are we going to do, Sarge?" asked one of the henchmen, confirming Roman's theory that this whole business had started between army buddies long ago, deep in the steaming jungles of an unwinable war. "Execute 'em?"

His heart bled for all the young kids whose lives had been lost, or changed forever by the horrors they had experienced—among them his own father. For the first time since learning of his dad's criminal activity, he thought maybe, just maybe, there was a reason for his father's descent into moral corruption. Not an excuse, never that—a person was always responsible for his own actions. But maybe a reason he could live with.

"He's right." Pritchett considered. "Shooting an FBI agent could complicate things."

Roman noticed the man didn't mention RaeAnne or Toby. Nor did he seem to have any ethical qualms, merely legal considerations. Both bad signs.

The lumberman regarded him. "I guess it's time to disappear, eh, Mr. Federal Agent Man?"

Roman stared right back. "Which one of us?"

"You tell me."

He was torn between suggesting a deal to allow the bastard to escape—he'd do pretty much anything to save the lives of RaeAnne and Toby—and telling the drug dealer he'd better kill him now, because there wasn't a place on earth far enough away to hide from justice. His justice.

Because a sick, clenching nausea had gradually seeped into his gut over the past few minutes along with the certain knowledge that Pritchett had been a factor in his father's fall into the dark side.

Oh, yeah. It was personal now. Very personal.

Standing right in front of him was the man who no doubt held the key to finding Roman's father—dead or alive. And if he was smart, he'd hand over that key without having to be persuaded.

"What's it going to be, Pritchett? Stupid or smart?"

Pritchett never got the chance to answer. They were both distracted by the far-off sound of a strange musical rhythm. Sort of like...steel guitars? The melody started softly, barely discernible above the normal sounds of the forest. Pritchett narrowed his eyes, sweeping his gaze over the sheer rock faces of the surrounding peaks, which echoed the jangly sounds back down at them.

Roman looked, too, wondering what the hell was going on. The three henchmen had frozen in place at the first notes, and he could see their eyes widen, a rabid look coming over them. The strange music grew louder and louder, accompanied by a deep, steady, *whoopfing* sound. *Whoopf, whoopf, whoopf, whoopf.*

"Incoming!" one of the men suddenly yelled, and all three dropped to the dirt, scrabbling for cover, waving their weapons crazily at imagined attackers. The only one of their captors who didn't move was Pritchett. He stood stock-still, white as a puff cloud, watching the horizon as if in a trance. Slowly, the whirling rotors of a helicopter appeared, rising heavenward over the trees, slicing through the air like the swords of retribution.

Roman's jaw hit the ground. Behind him, he heard RaeAnne suck in her breath and Toby give a low whistle. Then the air was rocked by a twangy voice singing out, *"Nevermore to go astray, this will be the end today of the wanted man. The wanted maaaan!"*

Roman couldn't help it. A grin split his face, and as he drew his weapon unnoticed, he laughed. Okay, so it wasn't Wagner, and the tiny sheriff's helicopter wasn't a Huey, but the result had been just as effective on the bad guys.

There was only one person on earth nuts enough to stage such a delightfully twisted rescue.

Bugs.

Hallelujah, they were saved.

And it was just chaotic enough for Roman to get away with murder.

From behind, he pressed the Python into Pritchett's neck and leaned his mouth close to his ear.

"Tell me where my father is," he hissed.

Chapter 15

To RaeAnne's surprise, Dawson consented to make the arrests jointly with Philip O'Donnaugh. Roman said it was only fitting—bringing full circle one of those cosmic coincidences he hated.

RaeAnne wondered. Roman seemed particularly anxious not to be involved in the final arrests. Considering he'd worked just as hard on the case as Dawson, she thought he deserved just as much of the glory. But she wasn't about to question it too much if he'd rather spend the day riding down the mountain returning the horses with her and Toby, than file reports in quadruplicate at the sheriff's office.

She hadn't been too shocked to see Philip's face peering down from the rescue helicopter. Roman had frowned when her ex-boyfriend jumped onto the ground right after Bugs, but she hadn't been able to disguise her smug smile. It would be so sweet tonight to have Roman admit aloud he'd been wrong about Philip.

The four of them and Toby were watching Dawson take off with the first two bad guys in the helicopter. They had several minutes before it returned and Philip made the second trip with the others, and Bugs hiked in to do an initial forensics check of the marijuana field.

"Man, was I glad to see you guys," Roman shouted above the racket as the helo took off.

"You'd already left for another case. What made you come back?" RaeAnne asked Bugs, prying her gaze from Roman's face. He seemed unusually preoccupied for some reason. And much more somber than he should be at the successful conclusion of his case.

She knew he was still upset about having put her and Toby in danger, but thought he'd be happier about everything being wrapped up neatly. Did he still harbor uncertainties about Philip? Or perhaps he was thinking he and RaeAnne would soon reach the conclusion of their time together, as well?

"The rescue was O'Donnaugh's suggestion," Bugs answered with an infectious grin.

If possible, Roman's face became even more dour.

"I tracked Bugs down, but getting here was a joint effort," Philip countered once the helo was out of sight. "We both figured things out about the same time and knew we had to find you quickly. But the music was *his* idea."

"Figured what things out?"

Surprisingly Philip looked none too pleased, either. What the heck was going on here? A scowl was frozen on his face and RaeAnne could swear wisps of the storm clouds from the mountains had gathered around his ears, though that was probably just an optical illusion.

"It was my father."

Roman's wandering attention snapped onto him. "Excuse me?"

"After you told me all that stuff last night, I realized the initials on those papers had to be my father's," Philip explained. "He was sheriff for almost twenty years before me, and must have been part of the poaching ring until he died some years back."

"Of course," Roman muttered. "A Philip Sr. And he had long gray hair, I suppose."

"Come again?"

Roman shook his head. "Never mind. I should have guessed. God knows where my brain was." She hid a smile as he gave her a look.

Bugs grinned wider. "Tell me about it. I only got suspicious when I ran the background checks on our prime suspects for Danforth's murder. When they all came back with combat experience in Vietnam—in the same year—I ran the other units in-country for the same area and time, and found myself staring at a couple other familiar names."

"The deputies?" Roman asked. *He knew it.* He'd known this whole mess had to be somehow tied together.

"You got it."

"Already arrested," Philip informed him tightly. "Two of them spilled their guts about the poaching, hoping I'd let them go."

It looked like it was on the tip of Roman's tongue to ask if he had, but apparently he thought better of it and said, "A man who'd admit his own father was a criminal? I doubt it."

A wave of sympathy swept over RaeAnne for both Philip and Roman. That was a situation she wouldn't wish on her worst enemy, yet here were two men she loved, both enduring it.

"I'm sorry," Roman said, and sounded like he meant it.

"No, I am. My third deputy—the young one—confessed to participating in the beating you took. I arrested him, too. For assault."

"I'm sorry for ever doubting you, Sheriff O'Donnaugh."

RaeAnne's eyes swam at Roman's words. She slid her arm around his waist and he pulled her close. Philip's gaze went to the proprietary hold on her for a split second, then darted away and he shrugged. *"De nada."*

"I still don't get it," RaeAnne said. "Why did they do it?"

Philip's mouth turned down. "The poaching or the beating?"

"Both."

His eyes went cold. "The lucrative poaching profits were one way Tecopa paid off the sheriff's office for turning a blind eye to the marijuana operation—that and a yearly sizable cash donation to the sheriff's reelection fund, which seems to have mysteriously disappeared from all the annual accounts."

"And the beating?" Roman asked, unconsciously reaching up to touch his ribs.

Philip shifted on his feet. "The VA's files on them described men who'd stop at nothing to protect their buddies and their turf. The deputies must have seen RaeAnne as a threat, knowing there was a very real chance she'd discover the body of the man they'd murdered. When you showed up at the site they probably got even more spooked, and used my relationship with RaeAnne as an excuse to get rid of you."

"Probably shocked the hell out of them when they found out I was FBI."

"You could say that."

"So when beating me up didn't work, they tried more direct methods—like shooting us."

RaeAnne frowned, trying to make sense of it all. "So your deputies were the ones who hired Toby to scare me off?"

"Not the Chairman?" Roman interjected with an oddly fierce look on his face. She glanced up, surprised.

"I don't see any motive for the Chairman," Philip answered. "But I'll be sure the question is asked during the deputies' interrogation."

"I think I'll ask the Chairman myself."

"Whatever you say."

Roman looked from Philip to Bugs and back. "Thanks for the rescue operation. Really. There's no telling what might have happened to us if you guys hadn't been so on the ball."

And then to RaeAnne's amazement, he stuck out his hand

to Philip and gave him a firm handshake. He even gritted his teeth and tolerated it when she joined in and gave both of the men grateful thank-you hugs.

She beamed at Roman. He could afford to be generous. She knew who was going to be lounging in the hot springs with him later on tonight. And so did he.

At least that's what she thought. Right up until the helicopter came back and they loaded up the remaining prisoners.

That's when Roman turned to her and said, "Can you and Toby make it down to Medicine Wind on your own? There's something I have to go and do."

Her heart clutched painfully.

So this was it.

She almost cried out in protest. It wasn't supposed to happen like this. It was too soon! It was unfair. She deserved a whole night with him before he left her! In her bed, in the hot springs, joined with him in his arms.

She didn't know what to do, what to say. It was a bittersweet irony—the knowledge that he was leaving her again, but that this time a single reminder from her about possibly being pregnant could make him stay.

Because he was all about honor.

But she didn't want him sticking around out of honor or duty because there may be a baby in their future. Or worse, because of his sense of guilt over their past.

She wanted him to stay because he loved her, and there was no place else on earth he'd rather be than by her side.

If she asked him to stay, he'd stay. But he'd resent her for it till his dying breath. Baby or no, he wasn't ready to love her. He had his rootless job. And his quest for his own father. To make him give up those things would be selfish.

She had her honor, too. She had to let him go.

She had to let him go.

She swallowed heavily and for both their sakes pasted a nonchalant smile onto her quavering lips.

"Of course," she managed to say without her voice cracking too badly. "No problem. Toby knows the way. Don't you, Tobe?"

"Sure thing, Miz Martin," Toby hurriedly assured. "Don't worry, I'll take care of her for you, Mr. Santangelo."

She gave a wobbly smile at the kid's obvious worship of Roman. She didn't blame him. She worshiped the man, too. But she was afraid nobody would be able to take care of her in the coming days and weeks well enough to avert the heartache that was slowly numbing her mind and body.

Oh, why did he have to find her again? Hating the boy he used to be had been so much easier than this powerful, overwhelming love for the man he'd become.

"Wait for me," Roman whispered as he took her in his arms one last time.

What choice did she have? She'd never love another man as long as she lived.

"I'll wait for you," she whispered back, and her heart broke even more. Knowing she could well spend the rest of her life waiting for this man to settle down and change his ways.

RaeAnne watched the helicopter take off with Roman on board and felt her legs threaten to buckle.

"Come on," she said to Toby before she could give in to the impulse to lie down on the ground and never get up. "Let's find the horses."

Thank goodness for the kid, who kept up a running chatter about the day's excitement. Even when the sky fogged up and it started sprinkling, his thrill over their experience went undiminished. If it weren't for having to keep up a cheerful face for Toby, she'd probably go crazy with sorrow.

When the corrals of Medicine Wind finally came into view, her stomach clenched, and it wasn't because a sudden flash of lightening split the clouds with an ominous roll of thunder.

Tonight would be the real test. Could she face the long night alone, without Roman by her side?

Would she survive?

*   *   *

Roman had the helo drop him in the meadow at Cleary so he could pick up his stuff and the Harley. After today's events, the idea of letting RaeAnne out of his sight held even less appeal than usual.

Unfortunately he had no choice. The helicopter had been ready to fly off and he'd had to be on it to catch up with the Chairman before O'Donnaugh started asking Pritchett questions. What the foreman of Tecopa Lumber had told him before being carted off to jail still burned like acid in his gut.

Knowing who held the secret to Hector Santangelo's whereabouts, the end of his quest was too close to turn back now. Roman had to put this thing with his own father to rest before he could even think about settling down and becoming a father himself.

But he was glad he'd given in to instinct and asked O'Donnaugh to check in on RaeAnne tonight. There was something at the back of his mind that wouldn't stop needling at him, though damned if he could put his finger on what it was.

Better to be safe than sorry when it came to his woman. And since O'Donnaugh had turned out to be one of the good guys after all, he figured there was no reason not to trust the sheriff to make sure everything was secure at the cabin tonight.

No doubt Roman was just being paranoid. She certainly hadn't needed his help staying safe for the past eighteen years. She'd do fine without him for one more night—or however long it took to find his father and throw him in jail. After all, the murderers had confessed, the drug dealers had been arrested. The bad guys were all caught. There was no one left to harm her.

Still, the thought of RaeAnne out at the site all alone with no phone really ate at him.

And not just because of the uneasy feeling he had. He also knew damned well what she was thinking. However wrong she was. That phony smile hadn't fooled him for a single second. She'd acted brave and unconcerned so he wouldn't feel guilty about leaving her, but he knew, deep inside he'd as good as cut her heart out.

Again.

As he strapped his pack to the back of the Harley and pointed the bike toward Bishop, this morning's insight about how badly he'd hurt her in the past returned with dismal vengeance. And now he'd done an encore.

Would she understand? Or would this only cement her determination never to trust him? Should he even try to fight against the tide and continue to woo her trust?

Did he stand even a small chance of succeeding? Or should he back out gracefully now, before he could hurt her even more?

A sudden chill wind made him zip his jacket to his throat and look up. A storm was brewing.

Not once had she told him she still loved him. What she *had* said was that she *didn't* want to marry him, even if she was pregnant. True, she'd wondered if he would consider moving to her town to be with her and their baby, but she'd never really asked him to do it.

Indications of success were depressingly absent.

He glanced over his shoulder. Giant black thunderheads had appeared out of nowhere to obscure both the sun and the top half of the Sierras. Still he kept the bike at a steady clip down the mountain.

The last thing he should do was push RaeAnne into something she didn't want. Marriage and family took a one-hundred-percent commitment. If she didn't have it in her, better to find out now. A baby would complicate things, but it could be handled. He knew she wouldn't exclude him from his child's life, she wasn't that kind of person.

From high above him, long tentacles of swirling mist crept down the sides of the mountain, as though reaching out to snatch him from the saddle of the Harley and toss him aside.

To where he couldn't hurt her anymore. A shiver worked its way along his spine.

Strange how just a few days with RaeAnne had shown him exactly how empty his life had been for nearly two decades. How incredibly he'd missed her. How enormously he'd loved her through all those solitary years of searching. And how far he'd strayed from fulfilling the hopes and dreams of his youth—dreams in which she'd always played an integral part.

A peal of thunder cracked through the air like a parting shot. Roman frowned angrily, glaring back toward the veiled mountain peaks. He wanted to shout at them to mind their own damn business. He *wasn't* leaving her. Not for good, anyway. They didn't have to act so condemning. But they just hid their barren faces from him, secreting themselves behind a curtain of roiling black clouds as streaks of lightning lit up the sky.

"Cowards!" he yelled into the cold mist, unable to keep quiet. But it only echoed through his helmet right back at him.

He thought about RaeAnne and Toby, by themselves on the trail to Medicine Wind in this weather. He hoped to God they were all right.

"Leave them alone!" he shouted at the spineless peaks.

Damn. He was really losing it. He raised a hand to rake it through his hair but hit solid plastic with his fingers. The day's experiences must have unhinged him more than he wanted to admit. His whole future was hanging in the balance, and here he was talking to the goddamn mountains.

He needed to get a grip, and fast.

He ground his jaw and spun the bike through the turn onto the highway, and threw it into high gear. The sooner he got to the Chairman, the sooner he'd be back with RaeAnne.

"What do you mean he's gone for a few days?"

Roman stared incredulously at the woman behind the desk at the Tribal Council. This couldn't be happening.

"It was fairly sudden," she said apologetically. "The Chairman got a phone call this morning. Apparently there was some urgent tribal business down at Pachenga Rez near San Dieg—"

"I know where the Pachenga Reservation is," he snapped. It was part of his old stomping grounds growing up on Rincon Rez, not ten miles away from his mother's home. Another coincidence? God, he was getting tired of this.

"Did he fly or drive?"

The woman balked at his question, so he slapped his FBI credentials on the counter in front of her. Then he moved the edge of his jacket to one side so she could see the Colt Python tucked in his waistband. Her eyes widened.

"T-two-thirty flight into O-Ontario Airport," she stammered.

"Thank you," he replied and checked his watch: 4:17. Surely there had to be another flight out of the small airport at Bishop tonight.

He didn't know why he felt this urgency to catch up to the Chairman as soon as possible. He'd waited all this time to find his father. A day or two more wouldn't hurt—especially since O'Donnaugh couldn't get to him, either, to question. And it would give Roman an opportunity to explain things better to RaeAnne.

But he had to obey his gut instincts. And right now they were telling him to get on a plane south. Immediately.

On his way out, an impulse made him stop and do an about-face. Quickly he strode to the Chairman's office, flung open the door and swept the room with a searching gaze.

"Hey! You can't—" The receptionist blanched at the look he drilled her with. "I mean, go right ahead. I'm sure the Chairman has nothing to hide from the FBI."

He stepped into the room and went straight to the desk. There was a modest scatter of papers on it, but he found nothing that might be a clue to his father's whereabouts. He opened the drawers, and again didn't spot anything of interest. Nothing left in the printer. Nothing written on the memo pad by the phone. The last thing he checked was the trash.

And that's where he hit paydirt.

RaeAnne took a deep breath and jumped over a rivulet of rain runoff, landing in the mud of the meadow on the other side. She had her yellow slicker pulled up over her head, but fat drops of water still ran down her face and throat, soaking the sweater beneath the thin plastic.

She didn't mind. She liked the rain. And it was good camouflage in case she started crying again.

Not that she would. She was doing okay.

Really.

Roman had asked her to wait for him, but had failed to mention whether he meant wait at the cabin, as in for a few hours or days, or that more general, royal-command wait for him that entailed another eighteen years.

She hadn't quite made up her mind which she opted to believe. She figured she'd give it tonight and if he didn't show up or get a message to her, she'd probably go for the latter. It was safest that way. For her heart, that is.

She slogged through the meadow and slip-slided up the muddy hillside to where she and Roman had left Great-great-granduncle Crawford Edisto under a tarp when the shooting had started.

It seemed like a lifetime ago since that had happened. She hoped ol' Crawford was all right. The wind might have lifted the protective covering to expose the skeleton and other evidence to the elements. Or who knew what the shooter might have done with the remains if he didn't realize it was an historical burial, and thought it might be more recent.

She swiped the rain from her eyes, staunchly ignoring the slightly salty taste of it on her lips, and took stock. The plastic tarp was still in place, if covered by a veritable lake of water that had been trapped in the three-foot-deep unit. She decided not to try to bail out the water. Its presence would keep the plastic from whipping about in the wind, thereby actually protecting the unit from worse damage.

She just wanted a peek. To make sure the skeleton wasn't in imminent danger from something she hadn't thought of.

Kneeling down, she lifted a corner of the tarp and carefully pulled it up, displacing the pool of water to the other corners. She peered in, shining her flashlight into the dark, shallow gap.

The dirt wall of the unit had been eroded by the rain, and instead of being perfectly straight, it now resembled a rough hillside. No big deal. With some careful measuring, she could reconstruct what dirt had been redeposited where, and what artifacts belonged to the unit and what had just been washed in.

She moved her hands on the tarp, easing the gap farther down the wall so she could see how far the damage went.

Suddenly her attention was caught by a shiny round object. In the light of the flashlight it looked gold. What the—?

She leaned down closer, and realized it was a ring, lying among the finger bones of the skeleton. A ring! Outstanding. Rings were often engraved. Or at least traceable. That should make identification a snap. Hopefully.

If this was Great-great-granduncle Edisto, she might be able to prove it. Yes!

Excited, she swept the flashlight beam around the small area, oblivious to the rain and the mud that soaked her knees and elbows. And all at once it hit her. There were too many finger bones. She reached down to delicately scoop away a shallow layer of mud. Revealing another wrist bone.

There were two skeletons, buried together, holding hands.

She sat back on her heels and slowly a smile played over her mouth. They were holding hands, their fingers knit like lovers, the shiny gold band declaring their devotion for all eternity.

Liquid filled her eyes, though she couldn't tell if it was tears or rain as drops spilled down her cheeks.

"Well, I'll be damned," she whispered. "I guess that explains what happened to Great-great-granduncle Edisto."

With great care she replaced the tarp, and in a happy daze strolled back to the cabin.

It wasn't until she'd reached the cabin door that she noticed the silhouette of a sedan parked out front, barely visible in the darkness.

Her heart leaped. Then slowed again. Not a Harley. A car.

She couldn't make out what type of car it was, so she had no idea who had come to visit. But whoever it was, she was glad for the company. She needed to share her discovery with someone, and frankly, any distraction from thinking about Roman was more than welcome.

She opened the door, and when she saw who was standing by the woodstove she gave a big smile and rushed into the room.

"Hi!" she said. "You won't believe what I just found!"

Chapter 16

Tucked into the farmlands halfway between L.A. and San Diego, Pachenga Rez was a haven from traffic, urban sprawl and cookie-cutter houses. Roman glanced one last time at the wrinkled, coffee-stained computer printout he'd fished from the Chairman's trash can just two hectic hours ago. *San Joaquin Street.* This was it.

At the end of the unpaved road in the middle of fragrant, moonlit alfalfa fields, he found a neat clapboard house surrounded by a narrow band of green lawn and brambly yellow climbing roses.

Thank goodness for caffeine addiction. If it hadn't been for the large brown spot nearly obscuring the address, the Chairman would probably not have tossed the paper out and Roman would never have found this place.

Stepping from his rental car, the sweet spice of old rose blindsided him, and for a brief, intense moment Roman was four years old again, back in his garden at Big Pine, helping his father cut a bouquet of Sutters Gold for his mom.

He beat back the piquant memory. The last thing he

wanted was a soft spot in his heart if he was about to confront his father. The man was a criminal.

Squinting into the darkness, he glanced around. There was no sign of either his father or the Chairman. No sign of life anywhere on the shadowy, rather desolate property. Other than his own, no car occupied the gravel driveway.

The front door, however, stood ajar.

Roman drew his weapon, visually rechecking the areas close to the house. Still nothing. He sidled onto the front porch and peered around the doorjamb. He couldn't see squat. The only illumination in the modest living room was a dim ray of moonlight filtering in through crooked Venetian blinds.

He withdrew his head, leaned himself next to the door and took a deep breath. He didn't like the smell of this. It smelled rotten, like a setup. Or…God only knew.

He realized his hands were shaking. Shaking and sweating. *Hell.* That had never happened before. He'd always been Mr. Cool…yeah, Special Agent Imperturbable, that was him.

Definitely time to get out of this damned cop business.

Just then a small, kink-tailed calico cat jumped up onto the porch and trotted over to him, rubbing up against his legs. Roman blinked, resisting the urge to bend down and pet the scraggly thing. Maybe dig something out of his pocket for it to eat.

Too many distractions.

He shook his head to clear it, and reached around the door frame, feeling for a light switch as the cat beelined it into the house. *There.* He found the switch and flipped it. The cat screeched and his heart stopped for the split second it took to kick the door wide-open, crouch down and aim the Python into the murky unknown.

A single floor lamp in the corner of the living room had clicked on, the light bringing into relief a nicely upholstered sofa and easy chair, loaded bookshelves and a high-tech TV setup. The recently vacuumed carpet was beige—except for a large red stain flowing around the side of the couch. He heard a low moan.

With a harsh oath, Roman sprinted through the room then dropped into a roll, coming up on one knee, weapon pointed two-handed at the open space behind the sofa. An old man lay there in a pool of blood.

His father.

Too stunned to move, Roman just stood staring for a full five seconds before another moan from the body snapped him out of it.

"My God," he swore, springing into action.

His training took over. He checked the old man's pulse and breathing—weak but there—ran his hands gingerly over the thin frame—and came away with two palmfuls of blood. Afraid to disturb the wounds which seemed to have slowed to a thick ooze, he vaulted into the kitchen seeking a phone.

Three minutes later an ambulance had been summoned and he'd put in a phone call to his boss. Help was on the way from all possible fronts.

So, he'd been right. Hector Santangelo was alive and, up until a few minutes ago, apparently doing well. It was like a slap in the face—no, a slap to his whole being, an electric shock, and a shower of ice water all at the same time.

Roman paced back and forth like a caged tiger. A groan from the floor brought him to his knees beside the man whom he had once called dad.

"Son?" the old man said without opening his eyes.

"I'm here," Roman forced past the melon in his throat. The admission almost strangled him, but he couldn't stop it from being true no matter how much he wanted to. "Who did this to you?"

A deep sigh wheezed from the injured man's chest. "Campanelli...finally made good...on his promise."

"Campanelli?" Why did that name have a familiar ring to it? Roman racked his memory for a possible reference. "Who's—"

"He's coming for you. Be careful." His father opened his eyes and pain filled them as he searched Roman's face. "Promise me."

His vocal cords temporarily paralyzed, Roman just nodded. He could have sworn he'd seen concern in the old man's expression. But that was impossible. A man who deserted his own son for thirty years didn't care what happened to him.

"I thought...you were a dream," his father rasped.

"Don't try to talk," Roman urged, fighting the wellspring of emotion threatening to surface. "Save your breath."

"Gotta tell you—"

"There'll be plenty of time for true confessions later." He didn't think he could handle both blood and betrayal at the same time.

But his father wasn't going to give up. "FBI," he said, then started coughing.

Still running scared. Well, that was too damn bad. His running days were about to come to an end. The old man lifted his hand, reaching for him. A familiar silver bracelet graced his thin wrist. After a long hesitation Roman grasped the hand between his, holding it as his father caught his labored breath.

"You should know, I work for the FBI," Roman said, needing to set the record straight, even under such dire circumstances.

Hell, especially under such dire circumstances. He didn't want to hear anything his father would regret telling him tomorrow. Or that would prevent him from putting the old bastard away for good.

He steeled his heart. "Anything you say could be used against you."

To his surprise, his father grinned weakly. "Arresting me, son?" Pride shone in the pain-clouded eyes.

Roman's mouth dropped open from total confusion. He had no idea how to respond to a reaction like that. Luckily he was spared.

"Jordan," his father wheezed out.

"Special Agent Jordan?" Roman asked. Jordan was the suit in Washington who'd blocked him from seeing his father's files and had shut him down without explanation when he'd started asking questions. "What about Jordan?"

"Call him," the old man said haltingly.

Roman didn't have time to ponder the significance of that bizarre request, for just then the ambulance screamed up to the house, followed by two cars of uniformed cops.

"You Santangelo?" the cop in charge asked, looking him over skeptically.

He was used to it. He automatically went to toss his long hair as he nodded, then remembered RaeAnne had cut it all off.

Suddenly a pain knifed through his chest.

RaeAnne.

For a few terrible minutes of turmoil, seeing his father for the first time since he was six, he'd forgotten about her and the arrests at Tecopa.

Could his father's shooting somehow be connected with Pritchett and—

The Chairman.

He swore vividly, pieces falling into place like cherries on a slot machine.

"You coming?" a medic shouted.

The ambulance was about to hustle his father off to the hospital. Roman reluctantly jumped onboard—to make sure the old man didn't disappear for another thirty years.

"Got a phone? I need to make an urgent call," he demanded, buckling into the side bench.

"Sorry," the EMT taking his father's vitals answered calmly. "Just the radio. You'll have to wait till the hospital."

Roman thrummed with anxiety. If anything happened to RaeAnne he'd never forgive himself. He had to find out—

"Roman," the old man mumbled.

"Right here." He brushed aside the EMT's protests and this time didn't pause before grabbing the trembling hand that was stretched out to him between the IV bags.

"Dad—" He swallowed twice as the word inexplicably swelled up and broke apart in his throat.

He tried again. "Dad, you've got to help me. The Chairman—the Paiute Tribal Chairman up at Bishop—is he involved in all of this?"

His dad swallowed, too. "Campanelli," he whispered threadily.

"Not Campanelli, the Chairman. Try to focus."

The old man's breath sounded like a door creaking in the wind. "Campanelli *is* the Chairman," he managed to whisper before passing out.

Roman's stomach wrenched so hard he had to grab the side of the ambulance to keep from doubling over.

Campanelli was the Chairman. And he'd just attempted coldblooded murder.

Oh, God.

RaeAnne was out there all alone.

The man was sure acting strange.

RaeAnne's visitor hadn't said a whole lot, other than to insist on sitting so he had a clear view of the front door. He just sipped his tea and smiled as she'd rambled on and on about Crawford Edisto, extemporizing about how he must have met a beautiful Indian maiden, married her and lived happily ever after right here in the Sierras, instead of going on to San Francisco with his brother.

Of course, it was all conjecture. But a proper analysis of the gold ring and skeletal remains should settle a lot of her theories one way or the other. She hoped in favor.

"Don't you think it's exciting? I think it's just so incredible."

He nodded. She could tell he was just humoring her.

So why was he sticking around if he found her conversation so uninspiring? Unfortunately she had a feeling she knew.

"I'll be fine, you know. You don't have to stay with me. This morning wasn't *that* traumatic."

Philip leaned back in his chair and regarded her. "I promised Santangelo."

She leaned back in her own chair and looked him in the eye, suppressing the involuntary spurt of pain and hope at the mention of her lover's name. "Promised him what?"

"To keep an eye on you till he gets back."

"Oh, really? And when will that be?"

Philip shrugged. "Dunno."

"Where did he go?"

Another shrug. "No idea. Thought you might, though."

"Afraid not."

He gazed at her over the rim of his cup as he tossed down the last of his fresh mint tea. "Seems to me your new boyfriend makes quite a habit of taking off without telling you where he's going or when he'll be back."

She picked at a knothole in the crude wooden table with a fingernail, resisting the urge to agree. "I don't suppose that's any of your business."

He carefully set down the mug. "I could make it my business if you let me." His hand reached across the table, capturing hers. "RaeAnne—"

"Don't," she quietly said, withdrawing her hand. "Please."

"And if he doesn't come back?" he asked, voicing her greatest fear.

"That's just something I'll have to live with. I'm sorry I hurt you. But I've made my choice."

He looked at her for a long moment, his expression gradually going cold and hard. "I'm sorry to hear that," he said. Then he pulled a gun from the back of his waistband and leveled it at her chest.

"Sweet Jeezus, can't you make this crate go any faster?" Roman demanded of his good buddy, U.S. Customs Agent Dave Granth, who'd graciously consented to fly him up to Bishop in his Cessna. Thank God for interagency cooperation. The FBI planes had all been out on jobs.

He was going crazy thinking about what might be happening to RaeAnne while he was still a hundred miles away, unable to help. He hadn't been able to send Dawson or Bugs to the rescue, either—they'd both been called off to that other job down south, hours away. And nobody seemed to know where O'Donnaugh was. Roman hoped to God he was at Cleary checking up on RaeAnne as he'd asked.

Dave's cell phone rang, and at a nod from his friend, Roman answered it. It was Special Agent Jordan returning his call. Finally.

"I hear you found Hector Santangelo," Jordan said without preamble, "and that he's been shot. Dead?"

"No," Roman answered. "I just checked with the hospital and it looks like he'll recover."

"Thank God."

His brows rose at the obvious relief in the man's voice. "I'm surprised you care. He is wanted for shooting two FBI agents."

There was a pause.

Oh, great. Whatever was about to come down the pike at him, he didn't want to hear it.

"Uh, look, Santangelo. There's something you need to know—"

Now he was really worried. "Wrong, Jordan. The only thing I need to know is that the boss has someone waiting at the hospital to arrest Hector Santangelo when he gets out of the ICU."

"That isn't going to happen. You see—"

"I don't care what kind of a deal he's made with some scumbag prosecutor. Do I have to remind you he *murdered* two of your own men?"

"He didn't kill them."

There must have been static on the line. "What did you say?" he calmly asked. There was no way he'd heard correctly. No way in hell.

"He didn't shoot those men."

Roman's brain pretty much shut down. *This couldn't be happening.*

"In fact, he's the one who caught the real killer." Jordan's deep sigh wafted through the phone line. "We couldn't tell you this before, but...Hector Santangelo is also a special agent. He works for us."

"Philip, what the hell is going on?" RaeAnne stared wide-eyed at the gun pointing right at her.

"Get down," he ordered. "On the floor! I think I heard footsteps on the porch." He flicked the gun impatiently, indicating the door directly behind her.

"So what?" she said, and realized to her annoyance she was whispering, too. She stood and moved out of the way, just in case Philip got trigger-happy in addition to being paranoid. "They've arrested all the bad guys."

"Are you sure about that?"

"Of course I'm sure." A shiver suddenly ran through her and she rubbed her arms. "Aren't you?"

He shot her an unnervingly strange look, but remained silent as he rose and braced his feet apart, standing like some Old West gunslinger, six-shooter trained on the front door.

There was a knock.

So much for ruthless criminals with revenge on their minds.

"Come in," she called, leveling a withering glance at Philip, who reluctantly shifted his weapon behind his back, though he didn't tuck it into his waistband. The door swung open, and so did her mouth—from surprise.

It was the Chairman. What could he possibly want this late in the evening?

"Is something wrong?" she asked, at once jumping to unpleasant conclusions. His start at seeing Philip in the cabin registered minimally, but she dismissed it. No doubt he'd presumed she and Roman were an item.

"No," he said. He seemed somehow...unsettled.

She frowned. "No?" When he just stood there, she added,

"Um, well then, how about some tea?" He glanced from her to the other man and back. "Sheriff O'Donnaugh was just goi—"

"Just going to make some more," Philip interjected before she could finish her sentence, then grabbed the teapot from the table and carried it to the woodstove where the kettle sat simmering. "RaeAnne picked fresh mint. Very calming."

What the heck was going on? She was practically getting electroshock therapy from the undercurrents zapping between the two men. After the day she'd had, this was not what she needed.

"I don't mean to be rude," she said, motioning the Chairman to a seat. "But was there something you wanted?"

His gaze jerked to her. "I'm looking for Roman Santangelo. I thought…"

She cleared her throat. "Sorry, he's not here."

"But he has to be! Where is he?"

She didn't much care for his tone, but decided to give him some leeway. "He's taking care of some business."

"Business he'll regret," the man muttered.

That definitely sounded like a threat. "I beg your pardon?"

She could see his jaw grind. "I assumed you knew," he said.

"Knew what?"

"He found his father. That must be where he's gone."

RaeAnne wasn't sure how to react to that bit of news. On one hand, she was jubilant, because it meant Roman could finally put that whole situation behind him. On the other hand, she knew no matter how much he denied it, turning in his father to the FBI—again—would rip him apart. Regardless of what his father had done, he was family, and Roman didn't betray family. Roman didn't betray anyone.

At least not like this—deliberately, fully aware of the consequences.

That realization hit her full force. And its significance to their own circumstances didn't escape her.

"Where?" she asked.

The Chairman's gaze slid to the sheriff.

"It's okay," she said. "Roman plans to turn his father in to the FBI."

That required a brief explanation. While she gave it, the two men focused on their tea mugs, almost as though avoiding her gaze.

"So you see, you can tell me where he is."

The Chairman seemed to weigh his options, then finally said, "Hector has been living on Pachenga Reservation for about ten years."

"And how do you know this?"

"Back in '73, I was the one who hid him from the authorities and helped him escape. I am the one who told the media he killed those men in self-defense. I made him into the hero he is today, a martyr to the cause."

"Hero?" Philip said, derision evident in his voice. "That depends on what side of the Red Road you walk on."

The Chairman straightened, his eyes narrowing. "What would you know of these things?"

"I know the poor sucker went into hiding and lost his family, while you launched your own political career."

"Poor sucker?" The Chairman sneered. "He owes his good name to me. The man was a pathetic drug addict. He'd been hooked on heroine since Nam and had already lost his family. His wife started divorce proceedings weeks before the shooting."

"What?" RaeAnne asked, astounded. Roman had never mentioned any of this. *Perhaps he didn't know.* If this was all true, it explained why his father had decided to play dead and disappear from their lives forever. He must have thought they'd be better off without him.

Man, did that sound sickeningly familiar.

Damn Santangelo honor.

Suddenly the deep rumbling sound of a motorcycle engine

seeped in through the windows and the crack under the wooden door. *Roman!*

The three of them froze and looked at each other. Then RaeAnne sprang to her feet. Philip drew his gun.

"Put that thing away," she said. "It's Roman!"

"You don't know that," Philip said, obviously with no intention of holstering his gun. On the contrary, he steadied his aim at the door.

"Philip! It could go off accidentally. You could kill him!"

"I do not discharge my weapon accidentally," he said with an edge to his voice.

She felt a hand on her shoulder and practically jumped out of her skin. The Chairman pulled her firmly backward when she would have run to the door. "He's right. You must wait and see."

"But—"

"Shh." She heard the thunk of something heavy on the porch and Roman's voice call out, "*Cara,* I'm back."

It was him! Her heart leaped in her chest.

But why weren't Philip and the Chairman standing down? She opened her mouth to return his greeting, but a stealthy hand snaked over it.

"I see you've got company, but I'm a mess from the drive," Roman called through the closed door. She struggled against the Chairman's hold. The nerve of the old gaffer! What did he—

"I think I'll just run on up to the hot springs," Roman shouted, his footsteps turning away. "For a quick bath."

And if the hand gagging her mouth hadn't told her, that simple statement along with the sharp bite of a cold blade against her neck certainly had…

There was something terribly, terribly wrong.

Chapter 17

Roman was about to keel over from sheer panic. RaeAnne hadn't answered him. There was somebody in the cabin with her—the car outside told him that much—but she hadn't come out to greet him, nor had she said a single word. Not even when he'd mentioned the hot springs.

There was no way she'd have let him go up there without her. They'd made plans for those hot springs.

Campanelli must be holding RaeAnne hostage. Somehow, Roman had to lure him away from her.

He loosened the snap on his boot knife, cocked the slide on the Python and prayed the damned bastard would follow him up the hill to the hot springs.

Where the hell was O'Donnaugh?

Roman lifted his eyes to the mountains, as he felt the hot rush of adrenaline in his blood. It was showdown time. Would the silent sentinels be with him, or against him? Clouds parted, and light from the moon poured down the hillside like golden honey. He smiled. *With him, then.* When had they changed their minds?

He could hear the heavy plodding of boots on the trail behind him. Campanelli was awfully sure of himself, not bothering to conceal his approach. When Roman reached the hot springs, he turned, ready to face the devil his father'd said had vowed to see both of them dead.

"You think like an Indian," the Chairman said, folding his hands in front of himself.

Implying the Chairman didn't? A week ago that revelation might have surprised Roman, but not today. Revenge was a white man's game. And what could this be other than revenge? Though for what, he still wasn't sure.

"You got it backward, old man," Roman said, nodding at the thin dagger tucked in the Chairman's belt, which appeared to be his only weapon. "It's just like an Indian to bring a knife to a gunfight."

The Chairman's teeth glinted in the moonlight. He seemed disturbingly unperturbed by having the Python leveled at him. "I once told you appearances aren't always what they seem. You underestimate me, my son."

"I'm nobody's son, not after today, and especially not yours. Get to the point, Campanelli."

"You haven't asked about Miss Martin. Aren't you concerned she isn't with me?"

Roman's eyes narrowed. "What have you done with her?"

"Don't worry. She's safe with Philip O'Donnaugh down at the cabin."

"O'Donnaugh?" Suspicion suddenly slammed into him. Had he been blinded by sympathy for the sheriff's all-too-kindred plight? "What the hell is going on?"

"What do you think?"

Admittedly Roman wasn't in the best of moods. He took a step forward, extended his arm and planted the Python's muzzle firmly in the middle of the old man's forehead.

"Talk. *Now.*"

The glint wavered. "O'Donnaugh's running the poaching ring, of course. Has been since his father died."

Damn it to hell. He'd been right all along. "If he's harmed her—"

"Don't worry. If she doesn't try to leave the cabin, she'll never even know O'Donnaugh's holding her. Not until—"

"They find me with my throat slit?"

The other man's eyes said he'd guessed correctly. "But if he hears any shooting, or if I'm not back in five minutes, he'll kill her."

Roman figured the plan was to kill her regardless. They'd both rot in hell; he'd make that happen personally if he had to.

"I see." He lowered his weapon, playing along for the moment. "So, what's your role in all this, Campanelli? Distributor for the poaching spoils?"

The old man looked down his regal nose at him. "I'm the brains behind it. All of it. It was my operation from the beginning."

Roman wasn't impressed. "So you killed Danforth?"

Campanelli made a deprecating noise. "Those idiot deputies shot Danforth when he stumbled onto them during one of their hunting expeditions on Tecopa lands."

Normally Roman enjoyed when his hunches were right, but nailing this case gave him no pleasure. "You must have been nervous when RaeAnne started digging at Cleary."

"Not me. I didn't have anything to do with the game warden's death."

"So it really was the deputies who hired Toby to scare her off?"

"Yes," he said impatiently.

"And shot at us last night?"

The Chairman nodded, slashing up with a hand. "But all this could have been avoided if you'd just have taken your woman to safety as I told you," he hissed angrily. "You should have heeded my warning!"

"You mean at your office? Or the box with my father's regalia, and the eagle feathers?"

"Both! You should at least have arrested the morons for

poaching! The boy gave you the envelopes and notes with all the information. That should have been evidence enough."

"Sorry to disappoint you. We need more than a list of names made more than three decades ago for an arrest." The thought of his father brought renewed fury over the whole situation. That he'd been alive and innocent all these years. "Where did you get those notes, and the things in the box? My father's things?"

"He left them behind when I helped him disappear."

Roman's banked rage burst into flame. "So it's you I have to thank for that, too." He leaned right into his face. "Too bad I already knew he was alive by that time. You should have understood a few feathers weren't going to stop me from finding him."

Campanelli made a fist and shook it. "He's been dead to you for thirty years. Why couldn't you let him stay that way? Why did you have to come back and dredge up the past? Ruin everything?"

"Balance. Honor. You should understand those concepts."

"You're too philosophical for your own good, Santangelo. And this time your outdated cultural idealism is going to cost you."

Roman barely resisted pressing the Python's muzzle back into Campanelli's skull and pulling the trigger. The arrogance of the man was truly astounding.

"Is that right?"

"But it doesn't have to cost Miss Martin. Give me your gun right now, and I'll see that her life is spared."

So that was his game. Roman pretended to consider. "There's just one thing I have to ask. Why kill my father? Why now, after all this time?"

Caught off guard, the old man's gaze focused on the darkness between them, as though looking into the distant past.

"Hector was the only one who could link me with Pritchett. The three of us had done some...business together in

Nam.'' His eyes came up. "But now that he's dead, nobody'll ever be able to connect the dots.''

He decided to let Campanelli's slight miscalculation go uncorrected and not inform him his father was alive yet.

Instead he did his best to sound outraged. "You murdered him over something that happened *thirty years ago?*''

"But you'll never be able to prove I did it,'' the Chairman said. "You'll never find the shotgun.''

He'd heard enough. He had to get to RaeAnne. Every minute of not knowing whether she was okay was shaving years from his life.

He raised the Colt. "We'll see about that, old man. Dave!'' he called, summoning his friend who'd been concealed a few feet away the whole time with his own weapon trained on the Chairman. Just in case.

Dave emerged from the shrubbery next to Campanelli and slapped a handcuff around his wrist before he could reach for his knife.

"You hear his confession?''

"Every word. What's the plan?''

"O'Donnaugh won't be expecting two of us. Reckon I'll just walk in and see what happens. Try to distract him, so you can grab him from behind.''

"Got it.'' Dave pushed Campanelli over to a tree, and cuffed the other wrist so he was left hugging the pine's trunk. "And Miss Martin?''

"I'll take care of her,'' he snarled as he thought of RaeAnne in the clutches of that corrupt, deceitful—

"Easy, man,'' Dave said. "I'm sure she's fine.''

"She'd better be,'' Roman muttered.

If she wasn't, he wouldn't be responsible for his actions. It had taken him eighteen years to find her, and he wasn't about to lose her again. Not to anyone or anything.

They'd have to kill him first.

Roman and Dave scoped out the cabin from the forest fringe, and when all seemed quiet, they scooted up to the windows. Sheets or some kind of cloth had been draped over them on the inside so it was impossible to see into the room.

Suddenly there was a loud crash in the cabin, along with a muffled scream.

"RaeAnne!"

All procedure and caution flew to the wind as Roman flung open the door, weapon cocked and ready to blast holes in the man who was hurting his woman.

He stopped dead, taking in the sight of RaeAnne and Philip, both gagged and bound, back to back on chairs which had crashed to the floor, presumably as they'd struggled to free themselves.

Two pairs of eyes blinked up at him, one filled with joy and relief, the other sheepish embarrassment.

Roman let out a long breath.

The bastard had lied.

RaeAnne glanced uncertainly at Roman as he pulled the Jeep back up beside the old stone cabin at Cleary with a jerk.

They'd spent most of the night at the sheriff's office giving statements about Chairman Campanelli and making sure he was locked up tight with no possibility of escaping justice for all he'd done, both in the past and the present.

In the driver's seat, Roman looked as broody as the mountains storming above them, clouds obscuring the sunrise. He'd had that same look on his face since finding her manacled to Philip on the floor of the cabin last night. He said he was upset about having left her in danger, but she suspected there was something more that lay beneath his moodiness.

Slamming on the brakes he reached for her. "Come here," he said, his voice rough with an intensity she'd never heard from him before. "I need to feel you close. Know you're safe."

In a single motion he unfastened her seat belt, sweeping her into his arms and embracing her with an almost desperate quality. She yelped in surprise when he stumbled from the Jeep, landing on certain feet.

"I'm safe now," she whispered against his shoulder, holding him tight. "And you are, too."

She sent up a silent prayer of thanks, knowing how close she'd come to losing him over something he'd had nothing to do with. Something that had happened so long ago.

Tears sprang to her eyes at the parallels to their own situation. How foolish she'd been to have run away from home those many years ago, refusing to hear his explanation if he'd chosen to come back and give it. How much they'd both lost because of a lack of trust!

With an arm under her knees he picked her up and made straight for the cabin, all the while kissing her like there was no tomorrow. Her heart nearly broke, knowing that it could well be true. For them, there would probably not be a tomorrow.

She met his thrusting tongue, grappling with his flannel shirt, tearing at the buttons, tugging up on his T-shirt when he set her down to unlock the cabin door.

In their flurry, she reminded herself this was just physical. They couldn't keep their hands off each other, but for her own sake, she must try for some kind of emotional distance.

They tumbled through the door and right onto the bed, and suddenly she was naked and so was he, and he was over her.

In her.

He slid home and for a brilliant second neither moved.

He'd be leaving her again soon. This time for good. His case was solved, the bad guys all in jail. He'd found his father. He had to get back to work.

"This is how I need you," he said between harsh breaths. "Under me. Around me. Holding me tight. So I know nothing can hurt you."

It was no use, she couldn't do distant. Not in the face of the overpowering emotion spilling from his every word. She wrapped her arms around his neck, her legs around his waist. Wanting so badly to believe he needed her. It might kill her tomorrow when he left, but she couldn't deny him the depth of feeling he so obviously sought tonight. Not when she felt it to her very soul.

He made love to her ferociously, almost savagely. And she reveled in it. In the pure, raw emotion. The primitive contact. The intense need between the two of them.

She felt claimed. Taken. They were one as she'd been with no other man, and it was all she could do to hang on to the roller coaster her heart had become. He took possession of her, body and soul, not allowing her any quarter. Again and again he thrust into her, eliciting a fireball of sensation between her thighs and through her whole being.

"Roman," she cried over and over, unable to form a single thought that wasn't of him.

He kissed her mouth and suckled her breasts and touched her in places no one else ever could. She was his. Totally. Completely. Without reservation.

She came apart under him in sweet surrender, giving him everything that she was and all that she would ever be. And then he rolled her on top and she did to him what he'd done to her.

And when it was over, and she lay panting, slicked with his sweat, covered with the scent of his sex, she thought she had never lived before this moment. Never experienced love. Never been in love. She ached with it, with the sheer intensity of the sweetness and the sting.

The night he'd left her those many years ago, she'd had a similar feeling—after the prom when they'd made endless, young love on this very same blanket, nestled under a warm, star-strewn quilt of desert sky.

Then, as now, she was overwhelmed with the fathomless depth of her feelings for this man. In that long-ago moment, she'd thought they were invincible. That nothing could ever mar the perfect love she'd carried for him in her heart.

She'd been wrong, then. And she wanted to weep, thinking she could be so wrong now, too.

But the difference was, tonight she was acutely aware of what would happen in the morning.

But it didn't matter. She would give him a lifetime of love tonight, while she still held him in her arms.

And face tomorrow when it came.

Much later RaeAnne dozed, but Roman's mind was too full to sleep. He lay for a long time with his arms around her, his leg draped possessively over hers. Their hearts beating as one, within inches of each other.

He was lost. Utterly lost. Desperate in his feelings for this amazing woman who tonight had given him what seemed to be her very soul. His own heart lay prostrate before her, basking in the glow of her blissful surrender.

He drew in a deep breath, smelling the poignantly familiar peach blossom scent of their passion, and trembled with fear.

Would she still send him away, even after a night like this?

She smiled, meeting his eyes.

"You're awake," he whispered.

"Mmm-hmm." She snuggled closer, tucking her body under his in a way that never failed to arouse him. "You?"

"Never slept."

"No?"

At her worried expression, a frisson of something warm and fuzzy spread through him. He shook his head. "I wanted to watch you sleep."

Her mouth formed an O of surprise. "You did?"

She looked adorably rumpled, and wonderfully, thoroughly loved. And he did—love her. To distraction. That had been the one constant certainty in his life since the first moment he'd noticed her in that junior high school bus. But did she love him? Could she learn to trust him? He was so afraid he knew the answer.

He kissed her hair before tears could well up. "I've always loved watching you sleep."

Her smile returned. "Did I snore?" she asked, though a

shadow of uncertainty underlay her teasing banter. Did she sense his inner turmoil?

His lips curved bravely up. "Only a little."

"Liar."

"Who, me?" *Only to myself.*

For he was deceiving himself if he thought he could ever make it through this life without her by his side.

She stretched under the blanket, and he loved the way her soft skin felt against him, all the way down. Not wanting to spoil the morning, he shook off the melancholy gripping him. He slid a hand onto her bottom, coaxing a sexy moan from her throat, and he wanted her all over again.

Then it occurred to him the moan could be in response to something other than his touch. He could feel the muscles in his own back and legs, and he'd only ridden half as long as she had.

"How's your backside? After all that riding?"

Throwing him a grin, she laughed and painted lazy kisses up his throat. "A bit sore, I'll admit. Especially after last night. A horse wasn't the only wild beast I had between my thighs yesterday. I could definitely use a hot tub."

He chuckled lasciviously. "Me, too."

"Guess we never made it to the hot springs."

"Then what are we waiting for?"

With that he scooped her out of bed into the chilly morning air, cutting off her surprised gasp with a thorough kiss. They gathered clean clothes and a thermos of coffee and hiked the quarter mile or so up the hillside to the bathing pool. Stripping bare, they slid into the hot water.

"Heaven," she sighed.

He grasped her fingers and tugged her onto his lap, not wanting to be farther away from her than skin to skin. "Oh, yeah. Definitely heaven."

He moaned as they sank neck deep into the hot, mineral-rich bubbles and relaxed, attempting to shed the stress and tension of a lifetime.

"What a day," he sighed, leaning his head back against

the stone rim of the basin, letting his fingers play over RaeAnne's smooth, bare skin under the water.

Hands down, the past twenty-four hours had been the toughest day of his life. Even worse than the terrible day he'd left RaeAnne years ago. Back then, he'd known she would be safe—or at least thought she would. Back then, Roman himself had been the betrayer. Today he'd been betrayed from all sides. All, that is, except RaeAnne—the one person who would have been entitled.

"On a scale of one to ten, I'd give yesterday a minus fifty-eight," she agreed, idly stroking her hand down his chest. "Still, at least something good came of it."

He ran the day through his mind. Other than waking up in that sleeping bag with his arms around her, he came up empty. "Oh? And what would that be?"

"Your father. You found him, he's alive, and he's not a murderer."

Unable to hide the scorn in his voice, he commented, "No, he just abandoned his son at six years old and didn't give a rat's butt about what happened to him for the next decade or three."

RaeAnne kissed his jaw and tightened her hold around him. "That's not true," she murmured. "He moved to Pachenga just to be near you and your mother, and remember—"

"Yeah, yeah. Campanelli swore to kill us both if my father told anyone he was alive… He was that determined to keep his connection to the drug ring secret and his name unconnected to Pritchett's." Roman closed his eyes, rent by the pain that squeezed his heart. Threatened or not, how could a man do that to his own son?

"Campanelli obviously meant it. The profits from the Tecopa drug operation were too good to lose if your father revealed his connection to Pritchett after they were all arrested."

"All this time," he whispered. "All this time my father's been alive and working for the Bureau. *Oh, God. I'll never* forgive him, or them. I quit my job, you know. I can't work for them anymore.''

"I know.''

And she did. She'd been there last night when he'd chewed out his boss on the phone as they sat in O'Donnaugh's office filling in papers. It had been an angry conversation, and he was sorry for coming down so hard on his boss, who probably hadn't even known about the situation. But he didn't regret the decision.

She was quiet for a few moments, the hush of the early dawn mountains cocooning them in a gossamer of birdsong and whispering leaves.

"Your father didn't betray you,'' she finally said. "He thought it was the right thing to do. He sacrificed his life to keep you and your mother safe.''

Roman had struggled to come to terms with this last inconceivable paradox all night. With no luck.

"You have to forgive him, Roman.''

Impossible. He grasped her face between his hands, forcing her to look up at him.

"Could you?'' he asked, certain of her answer. "Would you forgive a man who'd betrayed you that badly? Would you ever trust him again?''

Her lips formed a soft, knowing smile, her eyes filled with a love and wisdom he couldn't begin to fathom, and she simply whispered, "Yes.''

A sob caught in his throat when, with sudden, blinding insight, he realized she wasn't talking about his father at all, but about him.

The pure joy and amazement he felt nearly lifted him from the water.

"You do? I mean, you would?''

"Yes. Provided he was capable of the same forgiveness.''

He let go her face and pressed his hands to his temples. *Could he forgive? Was he capable of seeing things from his father's point of view?*

He thought back to that awful day he believed he'd contracted AIDS. To the anguish he'd felt, thinking if he so much as kissed RaeAnne goodbye she'd get the deadly disease. To the hopelessness of having to choose between abandoning the woman he loved more than anything, and saving her life.

In his mind, there'd been no choice. Not at that time. Could it have been the same for his father?

"We did exactly the same thing, didn't we?" he said, and wanted to laugh out loud at the cosmic justice being served up to him on a platter of retribution. Laugh—or he would start to weep and never stop.

"Yes."

All those years wasted.

It was a hard lesson.

But one he'd never, ever forget. Or repeat.

He glanced upward, to the high granite peaks blazing in a bright wash of orange light from the rising sun. It was as if they were holding their breath, waiting for his next words.

He turned to the woman in his lap, in his arms, the only woman he had ever wanted in his life, the woman he would never again let go.

"Do you have any idea how much I love you?" he whispered.

Her eyes sparkled with unshed tears. "Yes," she answered. "Because I love you just as much."

"Marry me," he said. "Marry me, and have my babies, and stay with me forever," he said. "Can you forgive me? Do you love me? Will you marry me?"

"Yes," she answered. "Oh, yes, yes, yes!"

And he swore he heard the mountains sigh.

Epilogue

Three Months Later

RaeAnne Santangelo slipped her hand through the crook of her husband's arm and leaned into him. A tear slipped down her cheek and she quickly wiped it away. She didn't want the others to know what a silly, sentimental fool she was, crying at the funeral of people who'd died over a hundred and fifty years ago.

Still, it was amazing she even remembered how to cry, she'd been so incredibly happy for the past three months.

She glanced up at Roman, the source of her greatest joy. He was watching her, and winked when she looked up.

Caught.

Oh, well. It wasn't as if he didn't know every last detail about her anyway by now, including her embarrassing propensity for misting up over old movies, greeting card commercials, weddings—especially her own—and apparently funerals, too.

He pulled her closer as they watched his father, Hector,

chanting over the grave of Crawford Edisto and the Indian woman he'd spent his life with. It was sad that they'd been taken at the same time by disease, probably yellow fever according to Dr. Cooper, the forensic anthropologist from Berkeley. But the couple had been old by then, and if they loved each other even half as much as RaeAnne loved Roman, one wouldn't have lasted a week without the other.

Hector Santangelo's voice was deep and clear as he sang a Paiute prayer over the grave. RaeAnne was pleased he'd consented to do the ceremony. There had been more than a few rocky conversations between him and Roman after they'd found each other. But she was so proud of the way Roman had kept his promise to forgive his father.

The two had talked endlessly about the past, sharing memories and stories of the years they'd missed. He'd learned how Hector had been recruited by the FBI, how he'd kicked his heroin addiction, then spent many years after his "death" working undercover, fighting the South American drug war, because he was so angry over what it had done to his life, and what it had cost him.

RaeAnne smiled up at her husband. Like father, like son. They were so much alike it was almost scary.

The soft, repetitive words of the Indian song flowed up through the fall-scarlet trees of Cleary Hot Springs as the great-great-great-grandnieces and nephews of Crawford Edisto solemnly poured shovels full of dirt over the grave of their ancestor and his bride. They'd been delighted with RaeAnne's discovery, to the tune of a hefty bonus check—enough for a nice down payment on an old Victorian fixer-upper nestled along the Russian River, that Roman was restoring in-between his veterinary studies.

Not that they needed the money. It turned out Roman had saved twenty years worth of Navy and FBI paychecks, invested wisely and could easily afford to retire and fulfill his dream of becoming a small animal vet.

"Hi Miss Martin—I mean Mrs. Santangelo," whispered

Toby as he handed her a shovel when it came her turn to help fill. "This is so great."

"It was a good idea, wasn't it?"

Everyone had debated about what was the best thing to do with the remains. Back in May, RaeAnne had elected to leave them exactly as they were and not excavate more than a few sample bones for Dr. Cooper to analyze and extract DNA from. Dr. Cooper had been able to prove they were indeed Crawford's remains. In the end, it had been decided to leave the burial site where it was, replacing the bones in their original positions, with the addition of two lovely headstones to mark the graves.

"Yeah," Toby agreed. "Very cool. Especially the Indian ceremony part."

She grinned. Toby had suggested it to her, and she had suggested it to the relatives. They'd loved the idea of a mixed-culture memorial service. So, over Thanksgiving vacation when everyone was able to get off work and school, they had all gathered together to celebrate.

"RaeAnne. Roman," Philip O'Donnaugh said as she passed her shovel to him, giving him a quick hug as she did so. He accepted Roman's slap on the back with a good-natured smile.

Now, that was the weirdest thing of all—Roman and Philip's friendship.

She suspected it had been mostly guilt that had driven Roman to invite him out for their first beer. Guilt that he'd believed Philip to be the perpetrator of all sorts of vice, corruption and nefarious reasons for courting her. But, somehow, in the weeks since the sheriff's office had become the center of the biggest scandal to hit Inyo County since…well, since ever, he and Philip had become fast friends.

Philip had been exonerated of all wrongdoing, of course. She'd never doubted it for a minute. But despite that, right after the Grand Jury investigation, he'd resigned his job as sheriff. Roman had invited him to fly up to Sonoma, and to her surprise, he'd accepted. To her even greater surprise, he'd left their place two weeks later riding Roman's Harley.

Roman had claimed he didn't need it anymore. He was buying a Volvo.

The baby-blue station wagon was now parked down by the cabin, sandwiched between the Harley and Toby's old rust-bucket truck.

"Let me borrow the bike," Roman asked Philip when the ceremony was over and everyone had shared a feed around the river-cobble fire ring in the meadow. "We won't be gone long."

"Sure," Philip said, tossing him the keys.

"Come on," Roman urged RaeAnne when she hesitated.

She glanced uncertainly at the sputtering machine, but then hopped on behind him. What the hell. She'd been taking chances ever since he'd cut her down from that stupid tree Toby'd tied her to. What was one more?

"Tuck in your chin, it's going to be windy," he advised, then pulled her hands around his waist and leaned around to kiss her. "Hang on."

The bike leaped forward. She slipped her hands under his leather jacket and held on tight.

It was the first time she'd ever been on a motorcycle. On the twisty mountain road he didn't drive fast, but it was exhilarating nonetheless. Just as all the firsts she'd shared with her new husband had been.

The smell of warm leather and hot man tickled her nose, the feel of firm muscles tantalizing her fingers. Lord, he turned her on. He could just walk by, and she would melt at the man's feet. She nestled against him and kissed the back of his neck, lingering with her lips and tongue so he'd be sure to notice. She wasn't disappointed. He swerved the bike into a cutout and parked it, pulling her off the seat and into a hot kiss.

"We don't have enough time for this," he said on a half laugh, half moan, after he'd kissed her thoroughly. "I promised Phil we'd be back soon."

That's when she noticed where they were. Her thinking spot.

He led her by the hand along the path, taking them out onto the huge granite boulder where they'd already shared so much.

"What's going on?" she asked as he took her in his arms, turning her so they both faced the towering mountains.

"There's something I've been wanting to do."

She could hardly wait. Usually those words were followed by a new, breathtakingly erotic experience for both of them.

She glanced up, puzzled, when he took a big breath and shouted to the peaks at the top of his lungs, "Thank you!"

What on earth?

"Is this some weird Indian custom I don't know about?" she asked. "Or should I be worried about you?"

He chuckled, nuzzling her cheek. "I'm not sure," he said. "But I'm not taking any chances."

"On what?"

"We never did find out who sent me that copy of your Forest Service dig application. Tanya swears it wasn't her."

She digested that for a second, unable to make heads or tails of his logic. "So you're saying…the mountains sent it?" She grinned, expecting him to laugh out loud at her outrageous suggestion.

But he just grinned back and shrugged. "It certainly wasn't O'Donnaugh."

"Your dad did it. I'll bet anything."

"Anything?" He lifted a brow suggestively.

She should know better than to bet with him. She'd lost on several memorable occasions. But truth be told, she hadn't minded a bit when he collected his winnings.

"Anything," she assured. "You be sure to ask him."

"Oh, don't you worry, I will. In the meantime…" He cupped his large hand gently around her head and drew her lips to his. "A kiss to seal the bargain."

"I thought you'd never ask."

She melted into him, flowing into his embrace like a river

to the sea. His tongue was slow and sensual, his lips warm and tender. Her heart did an endless, dizzy spiral, beating to the pulse of her boundless love for her man.

"Have I told you lately how much I love you?" she whispered.

"Not nearly enough," he murmured, despite her reminders at least a hundred times a day.

His lips caressed hers, his hand stealing under her blouse. It sought her belly, and settled there, gently possessive in its touch.

"Tell me again."

She obliged, whispering the words over and over as she kissed each precious inch of his mouth and cheeks and nose. "I love you. I love you. I love you…"

They'd waited until after they'd gotten married in Las Vegas—the same day he asked her—to buy a pregnancy test kit. She hadn't been carrying his child then, but they'd had three months to remedy the situation. This morning the stick had turned pink.

"You've made me the happiest man in the world," he said, gazing into her eyes, and she knew he'd left the past completely behind.

As had she. They'd both come a long way, their future bright, based on a foundation of love and commitment.

"I've always loved you, and I always will," he promised. "No matter what life throws our way, I'll never leave you."

Her eyes filled with tears, her heart with joy, and her life flowed with a sweetness she never thought possible.

"I know," she said.

And this time she truly believed.

* * * * *

If you enjoyed what you just read,
then we've got an offer you can't resist!

Take 2 bestselling love stories FREE!

Plus get a FREE surprise gift!

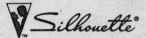